Crucible

Also by Ian Hecht
Soul Survivor (coming 2014)

Crucible

IAN HECHT

Marturia Media
MMXIII

ISBN 0-9920086-0-3
ISBN-13 978-0-9920086-0-4

Cover photos:
Luna Creciente by Santi LLobet
Eta Carinae by Emilio Küffer
Cracked Mud by Belle Dee

For Mandi, who believed I could,
and made me believe it too.

Table of Contents

Excerpted from "Welcome to the Moon: A Travellers' Guide" published 2135 by the Tranquility Press Office

Your first encounter with Lunar personnel will be Midway Station, the stopping point on the way to the moon. The station orbits the Earth-Moon L1 Lagrange point and is the place where you and your cargo are transferred from Earth-safe vessels to Lunar landers and vice-versa. It is approximately 56,000 km from the surface of the Moon, on average. Midway's gravity is set to 50% Earth normal, to help acclimate travellers in both directions.
***

Your next encounter with Lunar personnel will be Lunar Entry Control (LEC), the agency responsible for keeping track of comings and goings on those lunar bases open to the public. Make sure you have all your documentation prepared in advance to speed your entry to Luna. Make sure your wrist comm resets to UTC+0: because our day is 29 Earth days long, we set all our clocks to the same time.
***

Once past LEC, you'll find yourself in Tranquility Station, our first and largest settlement. Our population is about 1 million people, split between the 20 domes that make up the Station. We build all our Lunar cities as domes for the structural reinforcement the shape provides.
***

If you're not staying in Tranquility during your visit, there are some other excellent places to visit on Luna. From North to South, Nearside and Farside, here are some of the places you might visit:

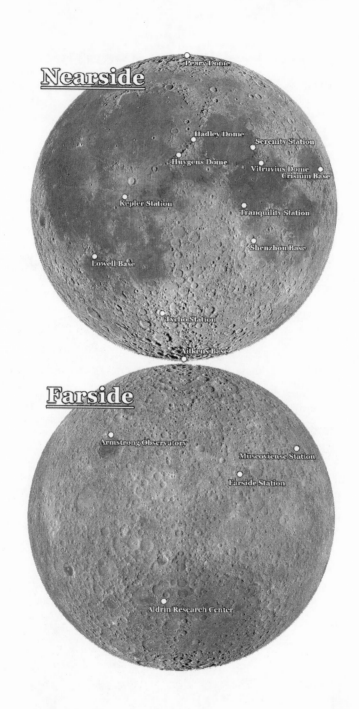

Nearside

Peary Dome

Hadley Dome

Serenity Station

Huygens Dome

Vitruvius Dome
Crisium Base

Kepler Station

Tranquility Station

Shenzhou Base

Lowell Base

Tycho Station

Aitken Base

Farside

Armstrong Observatory

Muscoviense Station

Farside Station

Aldrin Research Center

Peary Dome is a singular-dome center, enclosing approximately 37,000 inhabitants. Peary's biggest attraction is the 24 hour sunlit Park at the center of the Dome.
***

Serenity Station is located in Mare Serenitatis, very near the landing site of Luna 21, on the south-east edge of the base. While it was originally designed as a retirement facility for low-mobility seniors, because of its location reasonably close to Tranquility Station, it has become a recreational facility for all our Lunar residents and tourists. You'll enjoy all the recreational opportunities available at Serenity!
***

Tycho Station is a retirement community with a population of around 80,000. Located inside Tycho Crater, it is home to some of the finest amenities on Luna. It is made up of two domes with a large connecting tunnel.
***

Just as the North Pole of Luna has areas that are perpetually lit (like the location of Peary Dome), the South Pole has areas that are in constant, or near constant, darkness. Many of the water deposits and deposits of other outgassed substances are found in the shadows cast by crater walls of the South Pole-Aitken Basin, the largest impact crater in the solar system. The South Pole-Aitken Base is at the base of the Leibnitz mountains, and is a cluster of domes that house ½ million people. The main purpose of the base is exploitation of the estimated cubic kilometre of water found there, but other substances are also mined. Because of their ice mining, the South Pole-Aitken Base is home to the finest aquatics facility on Luna.
***

Farside Station: Get As Far Away From It All As You Can! Farside Station got its start as an observatory, since telescopes built on the far side of Luna do not have to look past Earth to see objects. With the construction of Armstrong Observatory, Farside Station became our premiere tourist destination, with theatres, casinos, low-grav sports arenas and anything else you could imagine!
***

There are, of course, some bases on Luna not open to tourism:

Aldrin Research Center is located on the Lunar Farside. It has a population of around 20,000, largely scientists and their support staff. The ARC does mostly materials research on the side of the moon perpetually facing away from Earth.
***

Shenzhou Base is one of two bases established and still maintained largely by one country. Like Moscoviense Station for the Russians, Shenzhou provides a secure base from which the Chinese launch their space exploration program. The base is located in Mare Nectaris, the location of the first Chinese moonwalk in 2024.

Part One
The Accident

Chapter One

There was a man lived in the moon,
lived in the moon, lived in the moon.
There was a man lived in the moon,
And his name was Aiken Drum.

Aiken Drum hated living in (or rather, on) the moon. He hated the cold, lifeless view out every thick window. He hated the dry, recycled air in his home dome, and the way it made his dark hair stick up in odd places. He hated the 3 second delay in communication to Earth – and that communication was probably as close to Earth as he would get, given that his lanky six-foot-one-inch frame wouldn't be able to support his weight on the larger planet, since his body had adapted to the Moon's gravity. Most of all, he hated The Park.

The Park was a little indoor garden at the center of the fifth level of the six-level dome (well, seven if you count the level below the surface where the mechanical air movers and water reclamation machinery dwelled) where trees and flowers and grass grew and produced some of the oxygen that everyone used. Because the dome was situated on the rim of the Peary crater at the north pole of the moon, there was near constant sunlight for the plants and the hydroponics bays that supplied the dome with most of their food. It was always noon in the Park. No matter what part of the lunar day cycle they were on, you could always go to the Park and see the light streaming in the transparent part of the dome. The carefully manicured lawns and rows of trees planted at precisely one and a half meter intervals knew darkness only during a lunar eclipse or when there was repair work being done on the dome above. The only concession to actual wilderness was a grove of bushes slightly to the west of the center of the Park, which provided some reflective privacy.

The administrators of the dome touted The Park's (it was never just "the park") twenty-four hour availability as a perk, but Aiken hated it. What better way to make everyone realize that it was all fake than to have a bright, sunlit recreational area all day and through the night. Aiken hated the Park's obvious falseness. Unfortunately, it was one of the few open areas in the dome available for meeting with people, so he spent more time here than he'd like.

Today he was walking through the center of the greenspace on his way to meet with his physics instructor, Mr. Bertram. His teacher had asked to meet Aiken's class on the periphery of the Park for today's lesson. Aiken was mystified. Mr. Bertram was usually so staid. He insisted Aiken and the other students sit in desks placed in rows in the small classrooms that Peary Dome used to instruct its next generation. What could possibly have compelled Mr. Bertram to allow them out of their stuffy little room into the open center of the dome?

Speeding up in curiosity, Aiken spotted the dirty-blond tousled hair of his friend Connor trudging along the path ahead of him. The two friends were opposites in a lot of regards. Where Aiken was tall and stringy, Connor was shorter and broad. Where Aiken's hair and eyes were dark brown, Connor had light blond hair and blue eyes. When Aiken got too introspective and withdrawn, Connor's gregariousness and easy humour usually managed to draw him out. They'd been friends since Connor had moved to Peary Dome when they were just kids. Aiken sped up a little more to catch up to him.

"Hey man," he called out.

"Hey, spaghetti-head," came the expected response.

"Any idea what we're doing out here in the wild green yonder?" asked Aiken.

"Nada"

"Maybe we're trying out some new physics experiment," he suggested.

"Are you nuts?" Connor replied. "Bertram would never let us out of the classroom to do something fun. It's probably community service or something boring like that."

Aiken considered that as he and Connor rounded the last corner of the pathway before the agreed upon meeting place. His breath caught in his throat and his step faltered for a minute when he saw who was with the group already gathering. Diana, her blonde locks radiant as always, was seated next to Ethan. Diana Lafontaine was in the class ahead of Aiken, so he didn't see her very often. Each time he did, he marvelled that so lovely a creature could exist in such an arid and sterile place. It wasn't just that her hair shone like spun gold, but that it perfectly framed her perfect face, blue eyes looking out from a visage the colour of alabaster. Her ample lips shone ruby in the sunlight of The Park, and when they smiled, her whole face lit up. Aiken could spend all day just looking at her face, but that would be to ignore the rest of her perfect petite form. Aiken was equally entranced by her bright mind as he was by her enticing physical presence. As he recovered his pace, a knowing chuckle came from Connor.

"See something you like?" he inquired.

"Shut up, you," groused Aiken.

Connor was well aware of Aiken's attraction to Diana, but was sure, and had repeatedly voiced to Aiken, that Diana was out of his reach. Her parents, who had immigrated to Luna only a few years ago, were administrators of the Peary dome.

"Don't let the virgin huntress catch you staring," Connor teased.

Aiken gave his friend a little shove, "Don't call her that."

"Why not? It's not like you're going to do anything about it."

"Because," Aiken responded, "it makes her seem so cold and remote and she's not really."

"How would you know – you've never said more than two words in a row to her."

Aiken could tell his friend was just bugging him, but it still got to him. He thought he knew Diana better than a lot of people – he was convinced that under the aloof front she put on, she was warm and gentle and just a little shy.

Anyway, Connor was right – he was mortified to go up and talk to Diana. He was even slowing his pace as he drew near the group around Mr. Bertram. Connor noticed and gave him a little shove in the back. Aiken stumbled forward and tripped, landing in a sprawl at Diana's feet. He glared at Connor as he got up.

"Nice landing, Drum," laughed Ethan, one of the oldest in the class. Ethan was solidly built, with dark hair and eyes that attracted the attention of the girls in their class. He radiated self-confidence and charm, and was always surrounded by a group of friends. Often enough, Aiken found himself to be the butt of their jokes, his "celebrity status" as the person who'd lived the most of their life on the moon not helping one iota. He was sure there were going to be some dig about his less than spectacular entrance, but with Mr. Bertram there, Ethan didn't seem inclined to poke too much fun. Aiken composed himself, then sat down across from Diana in the small circle that had formed on the green.

More students were gathering now, until there were about fifteen all told, besides Mr. Bertram. As the last found seats, Mr. Bertram cleared his throat.

"Today is an historic day for the human race," he began. Snickers from some of the students drew a glare. "Today marks the first test of a faster than light spacecraft."

Chapter Two

2:30pm Monday, May 18th, 2139

The students looked at him, dumbfounded. "How do you know?" asked Connor, recovering quickly. "A project like that would be top secret."

"An old college friend of mine is one of the scientists working on the drive casing," replied Mr. Bertram. "This isn't quite the Manhattan Project – it's so expensive, there's a multi-national conglomerate doing most of the contracting. The drive is an open secret at certain levels in the government. Needless to say, I don't need you spreading around that I got access to classified information."

The class nodded in agreement.

"Anyway," Mr. Bertram continued, "all we're going to do is watch the test. That's why I asked you to come here, where the dome gives a clear view of the area where the test will occur."

The students started whispering among themselves. "Do you think he's serious?" Aiken asked Connor.

"I don't know," came the reply, "but do you think Mr. Bertram would be the kind of person to set it up as a joke?" Aiken thought about that for a moment, then shook his head.

"I guess not."

Mr. Bertram was holding up a stellar cartography sheet – the sky as it appeared from the moon. He was trying to line up the e-paper document with the sky outside the dome, but the sunshine was making a hard job of it. As he became more and more confused, Diana stood up, turned the sheet the right way and lined it up for him.

"Thanks," breathed Mr. Bertram. He lifted his arm and pointed to a spot in space. "In about twenty minutes, you should see something right up there in the L4 Lagrange point." Aiken turned with the others to look at the spot where the instructor was pointing. He filed it away so that he would be able to find it when the time came, and turned to start talking to Connor again.

"Where do you think they're sending it?" Connor asked, face still turned up to the sky.

"What?"

"It's a faster than light ship, right?" Aiken nodded. "Then logically, if it's a ship, it will have a starting point and an end point. Where do you think they're sending it?"

Aiken shook his head. "I don't know – outer edge of the solar system, maybe?"

"Yeah," Connor enthused. "That'd be far enough to see if the drive works properly, but not so far that it would take forever to find out if something went wrong."

"What do you mean?" frowned Aiken.

"You should pay more attention in this class," laughed Connor. "Here's how it works – light and radio take a certain amount of time to travel a certain distance, right?"

Aiken nodded, "I'm with you so far."

"Well, the farther they send the ship, the longer it will take for the signals from the ship to come back to the observers here."

"I see."

"Even if they sent the ship to Proxima Centauri, the closest star to Earth, it would still take the signal more than four years to get back here – that's a long time to wait for the test results."

"You got that right – can you imagine what they'd be doing in the mean time?"

"Anyway, if they send the ship out to Pluto, say, it's only a little over four hours for the signal to get back."

"Well, that would make the wait easier."

At that moment, Mr. Bertram, who had been listening in, spoke up. "While your suppositions are accurate, this test has no destination. They're only going to spin up the drive to see if it will work in space. It is analogous to revving the engine on a car."

"I see," Aiken said doubtfully. Truth be told, he'd never even seen a car in person, only in vids. Having been born on the moon (first moon birth, hence the heinous name), he'd never been any deeper in Earth's gravity well. His muscles wouldn't be able to stand the strain without some serious physiotherapy before heading dirtside.

Mr. Bertram wandered away as Connor rolled his eyes. Aiken and Connor spent the remaining minutes before the test chatting about the stars they'd visit if they had access to faster than light travel.

"You know," said Connor thoughtfully, "with a drive like that, you could almost see through time."

"How so?" asked Aiken.

"Well, remember that it takes light time to travel? Say you went a thousand light years away from here and turned a telescope back on earth, what would you see?"

"I don't know, Earth?"

"Right, but Earth as it appeared a thousand years ago, because the light reaching your telescope would have left Earth a thousand years before you got there. You could see into the past."

"Yeah and on the flip side," Aiken continued, "you'd be seen back on Earth a thousand years from now, if anyone had a telescope pointed in the right direction, so you'd travel into the future."

"Well, sort of," laughed Connor, "but you have the right idea."

Aiken was silent for a minute, and then asked, "Do you think there could be travelers from the future looking back on us right now?"

Connor looked startled for a second, then replied, "I don't know why not, but it'd be a pretty boring observation – you mooning over Diana and tripping in front of her."

"Yeah, well, I wouldn't have tripped if you hadn't shoved me," retorted Aiken.

"Sure, sure, blame the little guy."

"Anyway," Aiken continued, "today

could be an auspicious day for us... we're witnessing the dawn of a new age." He imitated Mr. Bertram's tone as he said this.

Connor laughed, "Yeah, I'm sure future historians will want to know where we were sitting when the world's first faster than light drive went absolutely nowhere."

At that moment, Mr. Bertram waved to get their attention. "The test should be starting shortly," he announced.

Aiken and Connor fell silent and looked up to the point above the dome that their instructor had indicated earlier.

"I don't see anything," came the voice of Ethan. "Are you sure you have the right day?"

The class laughed. Mr. Bertram waved his hand to quiet the class, but no one was looking at him, because at that very moment, something could be seen up there.

Chapter Three
3:00pm Monday, May 18th, 2139

It started as a soft glow, barely distinguishable from the background, especially with the sunlight still streaming in from the other direction. The glow grew so bright that soon the entire class could see that something was indeed happening. The glow changed from white through a rainbow of colours as it spread across the part of the sky they were watching. The light rippled as it spread and grew more intense. Aiken's eyes started to water, but he didn't want to look away and miss something. The light grew more and more intense until it rivalled the light of the sun on the top of the dome and still Aiken couldn't look away. He sensed those around him were equally drawn to the sight. After another stretch where the light intensified, it began to pulse subtly, in a rhythm that felt familiar to all who saw it.

Aiken recognised the two-beat rhythm of a heart in the growing intensity of the pulsation. He could feel his heart trying to beat in time to the strange, brilliant light. He gave himself over to the sensation and could feel that his classmates were doing the same to varying degrees. He thought of nothing else. The sight filled his mind. All other thoughts were pushed aside and he desired to join with the phenomenon. His whole being wanted to take part in the dance of light above. His eyes were watering more profusely now, but still he didn't look away. He knew, somehow, that the show would soon be over and that he would want to see the end of it. His breath came softly, as if he were afraid that by straining anything, he might break the spell the light had cast on him. He could feel himself drawn upwards and realized the he was standing on tiptoe as if to soar up away from the cold, dry moon and become one with the light.

Suddenly, wrenchingly, the light vanished and in the center of where it had been was a growing red and orange and yellow bloom. What felt like a pressure wave on his brain hit a moment later and he knew something had gone terribly, terribly wrong. Then he blacked out.

He came to in a daze and sat up. The bodies of his classmates were sprawled on the grass and stones around him. He glanced up to the spot on the dome that had so transfixed him and the others, but could see nothing, no light save a smattering of twinkling bits in an expanding sphere. A pounding headache was starting behind his eyes, and he could already tell that this was going to be a doozy.

He looked around him again and spotted Connor, lying awkwardly on the ground beside him. His face was pale beneath sweat-slicked hairs. He leaned over and shook his friend. "Hey."

Connor blinked his eyes and looked confused for a second. "What happened?"

"I think something went wrong with the test," Aiken answered. "It wasn't supposed to end like that."

"You could feel it too?" inquired Connor, putting a hand to his forehead.

"Yeah," Aiken replied. "You have a headache, too?" He saw that other students were stirring as well, and starting to sit up.

"Do I ever," Connor answered. "It feels like someone took a cheese grater to the back of my eyeballs."

The students were murmuring amongst themselves when a cry rang out.

"Where is everyone? Who turned the lights out?" It was Faith, the newest girl in the class. She was holding her hands out in front of her and waving them around. A couple other students tried to approach her, but were batted away by her flailing arms.

Someone called out, "It never gets dark in here, Faith – something must have happened to you." This caused Faith to flail even more frantically around her, as if to drive off the dark that only she could see. Then Diana was there and Faith calmed down as Diana spoke quietly to her. Mr. Bertram sat up just them and frowned, putting a hand to his head.

"Students," he called out. "I don't need to tell you that something went wrong, but until there is something in the news bulletins, please do not speak of this to anyone else." After checking on the rest of the students to ensure that they were okay, he went over to where Diana was still talking to Faith and led them both away, still holding his hand to his temple. The spell that had seemed to come over the students as they regained consciousness was broken and they started to drift away in small groups, talking quietly amongst themselves.

Aiken and Connor had left together, talking about the experience and what could have gone wrong with the experiment. They agreed that tomorrow in class, they would ask Mr. Bertram if there was any news regarding the failed experiment.

As Aiken left Connor and wandered alone in the corridor back to the apartment suite he shared with his parents (but only for two more years!), he replayed the experience over and over in his mind. No doubt something had gone wrong, but why did he get the feeling that it was more serious than a failed drive test? His growing headache was making it difficult to think coherently.

As he approached the door to his suite, he thought he heard someone talking inside. It was a voice that sounded familiar, but he didn't recognise it immediately. The voice sounded muffled and indistinct. He rounded the corner and saw that the apartment door was open. Startled, he approached the door cautiously and peered around it into the unlit apartment. He crept inside, trying to make as little noise as possible. A figure was seated on the sofa opposite the door, but in the dark, Aiken couldn't make out any features. The figure looked up as Aiken crossed the light from the corridor. It was his father.

Aiken heaved a sigh of relief – he must just be really jumpy from the events of this afternoon. He waved the lights on and smiled at his father. "Hi dad."

"Hey. How'd the class go?"

"Not that great," Aiken replied, mindful of Mr. Bertram's caution. "It didn't really turn out like we were expecting."

"Really," stated his father. "And here I thought you'd be happy to get out of that stuffy little classroom, especially for physics."

"Yeah, well," Aiken started, "It just wasn't what I had expected, that's all."

"Well, tell me about it."

"Nah, nothing to tell, really." Aiken knew that his dad wouldn't pry any further if he put on his usual show of teenage indifference. True to form, his dad dropped the line of questioning and went back to the tablet computer on his lap.

Surprisingly, all the students actually complied with Mr. Bertram's request to keep a lid on their speculations. Aiken wasn't the only one to pass off the extraordinary experience as just another day in class. The only ones who got a slightly different story were the parents of

Faith, who obviously had to be told something had blinded their daughter. However, since they were relatively new to the dome, they still kept mostly to themselves and didn't have an opportunity to pass on this information to the parents of the other students.

The students went to bed that night dreaming of a rainbow hued, pulsating lightshow.

Chapter Four
7:00am Tuesday, May 19th, 2139

The next day, Aiken woke up slowly to the sound of the alarm. He batted his hand at the noise to make it go away. The alarm's tone faltered for a second, then resumed its beeping. The strident tone irritated his already sensitive head. Finally, Aiken sat up and turned it off. He went through his morning routine and went down the hallway to the kitchen.

As he approached the turn to the kitchen, he thought he heard the voices of his parents talking.

"I wonder if he ever...," came the voice of his mother, strangely muffled, trailing away to silence.

"She's got such…," his father's voice, also sounding like it was spoken through heavy cloth.

Aiken turned the corner to find both his parents seated at the breakfast table, eating, and casting glances at each other.

"Morning sleepyhead," his father said. "What do you want to eat?"

"I dunno, toast maybe?"

"Bread's on the counter," said his dad. "Are you young ones heading back to The Park today?"

"Nah," Aiken responded. "It's back to the old grind today in the classroom."

"Well, just remember," his mother said, "you'll be done the Physics quad soon enough and you can move on to another subject that's more to your liking."

Aiken smiled at that – his parents knew how much he disliked anything involving math.

"Yeah," he continued, "like biochemistry or geology or something fascinating like that." He rolled his eyes. His dad, the biochemist and his mom the lunar geologist glanced at each other, then back at Aiken. They all started to laugh. As Aiken turned to make his toast he heard his mother say, "I wish he'd take his school more seriously."

I'm standing right here, thought Aiken.

"Oops," came his mother's voice.

Aiken finished off his breakfast, then headed out to see if he could find any of his friends. In the corridor that led to the area in the Park where they had witnessed the failed test yesterday, Aiken ran into Diana.

"Oh, uh, hi," Aiken stammered.

"Hi, Aiken," Diana said. "How are you doing?"

"Oh, uh, fine, I guess," Aiken blushed. This was not going well. "How are you?"

"Well," she started, "considering yesterday, I'm doing fairly well. Headache's almost completely gone. My parents were a little worried."

"They know about yesterday?" Aiken inquired.

"Well, not really," Diana continued, "but seeing as they're in admin, they know something happened, since Faith got hurt and all."

"Oh yeah," Aiken spoke. "How is she doing now?"

"Well, she still can't see at all, but the docs are hopeful that it's only temporary, caused by the bright light."

"Do they know what caused it?"

"No," she laughed. It was a melodic sound and Aiken wished he could hear more of it. "They think she was staring at the sun. Without the atmosphere here, it's more intense, so it could cause more damage."

"Yeah, but what kind of idiot stares into the sun?" Aiken asked.

"Well, I guess they didn't think about it too hard," Diana said conspiratorially. "I mean, they're looking for the easy answer, right?"

"I guess," Aiken replied dubiously.

"Trust me," Diana said, putting her hand on Aiken's arm. An electric thrill ran up his arm and into his head. "They're not going to look any harder for an explanation." She paused, "I'm guessing they'll keep Faith for observation for a couple of days, then let her go when her vision starts to come back." *If it does.*

Aiken started. The last phrase had come from Diana without her having opened her mouth. "What did you just say?" he asked.

"I said, they'll keep Faith for a couple of days, then when she starts seeing again, they'll let her leave the infirmary."

"No, after that," Aiken pursued.

"Huh?" Diana was confused. "Uh, that was it." *What?*

"What what?" Aiken asked.

"What?" This time, Diana formed the words with her lips.

"You said 'what'," Aiken responded.

"Uh, no I didn't," Diana countered. *He is weird.* Again, her voice came through loud and clear, but Aiken could see that she had definitely not moved her lips.

Aiken was taken aback. Something was going on, but he couldn't figure out what it was. Leaving a confused Diana behind, he trekked on toward the Park, aiming to cut through to get to class. As he neared the spot where the class had gathered the day before, he spotted a figure sitting hunched over on a bench, looking intently toward the ground. Aiken got closer and realized it was Ethan, the guy who'd mocked him yesterday when he'd fallen.

"Hey, Drum," Ethan called out as Aiken neared. He still had his face turned toward the ground, but Aiken realised that his eyes were closed.

"How did you know it was me?" Aiken inquired.

"I've been practicing," Ethan responded.

"Practicing what?" Aiken was confused.

"My gift," replied Ethan, clarifying things not one bit.

"Uh, could you start over from the beginning, and not just where I came in," Aiken asked.

"Ah, Drum," Ethan taunted. "Always so slow to pick up on things."

27

"Spit it out, Ethan."

"Okay, here it is, simplified for the moon man. That pretty little show in the sky yesterday did something to our brains. I'm not the only one, I've talked to others."

"What are you on about," Aiken was getting nervous. Some strange things had already been happening around him.

"How do you think I knew it was you coming?" Ethan probed. "My eyes were closed and there's no way that I would know that it was your footsteps."

"I dunno," Aiken guessed, "Maybe you saw me come into the park and are just having a go at me."

"Guess again, moon man."

"You know," Aiken started, "you live on the moon now, too."

"Yeah, well, I wasn't born here, and I'm not staying here forever either. Now guess."

"Lucky guess?" Aiken tried.

"Nope. I heard your thoughts. I knew it was you because apparently all you think about is Diana."

"You what!?" Aiken was shocked, but not that surprised when he stopped to think about it. That would explain some of the occurrences today.

"Well, now you just went dark," Ethan

said. "Guess I shouldn't have told you."

"So we can hear what people think?" Aiken asked.

"Oh, so you have noticed," Ethan chuckled.

"Yeah, a couple of times I thought I heard someone say something that they didn't say out loud."

"Well, we're the only two, then," Ethan said.

"I thought you said you weren't the only one," Aiken countered.

"Well, everyone was affected, just not in the same way."

"What do you mean?"

"Well, Gwen can lift things without touching them," Ethan began. "And Hugo can make himself disappear."

"What!?"

"Yeah, he just kind of fades out until you can't distinguish him from the background." Ethan laughed, "It's kind of creepy, but what guy wouldn't want that ability?"

Aiken snorted, then asked, "Anybody else?"

"No one's seen your buddy Connor since we all split yesterday, so he's maybe off somewhere figuring out his own talent."

"How did the rest of you figure it out?"

Aiken inquired.

"Well," responded Ethan, "some of us who left together started to get creepy feelings all at once."

The man in the apartment, Aiken thought.

"Yeah, I heard that thought," Ethan continued. "Anyway, I was like you, thought people were saying things that they weren't, but I figured out pretty quick that they were thinking it, so I mentioned it to a few of the folks there. No one else could do that, but they were already starting to figure out what they could and couldn't do. We all just knew somehow, that it's connected to that light we saw yesterday," Ethan paused. "To tell you the truth, I'm kind of glad I'm not the only mind reader."

Aiken started at that term.

"Yeah, that's kind of what I felt, too. Anyway, people seemed a little freaked out that I could hear what was going on in their heads, so I came here this morning instead of hanging out." Ethan waited a beat, then spoke again, "Now that there's more than one of us, though, maybe people will be more accepting. It's not like we're trying to listen in, right?"

"Well," Aiken started, "since I didn't even know I could do it until just now, obviously not."

"And there's evidently a way of stopping it," continued Ethan, "Since you're not radiating any thought at all right now."

"I can see why people would be a little put off by one of their friends being able to read their mind, though," Aiken mused. "I can't see my parents being too thrilled about it either. Or the school. Oh, god. Can you imagine being able to pick the answers out of anyone in the class's head?"

"We might not want to advertise what we can do to anyone else right off the bat," Ethan countered.

"Why not?"

"Well, it gives us a leg up on everyone else, right?"

At that moment, Connor appeared beside Aiken. Actually blinked into existence, with a little popping noise. Aiken jumped.

"Ha!" exclaimed Connor. "Gotcha!"

"Well," Ethan said laconically, "I guess we know what your gift is."

"What?" Connor looked confused.

"As I was just explaining to Drum here," said Ethan, "we're all experiencing a little weirdness today."

"Oh, so the rest of you can do it, too?"

"Not like that," Ethan answered. "Drum and me can read minds, and other people have other abilities."

"And here I thought I had something special going on."

"Don't worry," Aiken consoled his friend, "you have us all beat in the 'sneaking up' category."

Connor was silent a moment, then spoke, "Does anyone know what Mr. Bertram can do?"

Ethan swore feelingly. "Can you imagine a teacher that can read your mind?"

Both Aiken and Connor were disconcerted at that idea.

"It's almost time for class anyway," Ethan continued. "Let's go find out."

The three of them left the Park together, chatting animatedly about the abilities the group seemed to have been granted.

Aiken thought to himself, in the deepest recesses of his mind, where he hoped Ethan wouldn't overhear, *You know, Ethan's not so bad once you get to know him. Maybe his ability to hear what people are actually saying has put the brake on his usual obnoxiousness.* Ethan continued talking with Connor, and seemed unaware.

Chapter Five

The group was disappointed when they arrived at the classroom, though. They wouldn't have a chance to find out what ability Mr. Bertram had gained. There was a scrolling message on the electronic noteboard saying that the teacher was off sick today and class was therefore cancelled.

"Let's wait around for a bit and find out if everyone else can do tricks with their brains," Connor suggested.

"How do we know it's our brains?," Aiken asked.

"What else would it be?" Connor

answered. "It's not as if reading minds is a skin condition."

"Fair enough." Both Ethan and Aiken were also curious to know what feats their classmates were now capable of.

Isaac was the first one to arrive, his bald black head gleaming. Isaac was one of the best athletes in the class – he had the build of a track star and the reflexes of a fighter pilot, which made him a deadly opponent on any playing field. Fortunately, his athleticism was tempered by an easy humour and a willingness to poke fun of himself.

"Let's see what you can do," Ethan prompted. "We're all showing off our new abilities."

"Ha," Isaac laughed. "You're going to love this."

He ran at the door to the classroom, and just as the three were certain that he was going to do himself some grievous injury, he and the door seemed to shimmer and he passed right through the door.

"Whoa," Connor stated for all of them.

Isaac's head poked back out through the closed door. "You like?" he asked mischievously. "I figured out something was up when I reached *through* a cupboard door for a mug."

"Yeah," Ethan exclaimed. "I hereby invite you to join Brainiacs Incorporated."

All the guys laughed at this, and Isaac stepped the rest of the way out through the door.

Connor looked thoughtful. "How do you do that without falling through the floor?"

"What do you mean?" asked Isaac.

"I mean, if you can make yourself insubstantial enough to walk through a solid door, why are you still substantial enough not to fall into the floor?"

Isaac thought about it a moment, then shrugged. "Maybe I'm not making myself insubstantial."

"Okay, let's test it," Connor stated. "You do what you do at the door and one of the other of us will try to pass through it."

"I don't know," said Aiken. "What if he sneezes when one of us is only halfway through the door? I may not remember lots of Physics, but I'm pretty sure two things can't be in the same space at the same time."

"Well, I'm willing to try if you are," Ethan spoke to Isaac.

Isaac shrugged. "Sure."

"Okay, fire away," Ethan said, walking up to the door. Isaac frowned in concentration at the door. A patch in the centre started to shimmer faintly. Ethan pressed his hand up to this patch, then snatched it away as his hand started to sink into the substance of the door. As Isaac kept up his concentration, he screwed up his nerve again, and pushed his hand completely into the door.

"Hey, I can still kinda feel where the door ends and the classroom air begins," he stated. The whole door was shimmering now. Ethan drew his hand back, looked over at Isaac, then stepped forward through the door. A moment passed, then Ethan stepped back out through the closed door.

"Awesome," breathed Connor.

At that moment, both Aiken and Ethan straightened and looked down the corridor. "Someone else is coming," Aiken stated.

"Okay, that was creepy, you two," Isaac said. He stopped concentrating on the door and it stopped shimmering. Ethan turned back to it and rested his palm on the surface. It didn't sink in. He turned back to the corridor expectantly.

Around the corner drifted Jillian Finch, a good friend of Diana's. Where Diana's stunning good looks made her the envy of the other girls and the dream of the boys, Jill's classic girl-next-door looks made her more accessible to everyone. She was friends with almost everyone at the school. Her short brown hair, framing her wide-eyed look of innocence, seemed to swirl weightlessly around her head as she moved towards the group. She looked like she was walking, but her feet never touched the ground, floating a couple of centimetres above the floor instead.

"I see you've figured out your gift, Jill," Ethan called out.

Jillian looked down and swore, "Damn it! I can't seem to stay on the ground." She smiled ruefully. "I can't really tell the difference. It doesn't feel like I'm floating."

"How high can you go?" asked Connor.

In response, Jill floated up to the ceiling of the corridor, some three metres off the ground.

"Wow," said Aiken enviously.

"Well," Ethan said, "you too are officially welcome to join Brainiacs Anonymous."

"I thought it was 'Incorporated'," laughed Isaac, as Jill returned to the floor.

"I think 'Anonymous' will work better for now," Ethan continued. "Our parents would freak out if they found out what some of us can do."

Aiken had a thought, "Do you think any of them will have abilities, too?"

The others all glanced around at each other. Connor spoke for all of them, "Unless they were watching the light show, no. I mean, we're all pretty convinced that's what did it, aren't we?"

The others nodded.

"Should we tell someone, though?" Jill asked.

"Why?" Ethan answered. "You have a sudden urge to end up on an examining table in Aldrin?"

Jill shook her head, frowning. "You think even our parents would send us there?"

"Can we afford to run that risk? I mean, even one parent gets the spooks involved, and they'll start looking at all of us." Ethan looked at each of the others until they nodded agreement.

Aiken spoke again, "We need to find out what actually happened at the test."

"Why?" Ethan asked, "We know what it did to us, isn't that enough?"

"What if the effects are only temporary?" Aiken countered.

The others considered this silently.

"You know," said Jill, "that never occurred to me. I wouldn't want to be floating three metres up when I lost that ability."

"Yeah," continued Isaac, "or partway through a wall."

"What?" exclaimed Jill.

Isaac demonstrated his ability again for Jill's benefit. She was impressed, but stated that he better not use that to walk into the girl's change room. Isaac laughed, but then looked thoughtful. Jill swatted him on the arm.

"I think that's more up Hugo's alley," Ethan said.

"What do you mean?" Jill asked.

"Well, he can make himself invisible," Ethan explained. Jill looked disconcerted. "In fact," Ethan continued, "he's right over there, now." He pointed to a section of the corridor a few metres away.

A shape slowly made itself apparent against the drab colour of the wall. At first only an outline was visible, then it looked like there was a person shaped oily patch in midair against the wall. Bit by bit a face came into view – an aquiline nose, followed by dark brown eyes surrounded by olive-coloured skin, jet black hair and a knowing smirk. Finally, the familiar features of Hugo appeared completely, looking sheepish.

"How did you know?" he asked.

"I can hear your thoughts, remember? I was tuned into you the moment you showed up, or rather, didn't show up. I bet Drum, I mean Aiken, knew you were there, too."

Aiken started. Actually, he had though he'd heard something from that direction, but had dismissed it because he couldn't see anyone there. He needed to get used to paying attention to this new sense.

"Well," said Jill, nodding at Ethan, "I guess we'll need you in the girl's change room to make sure no one's spying on us." As she realised what she'd just said, she blushed. "I mean, I guess you could stand outside and make sure no one was in there, or in the walls, or..." she trailed off.

She was rescued by the appearance of Kaira Simon, who strolled around the corner just then. Spotting the group congregated around the classroom door, she paused. "Classroom not open?" she called out.

"Nope, no class," answered Isaac. "Bertram's sick."

"Oh, goodie," Kaira said as she walked up. "I was so not looking forward to this after what happened yesterday. Poor Faith." Her hazel eyes had a look of concern, drawing all her elfin features together in a look of apprehension.

"So what's your story?" asked Ethan.

"What?"

"What's your gift?" Ethan pursued.

"What are you talking about?" Kaira looked confused.

"You mean, you don't know?"

"Know what?"

Ethan turned to Jill. "Show her," he

stated. Jill shrugged, then gently lifted off the floor. Kaira shrieked.

"What the hell?!"

"You mean, you really don't know?" Ethan asked.

"Evidently not," Connor interjected.

"Okay, so in the aftermath of yesterday's incident," Ethan explained, "some of us have discovered some unusual abilities that we're sure are a result of the light show."

"What do you mean?" asked Kaira, troubled. Jill drifted back down to the floor.

"Well, so far, we've got a couple people who can read minds, walk through walls, make themselves invisible and," he continued, gesturing at Jill, "float."

Aiken spoke up, "also, you mentioned Gwen could pick things up without touching them."

Ethan nodded and turned back to Kaira, "so, we'll show you ours if you show us yours."

Kaira shook her head, "I can't do anything like that." She looked around at her classmates apprehensively.

I always thought she was a bit of a dud. Ethan thought. Aiken picked up this thought clearly, as it was forefront on Ethan's mind.

Now, now, he chided mentally, *she may just have a more subtle ability.*

41

"Whoa," Ethan exclaimed, "What did you just do there?"

Aiken looked confused for a second. "What do you mean?"

Ethan looked him over, "I mean, I didn't just pick that one up from your thoughts. It was like you put it in my head."

"What?" Aiken was confused.

"That thought just then," Ethan persisted. "You didn't just think it for me to hear, you actually put it in my head."

The other students looked disconcertedly at both of them.

"What's going on?" Connor asked.

"It seems like not only can Aiken read thoughts, he can send them, too," Ethan explained. "Try it on someone else."

Aiken thought for a minute then directed at Connor, *Can you hear me?*

Connor started, then replied out loud, "Yeah, I can hear you."

"Cool," Ethan exclaimed. "Let me try now."

He thought at Connor, *Can you hear me?* Aiken could hear him, but Connor didn't seem to be able to. Ethan tried again, *Can you hear me, Connor?* Aiken could sense that Ethan was getting frustrated.

"Are you trying to fake me out?" he asked

out loud.

"Check out his thoughts," Aiken said, "You'll see."

"Hey, wait just a minute," Connor started to object, but Ethan waved his hand at Connor impatiently.

He skimmed the surface of Connor's mind, and realised that his mental projection hadn't been received.

"Nuts," he said aloud, "that would have been a really neat trick. Better than passing notes on our tablets."

"Maybe you just need some practice," Aiken suggested.

"No, I don't think so," countered Ethan. "All of our abilities seem to have come out at the same time. If I can't do it now, I'm guessing I can't do it at all."

"Maybe," Aiken said, "but the headache I have from yesterday still is telling me we're not through yet."

"You still have a headache? Mine's gone." Ethan sighed, "I guess I'll have to stick with the receiving end."

"That's not so bad," Aiken tried to lift his spirits.

"What do you know, you can send and receive." Ethan would not be mollified.

"Hey, if Aiken got both abilities, maybe

the rest of us have others, too," Connor mused.

The students were all excited by this prospect, with the exception of Kaira. "I still haven't found my first one yet, let alone others," she complained.

"Don't worry," Isaac said, "If you were watching the test yesterday, something must have happened. We all felt it, right?"

At this all the students nodded. "See?" Isaac continued, "Nothing to worry about... you'll find out your ability soon enough."

Both Aiken and Ethan heard the thought that passed over Kaira's mind just then: *And be a freak like the rest of you?* They glanced at each other, then back at Kaira. *Well,* Ethan thought where Aiken could pick it up, *at least she has a healthy attitude about the whole thing.* Aiken chuckled, then sent back, *I can't tell if she's more worried about not having an ability, or finding out she has one.* Ethan laughed out loud, to the disconcertment of the others.

"Do you get the feeling," Isaac asked Connor, "That there's something they're not sharing with us?" Connor laughed, then his thoughts turned inward.

Aiken sent to him, *don't worry, man, I'm still your friend, even if you don't have my astounding command of telepathy.*

Connor startled, then thought *I'm not*

going to get used to you doing that, you know.

I know, Aiken sent back, *but you can still do something I can't.*

That's right, Connor thought proudly. *Just watch.* With that, he vanished, to the collective gasp of the other students gathered.

Hugo asked, "Can he turn himself invisible, too?"

"No," replied Aiken, "he moves himself around mentally."

At that moment, Connor reappeared. "Liam's on his way," he announced. "I was just back out in the Park and saw him. He should be here in a couple of minutes."

While the students waited for Liam to show up, they discussed the abilities each of them had. Isaac demonstrated again his ability to make solid objects insubstantial.

When Liam appeared around the bend in the corridor, he had a very serious look on his face.

"What's wrong," Jill asked.

Aiken and Ethan knew at the same instant. "Mr. Bertram is dead," they chorused.

Chapter Six
9:30am Tuesday, May 19th, 2139

Liam reacted with surprise to their pronouncement. "How did you know Mr. Bertram was dead?"

"It's our ability," Ethan said. "You were thinking about it, and we heard. How did he die?"

Liam responded, "Brain aneurysm."

The students were shocked. "This doesn't look good for us," Hugo said.

"What do you mean?" asked Jill.

"Well, we all know that something affected our brains while we were watching the test yesterday," Hugo explained. "What if the same thing will happen to us? I mean, what if our brains can't handle whatever happened to them?"

The other students fell silent and stared.

"Well," started Liam, "I don't know if it means anything, but the reason that Mr. Bertram cancelled classes today was because he had a splitting headache all night. It turns out that was probably a symptom of the aneurysm." He paused. "Any of you experience anything more than a mild headache right after the test yesterday?"

The students looked at each other and slowly shook their heads in relief, except Aiken. "Mine's still there, but I wouldn't describe it as 'splitting'." A thought occurred to him. "What about Faith?" he asked.

Liam responded, "No, her problem is something else. Her optic nerve seems to be degrading."

"Uh oh," Aiken said. "The docs are going to figure out that it wasn't staring at the sun that did that."

Ethan spoke up, "Well, we need more than ever to set up B.A., then."

"BA?" Liam asked.

"Brainiacs Anonymous," Ethan replied. "We need to sort out who can do what and keep it quiet from everyone else."

Liam looked around questioningly, "Who can do what?"

"Don't tell me you haven't figured yours out either," Ethan groaned.

"My what?" Liam asked.

"Your ability," Ethan responded. "Why do you think we called it Brainiacs Anonymous?"

"I don't know what you youngsters are all about," Liam joked. He was in Diana and Faith's class, one year ahead of the rest of them. As the oldest student in the combined Physics course, he was often looked on to lead, and he bore the responsibility well. His well-defined features tended to project reassurance, and his stature (as tall as Aiken, but broader) made it easy to put confidence in him. "As to my ability," he continued, "check this out." He frowned in concentration, and suddenly, a chair appeared in the corridor just next to where the group was congregated.

"Cool," exclaimed Connor. "Can you move yourself, too?"

"What? No...why?" Liam answered.

In response, Connor blinked out and reappeared sitting on the chair. Liam looked thoughtful, then frowned in concentration once more. Nothing happened for a sec, then Liam's face straightened out. "I guess not," he said, somewhat disappointed. "Can you move things around?"

Connor got up off the chair and looked hard at it. He looked up and sighed. "I guess not. I must be able to move some things, though, since I've never shown up without my clothes." His friends laughed as he sat back down on the chair, but suddenly it disappeared from under him. He fell to the floor in a heap. "Hey!" he exclaimed, looking at Liam.

The rest of the students laughed again. Connor blinked himself back to his original spot standing next to Aiken.

"Couldn't have just walked over here?" Aiken asked.

"Why bother?"

"Because we do want to stay anonymous for the time being," Ethan answered for Aiken. "We should all meet somewhere and figure out what to do. Especially now that we know that not all the changes are good."

This reminder of Mr. Bertram's death sobered the students up quickly. "Where and when?" Liam asked. "I can bring the folks from my year if you can find the rest of yours." He paused. "Oh, except Faith... they're keeping her in the infirmary."

Ethan thought for a moment, then said, "With Mr. Bertram's death, I expect they'll shut class down for at least a day. Why don't we meet this afternoon back in the Park where we were yesterday?"

"Can do," replied Liam, already turning to go.

Once they'd decided who would contact each of the absent students for the meeting that afternoon, the rest of the class dispersed as well.

Chapter Seven

10:00am Tuesday, May 19th, 2139

Connor and Aiken walked back together along the corridor leading to the Park.

"Do you think anyone else was affected?" Aiken asked his friend.

"Why not?" Connor replied. "I'm sure there were people who were watching other than us. The folks who ran the test, for one, and Mr. Bertram said it was an open secret in some parts of the government."

Aiken pondered this for a moment as they continued up the corridor. "Do you suppose then," he continued, "that all sorts of people are discovering abilities just like ours?"

"Well," said his friend, "we figure that people who weren't watching weren't affected, so it would be limited to those with the ability to see the event."

"Yeah, well, you said there could be lots of them."

"I guess we'll have to wait and see," Connor mused.

"Maybe someone should check the newsnets to see if anything's been reported."

"Good idea." Connor blinked out of existence.

Well, I didn't mean right now, thought Aiken indignantly. He continued on the path to the Park, assuming that his friend would find him there. He wondered about the other students' abilities as he walked the path to the spot they had been yesterday. He reached the bench where Ethan had been earlier and sat down. As Ethan had done, he lowered his head and closed his eyes. He strained with his mind to catch the thoughts of people walking by. No one was in the immediate vicinity, but Aiken could sense the minds of the people walking the periphery of the Park. He had a hazy mental image of his surroundings, with ghostly forms moving about, lit from inside by a warm, yellow light. When he concentrated on any particular mind, the thoughts of that person jumped into clarity. Aiken was bored by the thoughts that most of them had on the forefront of their minds. He felt somewhat voyeuristic, peering into people's minds, but it wasn't as if he was taking advantage of any of the knowledge he was gaining. He thought about adding some thoughts into their heads, but decided not to when he remembered Ethan's warning about staying anonymous.

Aiken wanted to test his projective ability, though. It seemed less fraught with privacy invasion than just reading people's minds. He would just have to find a suitable test subject. He lifted his head to look around him, but found that he got a clearer image of where people were when he listened in to their thoughts. He was looking for someone who was alone and not in a hurry. His consciousness flitted from person to person, hovering over each bright mind. A few minutes later, he found the person he was looking for. One of the administrative assistants had taken an early lunch and was on her way to a spot in the Park to enjoy her meal. She was walking fairly quickly towards one of the benches scattered along the paths throughout the park. Aiken thought at her, *Excuse me*. The woman looked around, startled, but there was no one near her. She lowered her head and continued to walk. *Excuse me*, Aiken tried again.

Once again, she stopped and looked around, puzzled. Seeing no one, she shrugged and continued on her way. Aiken tried a slightly different tone. *Stop*. The woman stopped dead in her tracks. She stood motionless as if waiting for something. Aiken was stunned. *Continue*, he thought at her. The woman walked forward as if in a daze. She was responding as if he'd given her a direct order. Aiken experimented, *Take off your shoes*. The woman stopped on the path and lifted her shoes off, then continued on her way. Aiken was amazed and slightly frightened. He wasn't sure this power over others was something he wanted. As he cleared his thoughts from the woman's mind, she shook her head as if to clear away mental cobwebs. She looked at the shoes in her hand like she was confused as to what they were doing there. Aiken could see that she thought about putting them back on again, then decided to continue in bare feet off the path, walking slower than she had been when she entered the park. He withdrew his mind from contact with hers and looked up to see where she was. He was startled to discover that he had influenced someone clear across the open space from himself. He could just make out the figure of the woman on the other side of the Park, heading towards one of the benches along the path.

Aiken mused that this new discovery should probably be kept to himself for the time being. Not only was he a little scared of the possible implications of being able to control people around him, he was pretty sure that if his friends were apprehensive about he and Ethan being able to see their thoughts, the knowledge that they could make people do their bidding wouldn't be warmly welcomed. As he thought about this, he heard a soft pop from beside him, signalling that his friend had teleported himself back.

Chapter Eight
10:45am Tuesday, May 19th, 2139

When Aiken looked around, Connor had a slightly startled look on his face.

"What's up," he asked.

"Oh, uh, just trying something new," Connor replied. "I wasn't sure where you'd be, so I put myself up at the top of the dome and looked around while I was falling to spot you, then moved myself here when I saw you."

"Wasn't that dangerous?" Aiken asked.

"Yeah, probably, but I had to try," his friend answered. "Wouldn't you try to find out the limits of your abilities?"

Fearing that he'd been discovered, Aiken

looked down.

"What?" His friend asked. "What'd I miss?"

"Nothing much," Aiken replied. "Just trying to see how far away I can do my thing."

"Your thing, as you call it," Connor said, "is telepathy. Mine is teleportation."

Aiken looked at him questioningly.

"Well, I had to find out what they're called before I could look up reports on the net about them, didn't I?"

Aiken shrugged, "I guess."

Connor continued, "There's actually nothing on the nets at all about yesterday's test, although a few nets mention the light phenomenon. About people with our kinds of abilities, nada." He paused, "Well, I shouldn't say absolutely nothing, but the stuff that's out there looks like a bunch of cranks."

Aiken smiled, "Don't you think people would think we're crazy if we announced what we can do?"

"Yes, but we're not announcing it, are we?" his friend pointed out. "Maybe the other people with our abilities are hiding them, just like us."

Aiken was dubious. "If it's as obvious as what we've seen here, they wouldn't be able to keep a lid on it back on Earth."

"I guess," Connor said thoughtfully. "Unless there really aren't any others with our abilities."

"How could that be?" asked Aiken.

"Well, there are reports about the light phenomenon, but none about special abilities, and yet we're pretty sure they're linked." Connor paused thoughtfully. "Maybe it was too far away from Earth to affect them there."

"I don't think so," replied Aiken. "I may not be the physics whiz you are, but I'm pretty sure the L4 Lagrange point is equally far away from here as it is from Earth."

"You're right," answered Connor. "Well, maybe they are just hiding out, like we are here. There'd be a lot more of them on Earth, though. Total Lunar population is around four million in all the bases, and as far as we know, there's fifteen of us that were watching the test."

"Sixteen, if you count Mr. Bertram," Aiken interjected.

"Yeah, but he obviously didn't get any abilities," continued Connor, unabated. "Anyway, fifteen out of four million is..." he tapped at his wrist communicator, "around one in twenty-seven thousand. If you apply that to the fourteen billion people on Earth, you should have around five and a quarter million people with abilities. Even halving that to account for only people on the side of Earth facing the right way, that should have made the news."

Aiken nodded, "You're right. So, assuming no one on Earth has new abilities, the obvious question is 'Why?'"

Connor thought for a minute. "You know," he began, "if it's some kind of radiation, it would make a whole lot of sense."

"How so?"

"Well, the Earth is protected from all sorts of radiation by its magnetosphere."

"Okay, you lost me just there," Aiken said.

"Alright," Connor sighed, "here's the 'dumbed-down for Aiken' version: space is full of radiation. The sun puts lots out, there's lots in space left over from the Big Bang. With me so far?" Aiken nodded. "So, what happens when that radiation gets to Earth?"

Aiken shook his head, "I don't know."

"Yes, you do," Connor said. "Some of it passes right through the Earth, some is absorbed by Earth's atmosphere in the ozone layer, and some is trapped in the Van Allen belts. If whatever-it-was was a kind of radiation, it could have been blocked before reaching anyone on Earth."

Aiken pondered this for a moment, then asked, "Aren't we shielded from radiation also?"

"Yeah," Connor replied, "but not to the same extent as Earth. Stuff like glass blocks UV from the Sun, but other types of radiation pass through."

Aiken and Connor sat for a while longer discussing this idea, then decided to go to Aiken's apartment for some lunch before the meeting with the rest of the students.

As Aiken walked along beside his friend, they chatted about everyone's newfound abilities. Aiken was envious of Jill's floating, especially, and said so.

Connor surprised him by saying, "Well, maybe you have that one, too, since you have a couple already and everyone else only seems to have one. Try it, maybe."

Aiken concentrated on floating and willed himself to fly, but his feet remained stubbornly attached to the floor. "Guess not," he said somewhat dejectedly. He brightened and turned to his friend, "Have you figured out how to, uh, teleport objects yet?"

"Nope," Connor answered.

"Well, there's got to be some kind of trick to it," Aiken enthused. "After all, as you pointed out, you always show up with your clothes and your shoes and wrist com."

Connor thought about this. "Maybe I have to be holding it. Be right back." With that, he winked out. A minute later, he appeared in the same spot with the same quiet popping noise, a tablet computer in his hands. "I'm a genius!" he exclaimed. "I just have to touch something to take it with me!"

"Hold on a sec," Aiken cautioned. "You're touching the floor, and you didn't take it with you, 'genius'."

"Oh, yeah," Connor replied. "Well, maybe it has to be off the ground, like it's only touching me or something. Be right back again." And off he popped. While Aiken waited for his friend to come back, he thought about Connor's ability. *Wouldn't it be nice to not have to walk everywhere?* I could just pop myself to wherever I wanted. Off to my room -- and suddenly, as he imagined his room around him, he was there.

"Whoa!" he shouted. "Awesome!" Carefully, he pictured the edge of the Park where he had been waiting for Connor to reappear. Nothing. He thought about how he'd gotten himself into his bedroom. *I pictured myself in the place I wanted to be.* He put himself in the mental image he had of the Park edge and -- pop -- he was there!

Connor was there, too, with a large box, and looked startled to see Aiken appear from thin air. "What did you do?"

"I'm not sure," Aiken replied. "I was

61

thinking about your ability, and I pictured myself in my bedroom, and then I was in my bedroom. Cool, eh?"

"Sure," Connor replied, looking dejected. Aiken could see the disappointment in his friend's mind that he was no longer the unique holder of his ability.

"Hey, you moved a box," Aiken said, hoping to turn his friend's attention to something else."

"Yeah," Connor started to warm up to him again, "I was right – if I can pick it up, I can take it with me."

"That'll come in handy," Aiken enthused. "I guess you'll have to start working out so you can pick up more stuff."

"Well, here on Luna, it's not all that hard," Connor said. "I could probably have brought my living room couch along." He smiled at that thought. "If I went back to Earth, though, I'd be hard pressed."

Aiken smiled at his friend, then froze as a thought occurred to him. "Have you tried going back to Earth?"

"Uh, no," Connor answered. "So far, I've only been places I can picture clearly in my mind."

"You should see how far you can go," Aiken encouraged his friend, all thoughts of lunch pushed aside. "We went on that trip to Hadley dome last year to see the Apollo 15 landing site. Can you remember anything from there?"

Connor thought for a minute, then brightened. "I remember their cafeteria. They had real cake out for us, not just reconstituted crap."

Aiken laughed, "Trust you to remember something involving food." They both chuckled at that, then Connor grew serious. He screwed up his face in concentration, then with a pop, vanished.

Chapter Nine
11:15am Tuesday, May 19th, 2139

A minute went by, then two. Aiken started to get worried when Connor wasn't back after five minutes. Just as he had convinced himself that he should try the trip to Mons Hadley himself, Connor reappeared with a louder pop that usual. He held in his hands two plates with cake on them.

Aiken rolled his eyes at his friend. "What?" exclaimed Connor. "They must get regular shipments of real flour, instead of always using reconstituted algae."

Aiken grabbed one of the plates from his friend. Connor shouted, "Hey, those were both for me – you want cake, go get it on your own."

Aiken shook his head, then pictured his kitchen around him and -- pop -- he was there. A second later, Connor appeared beside him. "Ha!" he said, "I knew you'd come here. Run off with my cake, have you?"

Aiken laughed and then said seriously, "Did you really know I was coming here?"

Connor knew what he was asking, "No, it was just a lucky guess."

"Pity," Aiken sighed. "Well, let's not waste this cake."

Connor laughed, "I was serious about getting your own."

"What do you care, now?" Aiken teased. "You can go get more anytime you want."

"And have you steal it? I don't think so."

Both friends sat down at the kitchen table to enjoy the treat. Aiken paused halfway through his cake and asked Connor, "Do you think you could make it to Earth? I mean, if you wanted to?"

"I suppose so," Connor answered. "It'd have to be a place that made a big impression on me, though. I haven't been on Earth since I was six. I'm not sure I could picture anything from that long ago clearly enough."

"Unless it involved food," Aiken teased.

"Yeah, unless," Connor took the ribbing

good-naturedly. "Now what else do you have packed away in this kitchen?"

The friends ploughed their way through a copious amount of food, then sat across the table from each other and chatted. "Do you think you have any more abilities in your noggin?" Connor asked. "You've already outclassed Ethan and me, so what else can you do?"

Aiken was uncomfortable with the question, given the experience that he'd had with the woman in the Park. "What do you mean?"

"Well," Connor explained, "you have both halves of telepathy, send and receive. You seem to have at least part of the teleport ability. I'm just wondering if you have the other half of the teleport, for starters."

"What's that?"

"You know," Connor continued. "Liam's ability to move things from place to place."

"Don't know," Aiken pondered. "Let's see." He concentrated on the loaf of bread he'd started for breakfast that morning, when things had seemed so normal. He wanted it to move over to the other side of the kitchen. The loaf twitched. He concentrated harder. The loaf wiggled around on the countertop, then sailed off into the air.

"Whoa," Connor exclaimed. Aiken lost

his concentration and the loaf dropped to the floor beside the table.

"I wasn't expecting that," he breathed.

"That one would be telekinesis," Connor said. "I saw that one, too, while I was poking around on the nets."

"Yeah," Aiken replied. "Ethan mentioned that Gwen was moving things around without touching them. I guess that's what he meant."

"Well," said Connor. "Aren't you full of surprises? That's not what Liam did, though." He picked the now slightly flattened loaf and put it back onto its spot on the counter. "Try again and this time, don't try to move it, just picture it where you want it to be, like when you teleported yourself."

Aiken closed his eyes to better visualize. He pictured the bread on the table in front of Connor. There was a soft pop, and Aiken opened his eyes. The bread sat just where he'd pictured it. "Don't touch it," he told his friend. "I want to try flying it back." With that, he mentally pictured his hand reaching out and picking up the loaf and putting it back on the counter. The loaf soared back to the spot it had come from.

"Wow." Connor seemed impressed, and no longer bothered that Aiken could perform his ability as well. "I wonder what else you can do."

As Aiken considered this, a thought occurred to him. He closed his eyes and pictured a hand reaching down and picking him up off the ground. When he opened his eyes, he saw Connor sitting across from him, mouth agape. Looking down, he saw his feet were no longer touching the floor. He was floating. He pictured the hand settling him back down to the floor and he drifted lazily down.

Connor was still in awe, "How did you do that?"

"It's the same as the flying bread," Aiken answered, "except instead of picking something else up, I picked myself up."

"Wow!" Connor exclaimed. "You're a triple threat: telepath, teleport and telekinesis."

Aiken smiled.

Connor said enthusiastically, "try something else."

"What, though?" Aiken asked.

"How about what Isaac does?" Connor answered. "Can you make something solid go all funny?"

"Go all funny?" Aiken laughed at his friend. "Is that the technical term you found on the nets?"

"No," Connor laughed with him. "I don't know what you'd call it... insubstantiation, maybe?"

Aiken chuckled, then turned around and focused on a cupboard door in front of him. He remembered what Isaac had said about just absent-mindedly reaching through to grab a mug. He thought about the substance of the door and could almost see the atoms aligning themselves into the pattern he desired. The cupboard door in front of him started to shimmer faintly, then the shimmering grew more intense. Aiken reached out his hand and put it on the surface of the door and pushed. His hand started to pass through the door and he snatched it back. The door snapped back to solid in front of him.

"Awesome," Connor breathed reverently. Looks like you got the mega dose of whatever it is the rest of us have, too." Aiken looked troubled. "What is it," Connor asked.

"Well, whatever 'it' is," Aiken answered, "it killed Mr. Bertram. If I got an extra-large dose, that can't be good. I mean my headache's mostly gone, but I don't want to take any chances."

Connor looked subdued. "Sorry." He paused. "You could head over to the infirmary and get your brain checked for bulging at the seams."

Aiken thought about that, then said, "And what would I tell them? 'Oh, by the way, I have these amazing mental powers, but I'm afraid my brain's gonna explode, so could you just give it a little scan for me'?"

Connor snorted. "You could just tell them you have a splitting headache and after what happened with Mr. Bertram, you're worried."

"I guess that would work," Aiken said thoughtfully. He looked at his wrist communicator. "Looks like we might have enough time before the meeting, if we hurry over there."

"Aren't you forgetting something?" Connor asked. "No need to hurry, we can just teleport to outside the clinic and walk in."

"Oh yeah," Aiken said sheepishly. He reached out with his telepathic sense to the area of the dome where the clinic was and checked to see if there was anyone around who would see their apparition. "All clear," he told Connor.

"What? How do you know?"

"Amazing mental powers, remember?"

"Oh, yeah." Connor paused. "Well, let's do it."

Aiken and Connor both pictured the hallway outside the clinic, then put themselves in their mental pictures. With two pops, they were there.

Chapter Ten
12:00pm Tuesday, May 19th, 2139

Aiken walked through the doors of the clinic and surveyed the waiting room. Only a couple people were there. It was, after all, the middle of the day. He walked up to the receptionist and gave his name and complaint. The reception told him to be seated and wait until his turn was called. He sat down beside Connor in an ugly green plastic chair.

"Man," he groused, "these chairs couldn't be more uncomfortable if they were designed that way."

Connor laughed. "I think it's a

psychological ploy to make you feel better when you get out of them to see the doctor," he surmised.

Aiken chuckled and reached for an out of date magazine on the table next to him. The magazine was just out of reach, but zipped into his hand anyway. Connor looked at him, then formed the thought where he knew Aiken would see it, *we're supposed to be **anonymous**, remember?*

Aiken thought back at his friend, *I couldn't help it, the magazine just came to me.*

Well, tone it down, Connor thought back at him.

They sat quietly for the couple minutes it took for Aiken's name to be called. As he waited, Aiken looked around. He chuckled to himself at the room. It seemed that every waiting room he'd ever seen, whether in person or an image tended towards the same décor. Plain coloured walls with a band of darker hue at about waist height. Uncomfortable seats locked together, with sticky residue on the seats and armrests. A monitor in the upper corner playing out some daytime drama, and a stack of magazines taken from the doctors' personal collections after they were sufficiently out of date as to be more or less useless. A desk behind which the receptionist could hide and read her own magazine, or surf the nets.

He left Connor in the waiting room and went back into the exam room, impatient to have the test, and more that somewhat apprehensive.

As he went over the story Connor and he had concocted, he was tempted to use his persuasive ability to make the doctor believe him, but he refrained. He didn't know what side effects there might be, and he didn't want the doctor to be shaking off his suggestion and realise what he'd done while Aiken was undergoing some test. He was pretty uncomfortable with the idea he just could just suggest something and people would hop to obey. Well, maybe it wouldn't work on a doctor the same way it had worked on the admin assistant earlier, anyway. He restrained himself.

The doctor thought the test was probably unnecessary, but Aiken wheedled a little more, and the doctor decided that discretion being the better part of valour, he'd order the test. Aiken was taken into the next room, where a bed lay under a large scanning device. Aiken lay down on the bed as the technician calibrated the device. Aiken heard him call out from the glassed-in control room off to the side that the test would begin shortly, so he should lie as still as possible.

Aiken heard a clunking noise above him

and the machine glowed to life. As it rotated around the head of the bed, a glowing 3D image sprang to life over Aiken's head. The machine completed its circuit.

The technician off to the side swore, "What the hell?" He called in the doctor to look at the results. Aiken grew more uncomfortable given the fact that there was evidently something wrong with his scan. The doctor ordered the technician to perform the test again. Once more, the machine over Aiken's head sprang to life and did its circuit around the top of the bed. Again, the image appeared floating above Aiken's head.

The doctor, more concerned this time, ordered the technician to perform a diagnostic test on the machinery.

"What is it?" Aiken called out. "What's going on?"

"Son, if you're playing some kind of joke or trick on us, you're going to be in a lot of trouble."

"No trick," Aiken replied, worried now. *What's wrong with me?*

"We're going to run the test one more time to make sure the imager is scanning correctly," the doctor answered as though Aiken had spoken aloud. "Please lie as still as possible."

The technician poked his head around the edge of the machine and confirmed for the doctor that the scanner was operating within established parameters.

A third time, the scanner traced a circle around the head of the examining table and the three dimensional image appeared in the air.

"Well, I never," the doctor trailed off. "You can sit up now, son."

Aiken swung his legs over the edge of the table and sat up. As his head passed through the floating image of his brain, the pattern of light projected on his eyes reminded him of the previous day's test, which he was certain was the cause of all that had followed.

The doctor and the technician were both looking at him strangely. Aiken saw fear and astonishment in their eyes.

"What did the test say?" he asked them.

"Well, uh, well, it's like this," the doctor began. "Your brain, uh, your brain's geometry... uh," he trailed off. "Where to start?" he mumbled to himself. Aiken was tempted to look into his mind to find the answers for himself. If any situation called for looking into someone's thoughts, even a doctor's, his own survival might be it. He refrained, since there was evidently something wrong and he didn't want to use his abilities until he knew it wouldn't kill him like it had Mr. Bertram.

"Can you tell me what's wrong?" he gently prodded the doctor. The doctor looked up, then reached down to the workstation where the technician was seated. Keying in a series of phrases, he glanced up with satisfaction.

"Mr. Drum," he started, "this is the image we recorded of your brain when you were twelve, at your last scheduled full work up." A colour enhanced image appeared in the space over the examination table. Aiken took a step away from the examination table to see more clearly.

"And here's the image we recorded today," the doctor continued, typing another command into the workstation console. The image that had been there earlier appeared beside the projection of his younger brain.

"I can't see anything," Aiken said.

"Wait," the doctor answered, typing yet again. The images moved together until they overlapped and finally rested right on top of each other. "I've adjusted these for size," the doctor said. Aiken could see that something was different.

"In the four years since we last imaged your brain, somehow the structures of your brain have been… altered."

Aiken knew it was a lot more recent than four years ago. "What's changed?"

"Well, basically, everything is just slightly... off, for lack of a better word. This is not what a sixteen-year old brain should look like." The doctor paused, glancing up at Aiken. "Also," he said after a beat, "there are far more connections than there should be."

"What do you mean?"

"Well, as I'm sure you know, it's the connections between the parts of the brain which give us our conscious thought ability. The average human brain has between ten and a hundred billion neurons, each connected to a couple hundred neighbouring neurons. If this scan is accurate, your neurons have forged connections on the scale of thousands, not merely hundreds."

"And?" prompted Aiken.

"And," the doctor continued, "If hundreds of connections give us thought, thousands of connections is, well, it's beyond imagining what someone with that amount of neural connectivity would be capable of."

Aiken was still somewhat troubled. "Am I healthy, though?"

"Oh, well, yes," the doctor responded, somewhat flustered. "I guess so."

"No aneurysms or embolisms or anything

like that?" Aiken pursued.

"No, no, nothing like that," the doctor assured him. "Other than the odd geometry and the stupendous increase of connections, your brain is perfectly healthy." He looked thoughtful, "Of course, you'll have to stay here or in the infirmary for a more complete battery of tests."

Aiken had no intention of doing any such thing. Armed with his newfound knowledge and anxious to get to the meeting with his classmates to pass on what he'd learned, he pleaded with the doctor to let him leave. "I'll come back later," he promised.

"You'll do no such thing," the doctor replied. "You can't leave until we've figured out what happened." *And how to fix it.*

At that thought, Aiken knew that he would have to use his newfound abilities to leave and prevent the doctor from testing any further. He reached out with his projective telepathic sense and felt around in the doctor's mind. He had a sense of what he needed to do. Instead of just sending a thought, he needed to overlay a thought on top of another, so as to block the underlying original. Hating himself for doing it, but mindful of Ethan's warning on secrecy, he worked his way through the minds of the technician and the doctor and overwrote the last half hour with an innocuous conversation between the two of them. They'd vaguely remember talking about something, but not specifics, and definitely not that he'd been there. Then, reading the technician's thoughts, he used the man's knowledge to delete the scans taken of his brain, as well as the record of the calibration. That should keep the students' secrets safe for the time being.

Aiken walked back out into the reception area where Connor was waiting for him. "What took so long?" his friend asked.

"Tell you in a sec," Aiken said, then turned to the receptionist. Once again using his projective ability, he overwrote the memory of him and Connor being there with a half hour of bored daydreaming. It disturbed him that it came easier each time. He released his hold on the minds of the three medical workers as he and Connor left the clinic.

"What was that about?" Connor asked.

"The meeting's about to start," Aiken reminded him. "I'll tell you there, and everyone else should hear, too."

He and Connor both teleported themselves to the vicinity of the meeting place, then walked the rest of the way there. As they arrived, they saw that almost all of the students had gathered.

Chapter Eleven
2:00pm Tuesday, May 19th, 2139

Faith was still missing, as she continued to be watched in the infirmary, but all the students that had been outside the classroom that morning had arrived as well as a couple others. Aiken recognised Mason Gabriel, Gwen's older brother.

He leaned over to Connor, "I wonder what ability Mason gained?"

"The ability to attract women?" Connor joked.

"Nah, even that's too much of a stretch," Aiken laughed. Mason was a bookish seventeen-year-old math prodigy. His dark brown hair stuck up in directions that didn't seem physically possible, and his plain brown eyes were hidden behind massive eyeglasses, although those were scheduled for demise on Mason's eighteenth birthday, when he'd be eligible for the surgery necessary to correct the defect in his vision. His fashion sense verged on the non-existent, and it was always kind of a laugh whenever he showed up for some event wearing mismatched, wrinkled clothes. His idea of dressing up was tossing on a sport coat with patched elbows over a t-shirt with the name of some obscure twentieth-century cultural reference on it. Today's read "Finger Lickin' Good." He was technically in the same class as Diana and Liam, but he spent most of his instructional time taking advanced classes over the netlink with Earth. He'd apparently been at the drive demonstration as a part of an advanced physics project he was undertaking for Mr. Bertram, or had been before Mr. Bertram's demise.

Just then, they heard a soft pop behind them. Recognizing the sound of a teleport, they turned and saw their friend Nicole glace around apprehensively.

"Relax, Nicky," Connor said. "No one here but us Brainiacs."

Nicole looked relieved. "You would not

believe the day I've had." Her normally lustrous curly brown hair hung lank around her face, framing her usually sparkling grey eyes, which now just looked tired.

Aiken snorted, "Try us."

Nicole laughed, then said, "Yeah, I guess you would believe it."

"So," Connor said, "you can obviously teleport yourself around. What else can you do?"

"Well," started Nicole, "I can also…"

She didn't finish that sentence, though, because at that moment a deafening telepathic hail silenced them all. *Hey!*

Diana and her two friends Olivia and Penny appeared from around the corner.

"Which one do you think that was?" Connor asked his friends.

"No idea," Aiken replied, "but we'll find out soon enough."

Just then, Liam stood up from where he had been seated with Ethan and Isaac. He waved to get everybody's attention, then spoke. "Welcome to the first meeting of what's been called Brainiacs Anonymous."

"First on the list of things to do," Connor muttered to Aiken, "is change that name."

Aiken chuckled, "Over Ethan's dead body, I assume."

"Since everybody already knows everyone else," Liam continued, "I say we start by listing off what abilities we've discovered."

"Who made you boss?" a voice called out. Aiken identified it as Olivia's.

"No one," Liam replied easily, "You want the job?"

Olivia glared for a moment, then backed down.

"See," Connor whispered, "she's spoiled, but not snotty."

"Yeah," Aiken replied sarcastically, "and there's air outside the dome, I hear." While Aiken didn't know Olivia that much, her reputation preceded her. Her parents were wealthy industrialists who moved to the moon to oversee their company's operation there. Olivia, as a child, had made it quite well known that it was not her decision to come, and given her choice, she'd have been back on Earth in a heartbeat. In the intervening years, she'd come to call Peary home, and had in turn been accepted by some of her classmates, but the lingering feeling of resentment still held sway in some quarters. Aiken, as a fully lunar child, had taken exception to some of her choicer remarks, even as some of them resonated with him.

Nicole shushed them both.

"Anyone else want it?" Liam asked. He

waited. "No, I'm serious... I'm not saying I should be in charge, but someone has to be."

"Go on, Liam," Hugo said loudly enough for everyone to hear. "You're oldest, why not?"

"Fair enough," Liam replied. "So, onto business. What abilities have we discovered? We'll start over there on my left."

He pointed to Gwen, who was seated between Hugo and Jillian. Gwen had, fortunately, taken more after her mother in the looks department than had her brother Mason. Her dark reddish-brown hair fell in waves around her freckled face, enclosing her green eyes and elegantly delicate features.

"Um, well," Gwen cleared her throat. "I can pick things up and move them around."

"Telekinesis," Connor said.

Liam turned to him, "What was that?"

"Telekinesis," he said more strongly. "I looked them up on the nets while we were waiting for the meeting."

"Fair enough," Liam answered. "Next."

Jillian, who was seated next to Gwen spoke up. "Well, I can sort of fly." The students who had not witnessed this gasped.

Connor spoke up again, "We think that's also telekinesis. Except instead of picking up other stuff, you pick up yourself."

"Who's 'we'?" Diana's voice asked.

"Well, me and Aiken mostly figured it out," Connor replied. "You've got your projecting and receiving telepaths, your self-telekinetics and other-telekinetics, and your self-teleporters and other-teleporters." With this last, he nodded to Liam.

"Looks like you have most of us covered," Liam said encouragingly. "Does anyone have an ability that Connor just listed?"

Hands went up around the group.

"How about something that's not on Connor's list?"

Hugo and Isaac both punched their fists in the air at the same time.

"Right," Liam said, "We've got Mr. Invisible and Mr. I-can-walk-through-walls." He nodded at each in turn. "Anything else?" He looked at Kaira. "Figured out what you have?"

"No," Kaira answered miserably. Aiken could see from her thoughts that she'd come around since the morning, and the side of her that wanted to be gifted like her friends had won out.

"Well, no worries," Liam soothed. "Everyone's got something so far, so yours will probably show up sooner or later."

"What about Faith?" Jillian asked. "Does she have any abilities?"

Liam shrugged then turned to the group

seated with Diana. "Well, you were the ones who were with her most recently. Did anything happen to her?"

Diana, Olivia and Penny shared a conspiratorial look. Penny spoke up, "Uh, yeah. She can see."

"Well, good," Liam said, "I guess that's encouraging."

"No," Penny shook her head. "You don't understand. She can't see with her eyes." A confused look passed between most of the students. Penny continued, "She seems to be able to see with her mind."

"See what?" Ethan asked.

"Basically," Diana interjected, "whatever she wants. She can focus on things small enough that you'd need a microscope to see them, or things so far away you'd need a telescope. She sees everything perfectly clearly." She paused. "Oh, and she can see through walls."

This latest pronouncement produced gasps from the gathered students. "Awesome," breathed Connor.

"You sicko," Nicole poked him, "It's a good thing that it's a girl that got that ability, because you know what a guy would do with it."

Connor and Aiken both laughed at this.

"It's true," Connor sighed, a mischievous glint in his eye.

Aiken thought quietly. So far, every ability he'd attempted, he'd succeeded at producing. Wondering if he could manifest the mental sight, he said to Connor, "That'd be useful for teleportation. No more having to mentally picture the place you want to be. You could just look there."

Connor nodded, "Yeah, you could go somewhere you'd never seen before that moment."

Aiken began to reach out with his mind to see if he could find Faith in the infirmary, so that he could observe her technique and try it. As his mental probe extended past the periphery of the group, he was once again mentally deafened by a loud pronouncement. *Check out what I can do!* It was Diana. Apparently, she'd gotten the projecting end of the telepathic ability.

Aiken withdrew his mental probe to watch more closely. Only he and the other telepaths sensed what Diana did next. Reaching out with her telepathic ability, Diana tweaked Mason Gabriel's mind. *Stand up*, she ordered him. Mason obeyed like an automaton, a confused look on his face.

"What's going on," Connor asked.

Aiken and Nicole chorused, "She's

controlling Mason."

Connor looked shocked. "You can do that?"

Once more Diana sent a telepathic command in Mason's direction. *Do a backflip.* To the astonishment of the gathered students, Mason crouched down, gathered himself, then sprang upwards in a tuck. At the apex of his flip, Aiken realized that Mason wouldn't make it all the way over and would probably land on his head. Reaching out with his telekinetic ability, he pictured a hand grabbing onto the upside-down student and gently lowering him to the ground.

Diana removed her commands from Mason's mind and he sat up, blinking owlishly. Aiken sent a telepathic thought in Diana's direction. *Careful, he almost hurt himself there.* Chastised, Diana sent back, *Sorry about that. I didn't realise until he was too far into it.* The intimate mind-to-mind contact with Diana sent shivers down Aiken's spine.

Connor watched the interplay with interest, surmising what had happened. Nicole asked, "Did you just catch him in midair?"

Aiken shrugged, "Yeah, he was going to land on his neck."

"Nifty," she said, "you'll have to teach me how to do that so fast."

"You mean you can…" Aiken trailed off.

"Yeah, I was about to tell you guys when Shouty McLoud Pants over there deafened us all."

"Don't call her that," Aiken responded hotly.

"Yeah," Connor chimed in, "It's 'Shouty McLoud Brain', duh." He and Nicole both rolled their eyes at Aiken's obvious discomfiture.

"Yeah, you're both hilarious," he said sarcastically.

"We try," Nicole smiled at him sweetly.

Liam was trying to regain everyone's attention. The trio turned to look at him as he waved his arms in the air. "Well," he said lightly, "That will certainly come in handy when you want someone to write a paper for you."

The assembled students chuckled uneasily. "Let's start again at the top, shall we?" he continued. "We know that Gwen has telekinesis, as does Jillian, though a slightly different manifestation. Hugo can make himself invisible and Isaac can walk through walls. Faith can apparently see anything she wants, including whether you're wearing boxers or briefs." Another chuckle.

Connor leaned over to Aiken. "A thong for me," he joked.

"Ew," Aiken grimaced, "Way too much

information."

Liam continued, "Diana can turn people into acrobats. I can, uh, teleport?" he checked with Connor. Connor nodded. "Teleport objects, while Connor here can teleport himself. Ethan is telepathic on the receiving end, while Aiken appears to have both projective and receptive telepathic abilities." At this, a murmur of interest swept over the crowd. "Anyone else out there with more than one talent?" Liam asked.

Tentatively, Nicole put up her hand, as did Diana's friend Olivia. Liam addressed the older girl first. "What can you do, Liv?"

"Well," she began, "I'm set up like Aiken there. I can send and receive thoughts." Another murmur of interest. Aiken could see in Connor's mind that his friend wanted to let everyone know that Aiken had more than just telepathic abilities. He reached out mentally and surreptitiously calmed Connor down a notch.

Liam turned to Nicole expectantly. "I have three tricks," she started. "I can teleport myself and objects, I can move things around without teleporting them, and I can send and receive thoughts like Liv."

The other students looked on enviously. "That's actually five," Connor clarified for her. "And I'll bet the self-telekinesis is hiding up there somewhere, too. It was for Aiken." The last part rushed out.

Aiken gave an annoyed glance at his friend, then looked around to gauge the reaction of his classmates. Some were clearly envious of his good fortune, others disgusted. Aiken wanted to disappear, but decided it would be a bad time to demonstrate that he also had that ability. He looked over to his right and saw a sight that made him feel a little better. Diana was looking him over with undisguised interest. Deep in his mind, where he hoped none of the other telepaths could seek it out, he thought, *Ha, at last I got her attention.*

Liam spoke into the dark silence, "Well, Mason, we haven't heard a peep from you. What did you end up with?"

Something really lame, no doubt. The telepaths in the group had no trouble identifying Olivia's tone.

Mason muttered something unintelligible. "Sorry, what was that?" Liam asked.

"I said," Mason murmured softly, "I can prognosticate to an extent."

"English please," Ethan joked.

"I catch glimpses of events that have yet to unfold," Mason clarified.

"Maybe I'm slow, but I'm still not getting it," Ethan responded.

"He can see the future, more or less," Gwen rescued her brother. "It comes and goes, and it's not very clear, from what I understand." Mason nodded gratefully at his sister, then sat back down to astonished glances from his peers.

"The question is," Connor whispered to Aiken, "can he tell me what's for supper so I know whether to come over to your house?"

Aiken snorted. "You will find a way to turn all of these abilities into something to do with food, won't you?" he replied softly.

"What else are we going to do with them?" his friend asked, only half joking.

Liam turned once again to Diana's group. "I nearly forgot about you, Penny. What's your deal?"

Instead of answering, Penny pointed to a nearby fountain. The whole group swivelled around to get a better look. At first, no one could see anything. Everyone craned their necks a little more in order to be the first to catch a glimpse. Nothing for a beat, then Jillian softly exclaimed, "Oh!"

More and more people began to see what Penny was doing with the water. Somehow, she'd fashioned the individual spouts into a braided pattern of water, individual streams flowing over and around and through each other to make an astonishing display of uncanny patterned beauty. One of the streams coming from a spout rose higher and higher than the braided trio until it looked like it was spraying off into space. As the water fell down from the heights, it moulded itself into contours and forms that no water had ever made naturally before. It started off with a series of simple geometric forms, a triangle, a bas relief pyramid. The water droplets flowed, recombined and formed new shapes. The students recognized the face staring back at them out of the spray. It was Penny's own. While the ebony skin tone was obviously absent, Penny's large brown eyes could be seen peering out from the mist, and even her ringlets were visible, bouncing around as usual. The face blinked and moved its watery eyes around in time with the flesh and blood Penny, then disappeared with a splash of the curtain of water.

When the little show was done, some of the students applauded. "Wow," breathed Nicole. "That was amazing."

Penny wasn't finished. Whispering in Hugo's ear, she stood him up facing her. "Are you sure?" Hugo asked her. She nodded, "When I give you the signal."

"I don't want to hurt you," Hugo persisted.

"Don't worry," Penny assured him. "I'll

be fine."

Hugo looked resigned, but lined himself up with Penny. Penny closed her eyes and composed herself. When she opened them again, she nodded at Hugo. He cocked his fist back and took a swing at Penny's midsection. The punch never landed. Instead, Hugo's knuckles skittered off Penny's abdomen, throwing him off balance. He caught himself, then smirked at Penny. Raising his arm again, he aimed for her shoulder and swung, much harder than last time. His fist stopped dead mere centimetres from her skin, but stop it did, like Hugo had struck a brick wall. He dropped his hand in amazement, shaking it ruefully.

The rest of the students clapped now. Penny mock-curtsied, then went back to her original spot and sat down.

"Wow," Aiken murmured.

"I'll say," Connor replied. "I thought for sure she was going to end up on her butt."

"Yeah," Aiken responded distractedly.

"Why do I get the feeling that we're not talking about the same thing?" Connor was curious now. "Spill it."

Aiken turned to him, "Oh, I was watching her mind when she did that. It was astounding. It's like the telekinesis thing, only on a much smaller scale. She manipulated the molecules of water and then air to do and be what she wanted them to be. I'd guess that's what Isaac's doing, too, when he does whatever it is he does."

Aiken screwed up his face in concentration. "Here, now try and pinch my arm," he said, holding it out to Connor.

"Okay," his friend responded to the challenge, "but don't whine if this hurts too much."

Connor first attempted to just grab onto Aiken's arm, but every time he felt that he was getting a grip on it, his fingers would slide off as if coated in oil. Next, Connor tried swinging his own arm into Aiken's arm. No luck. It was like hitting a wall. Connor shook the numbness out of his hand. Finally, Connor attempted flicking Aiken's arm with his fingernail. Once more, his efforts proved futile.

"Nifty," he remarked.

"I'll say," Aiken replied. "A person could stop bullets if their mind was up to it."

Nicole looked on in interest. "So you can do whatever you put your mind to?" She asked. "Literally?"

"More or less," Aiken responded.

"More or less?" Connor countered. "There's not a single ability that you've tried that you haven't been able to do. That's just a little more than 'more or less'."

Aiken shook his head, "Let's just keep some of that under wraps, shall we?"

His friends were apprehensive. "Got something to hide?" Connor asked.

"No, no, nothing like that," Aiken assured them. "Just some of the looks I was getting earlier, well, let's just say I have a feeling it would be a lot worse if we told them I can do almost everything that everyone else can do."

Connor nodded at that, while Nicole looked thoughtful. Liam cleared his throat to once more get everyone's attention after Penny's demonstration. "So by my count," the oldest student summarised, "that's all of us who were at the demonstration yesterday. Everyone's got something or other, except, it seems, Kaira."

Aiken put his hand up at that point. When Liam acknowledged him, Aiken said, "There may be a way to conclusively prove whether or not Kaira has some ability." This announcement raised eyebrows around the group.

"What do you mean?" Liam asked.

Aiken explained the situation with the brain imaging that he'd undergone, and the notion that the drive test or something related to it had somehow altered the underlying structures of their brains. He glossed over the part where he had overwritten the medical staff's memories. He was pretty sure that wouldn't go over well with everyone.

"Is it dangerous? Are we going to die?" the questions poured forth.

Aiken raised his hands, "As far as the doctor was able to surmise, there weren't any particular dangers tied into the changes. I specifically asked him about aneurysms and embolisms and he didn't find any." He paused, "So we're going to be okay. And Kaira can check to see if she's been affected."

At this, Kaira smiled tightly. She still looked somewhat apprehensive, but Aiken could tell that it was now apprehension that she wouldn't have a talent, rather than apprehensive that she would.

Don't worry, he thought at her, *I bet you have some amazing ability that no one else has.* Kaira started when his voice entered her mind, but when his message was complete, she smiled gratefully over at him.

"So, they know about us now?" Ethan asked uneasily.

Aiken had been dreading that someone might ask this question. "No," he stated softly.

"Why not?" Olivia was more belligerent.

"Because," Aiken confessed quietly, "They don't recall performing the test." As the implications of what he had said began to sink in, the students began to look nervously at one another.

"Can all you telepaths do that?" It was Isaac. "I mean, can you all mess around in our heads?"

Ethan fielded this one, "I know I can't... it may be a projective ability."

"Well," Isaac pursued, "that still leaves Aiken, Diana, Liv and Nicole. Can they all screw around with our heads?"

Nicole spoke up. "Honestly," she said, "I don't know. I've never tried. I'm kind of afraid to." She paused. "And I guarantee that I won't be trying it on any of you," she stated emphatically. Olivia nodded in assent. Diana looked deep in thought, and Aiken was looking around to see if there was still fear on anyone's face.

Olivia spoke up, "I propose a pact. We agree not to use our powers on each other without the express permission of the other person."

"How will we know if you have, though?" It was Hugo. "I mean, if Diana orders me to do something, I pretty much have to obey, right? Or if Aiken here can change my memories, how would I even know that I'd been messed with?"

Liam grimaced, but it was Diana who

spoke. "There's just going to have to be a level of trust, right? First, we don't want to end up at Aldrin because someone was using their ability and got caught at it, and second, you yourself have an ability that some of the rest of us are going to have to trust isn't being used on us."

The other students nodded at this. One by one, they each pledged not to use their talents on each other without permission.

"What about people outside the group?" Ethan asked. "I don't want to end up vivisected because someone decided to play a prank that went wrong."

"What, you want us to ask permission of other people before we use our secret abilities on them?" Connor asked.

"No, I'm just saying we need to be careful if we don't want to get caught."

"That's leaving aside the whole 'right and wrong' aspect," Nicole spoke up.

"What?" Connor turned to her.

"I mean, it's one thing to talk about not getting caught. It's another to talk about whether we should even be reading people's minds or getting them to do things in the first place."

Aiken was grateful Nicole had brought the subject up. He'd been having some doubts about how he'd used his abilities already that day, and it was only one day into having them.

Nicole continued, "These abilities aren't toys. We have the potential to cause a lot of damage if we're not careful, or even if we start thinking that we're better than other people because we have them and they don't."

Aiken could see some of the students considering Nicole's words.

Diana spoke up again, "I think it's going to come down to trust again. I'm not saying that we should just do whatever we want to people outside of the group, but I know I've used m ability without really meaning to, and it's brand-new to me."

The rest of the group nodded in agreement.

"We can't just not use them," Diana continued. "I'm not sure that we could, and I'm not convinced we should, either."

"That's not what I was saying," Nicole responded. "I just want us to be aware of what we're doing."

"Fair enough. Next up on the agenda," Liam was talking again, "What do we do now?"

"What do you mean?" Hugo called out.

"I mean, we've already established that we need to keep our abilities to ourselves for the time being. We have no idea how many more people there are out there with the same talents as we have, and we have no idea what side effects, if any, there are to using them." He looked at Aiken, "No offense, but one brain scan the day after the event is not that conclusive."

Aiken nodded his agreement. More scans were needed to produce a more detailed view of what was going on.

"I have an idea about that," Ethan spoke up.

"What's that?" Liam asked.

"Well, some of us have the ability to read thoughts. What if the receptive telepaths ferreted out the information we need from the doc's mind, then we could do our own scans in the clinic after hours with the help of the teleport crew." He had another thought. "Or," he continued, "Faith might be able to scan us if she knew what she was looking for."

The gathered students looked at each other with enthusiasm. "We'll have to get Faith into the loop," Liam mused.

Olivia lifted her hand at this. "Already done," she said. "I've been sending her all the goings-on here."

"Is she willing to help out?" Liam asked.

"For sure," came the reply. "We may need some memory redux on the infirmary nurses and a doctor or two though. If that's an okay use of our abilities."

Liam looked over at Aiken. "Think you're up to it?"

Aiken grimaced, and answered. "If I have to, I guess." He heard a couple of surreptitious sighs and chalked them up to relief that he wasn't enthusiastic to meddle with people's memories.

With a plan for action (or, rather, inaction), the students were much more comfortable about the state of things. They decided that since they didn't have class the next day either they would meet in the same place at the same time, once the possibility of scanning had been established.

The students drifted away in small groups, chatting animatedly everything that had just happened and all they'd learned. Aiken stayed behind with Ethan, Connor, Nicole and Liam to plan how they would accomplish the scanning of all the students.

Chapter Twelve
3:00pm Tuesday, May 19th, 2139

Aiken spoke first, "I think our first choice should be to have Faith scan us, if she's up to it. It avoids the possibility of getting caught breaking in to the clinic. Also we don't have to wait until evening to get the scan done."

"On the downside," Ethan countered, "we can't keep records of the scan like we could with the imaging machine."

Good point, Aiken conceded. *If we're going for longitudinal studies, it might be better to have a hard copy to compare.*

"Maybe we can do both," Liam mused. "We could use Faith's ability to get up-to-the-minute snapshots, and take scans more gradually on a more regular basis for comparison purposes."

"Yeah," Nicole added, "Faith can tell us if our brains are going to explode, and the machine can tell us if they're slowly turning to mush."

The others chuckled, then grew serious. "Are any of us actually worried about either possibility?" Connor asked.

"Not really, no," Aiken responded. "At least, I'm not."

"Well, you had your scan done already," Liam answered. "You can afford to be more cavalier."

"Well…" Connor started. Aiken moved to stop him, knowing what he was going to divulge, then relented. He had to start trusting someone. "Aiken seems to have gotten a larger dose of whatever it was that caused our abilities. He can do them all."

Ethan and Liam were stunned. "What do you mean?" Liam finally voiced.

"He can do everything," Connor repeated. "Telepath, teleport, telekinesis, and also Isaac and Penny's abilities."

"Wow," Ethan exclaimed. "No wonder you were worried about your brain, after what happened to Mr. Bertram."

Aiken demurred, "I haven't done Hugo's

invisibility or Faith's vision, or Mason's fortune-telling."

"Yeah, because you haven't tried," Connor shot back. Aiken inclined his head in concession. "What you need to do," his friend continued, "is take a peek inside their noggins while they're doing their thing, like you did with Penny. That should give you all the information you need."

"That aside," Liam said looking sharply at Aiken, "I think we're set up – Ethan, you and I will go get the information we need from the medical folks, and only that information, and Nicole, Connor and Aiken, you need to get Faith up to date. Once Ethan's got the necessary information from the clinic, we'll meet up with you in the infirmary, where Aiken can pass it from your mind into Faith's and remove any memories from the people there that might get them asking questions." He looked around and got everyone's assent. "If Faith can convince them that she's fine, she can get out of there, and start peeking at our brains."

The group split up and headed to their respective destinations. Aiken's group headed to the infirmary to see if Faith's situation required intervention. Because all three were teleports, they had Aiken peer ahead telepathically, then they popped themselves over to just outside the doors of the infirmary, which was located on the outer edge of the dome.

Aiken and Nicole both peeked inside with their telepathic senses and, registering nothing out of the ordinary, they both motioned to Connor at the same time that it was time to enter. "Okay," he teased, "that was creepy."

"Oh, like everything else that's been going on is perfectly normal," Nicole countered.

"Point."

"Can we just go in there?" Aiken asked them both. Laughing, the trio entered the infirmary section and headed for where the two telepaths knew Faith was resting. When they reached her bedside, the first thing they noticed was that her still clear-blue eyes weren't focused anywhere in particular.

"Uh, hi Faith," Connor began.

"Hey guys," she replied. "Don't worry about the eye thing. I can see fine without them. Apparently, my optic nerve has degraded enough that it won't carry signals either way, so they're basically out of my control."

Aiken and Connor looked at each other, slightly weirded out by the wandering eyes.

"Yeah, I get that a lot," Faith said, startling the pair. "Don't worry, though, I can probably see a lot better than you can, now."

She reached up and brushed a lock of red hair from in front of those bewildering eyes. She smiled impishly, winking at Connor, who looked more than somewhat flustered. Her freckled nose wrinkled in amusement at Connor's discomfort.

"Yeah," Nicole interposed, "that's why we're here."

"I know," Faith answered, sitting up. It was slightly disconcerting to see someone whose eyes were drifting reach out precisely for the pillow and fluff it up, without having to paw around for it. "Liv told me."

"So," Aiken asked, "You think you're up to it?"

"I'm willing to try, but I can't promise anything. I haven't tried looking at something in such a dark place before."

Connor looked thoughtful. "Have you tried viewing on anything other than the visible light spectrum? I mean, microscopic and telescopic vision are basically enhanced forms of the spectrum we can see already... Although," he said, answering his own question, "Your ability to see through things may not be."

"Actually," Faith corrected him, "I think seeing through things is a depth of field issue. Like lenses allow you certain focal lengths, my sight allows me to focus on something beyond an intervening object." She paused for a second. "Your idea about different wavelengths might be interesting, though. I'll have to try."

"I bet if you somehow loosened your sight from micrometer wavelengths to millimetre wavelengths, you could see into the infrared," Connor encouraged.

"I have no idea how to do that," Faith said dejectedly.

"You guys are such nerds," Nicole teased. "Micrometres and infrared... why not just try to see how hot something is?"

Faith brightened at this, and turned her head toward the light fixture on the wall. "Uh, you're not going to get much of a heat reading from that," Aiken reminded her. "We use mostly light emitting diodes on the moon to cut down on the amount of power we use. The lights that aren't LEDs are lightpipes from the exterior of the dome. No incandescents."

Faith reddened in embarrassment. "Oops. I keep forgetting little things like that."

"Well, you're still new here," Connor reassured her. "Give yourself another couple of months and you'll be an old pro at all our cutting-edge technology. And by cutting edge, I mean that it's so old you'll hurt yourself with it if you don't watch what you're doing... uh, so to speak," he said, gesturing at her eyes.

Once again, Faith looked around for a source of heat to zone in on. Finding a hot water bottle that another patient was using on his back, she tried to see how hot it was. With her permission, Aiken monitored her talent while she was using it to see if he could duplicate her feat. He noticed a subtle shift in the texture, for lack of a better word, of what she was seeing.

"Oh," Faith exclaimed softly. "I can see it all now... Wow." The texture changed again. "Now I'm seeing what looks like the EM fields of all the electronic gear in here. They're radiating out from each source."

Aiken was impressed that she'd so readily adapted her talent to a new use. "Now all we have to do," he said, "is find out what frequency that scanning machine is operating at, and you can tune your sight to that and check out people's brain structures just like the machine."

"First, though," Connor injected, "We need to bust Faith out of here. Would it be easier to convince the medical staff that nothing happened in the first place, or that nothing happened to improve Faith's vision?"

"Dunno," Aiken said thoughtfully, "I guess it depends on whether Faith wants to pretend she's blind, or pretend her eyes work properly."

Nicole nodded, "Either way, someone's going to find out sooner or later. I mean, on the one hand, look at her eyes. No one's going to figure out that she shouldn't be able to see with those? On the other hand, it will be fairly obvious that you can see if you start talking about the colour of things or where they are in relation to each other."

As the four of them were pondering this, Liam and Ethan strolled through the doors to the infirmary. Ethan had a cat-that-ate-the-canary grin on his face. Spotting the group around Faith's bed, the pair sauntered over.

"Easy as pie," proclaimed Ethan.

"What, you mean three point one four one five nine?" Connor joked. It was an old standby of his that he'd picked up from Mason Gabriel.

"You math nerds have a strange sense of humour," Liam said, having heard this one from Gwen's elder brother on more than one occasion.

"We try not to be too fractious," Connor shot back.

"That was terrible," Ethan groaned. "Stop, please."

"Fair enough," Connor conceded. "I take it things went well at the clinic."

"It was awesome," Ethan said. "I didn't even have to go inside. We just set up outside, with Liam standing watch. I felt around for a mind, then dove right in and found what I was looking for more or less right away."

Liam chimed in, "I was actually worried that something was wrong, it was so fast."

"Well," Connor mused, "I suppose it all happens at the speed of thought."

"Which is slower for some of us than others," Faith laughed.

"Let's not go there, shall we?" Nicole responded. "Have you made your decision, Faith?"

Both Ethan and Liam wanted to know what she was talking about, so Faith laid it out for them.

"What about something up the middle?" Liam proposed.

"What do you mean," Aiken asked.

"Well, what if you could convince the doctors that her optic nerve had partly regenerated, allowing her some sight, but not complete control of her eye movements?"

Aiken nodded thoughtfully. "If we're going to get them to believe something anyway, it might as well be something plausible, if not possible. As a bonus, Faith can 'get used to' her reduced visual acuity, and ease into using her mental vision."

"That's a great idea," Faith decided.

"Let's go with that. I've only been here for a day and I'm already sick of the beige on the walls."

"Yeah," Aiken wondered, "Why are hospitals and medical areas painted so drab?"

"Well, it because they don't want patients to have a reaction to a brighter colour," Connor answered.

"Not the time, boys, not the time," Nicole reminded them.

"Oh, yeah, I guess not," said Aiken sheepishly. He glanced over at Faith. "I'll need to know which people you dealt with, so I can modify them appropriately. Are any of them here right now?"

Faith nodded towards the nurses' station, "The cute one in scrubs over there."

"Uh, Faith... I'm a guy. I have no idea which one you're talking about."

Connor arched an eyebrow at him. "Okay, I'm a straight guy," Aiken conceded.

"The doctor with the brown hair wearing green scrubs talking to the nurse."

Aiken concentrated for a minute, his face tightening. "Okay, that's one. How many others were there?"

Faith thought for a moment, "I'm pretty sure there's only one other doctor, the eye guy. Also almost all the nurses. And my parents. Oh, and Diana's folks, too."

Aiken groaned as she listed them off. This could take a while. "Do we know where any of them are right now?"

Faith answered easily, "My parents are at work, and I'm pretty sure Diana's are too. It's still the middle of the day shift, so most of them should be at work. The couple night nurses might be at home, though."

"You'll have to get that information from one of the ones here before you clear them out, Aiken," Ethan said.

There's got to be an easier way, Aiken thought to himself. Then it came to him. *I'm going to get their images from your mind*, he sent to Faith. *That should speed things up a little.*

Faith nodded in assent, then prepared herself by scrunching her eyes closed and balling up her fists. Aiken laughed a little at the sight, but delved right in.

As he roamed the corridors of Faith's mind, he felt another mind's presence beside him. It felt familiar, then he recognised it as Nicole. She sent to him, *I want to see what you do, in case I ever need to.*

Fair enough, he shot back. *Follow me.*

He quickly found the memories he was looking for, since they were forefront in Faith's mind. Filing them away for reference, he withdrew his mental probe. Only seconds had passed, so Faith's face was still screwed up in concentration. He sent a light tendril of thought back in her direction. *All done.*

"Already?" she asked.

"Yep."

"What just happened?" Connor asked. Liam was also showing his confusion.

"I just decided to save a little time and go get the images of the people I'm looking for from the source." He indicated Faith with a nod.

"Okay, boy genius," Liam laughed. "Sounds like you're all set. You need any help chasing these folks down?"

Aiken shook his head, then reconsidered. "I wouldn't mind a lookout for when I'm rewriting their memories. I can't really focus on two things at once."

"Hey, he does have limits," Ethan exclaimed, teasing.

"Yeah, yeah," Aiken mock-groused. "Now, are you going to help me?"

"No, not me," Ethan replied, "You should take another teleport with you so you can get around faster. Either Connor or Nicole."

Aiken raised his eyebrows at those two. "Either of you interested?"

Nicole answered first, "I'm going to help Liam break Faith out of here. You boys go have your fun."

"Oh, fun. Is that what we're calling it?" Aiken asked sardonically.

"Hey," Ethan retorted, "we are the most powerful people in the dome right now. On all the Moon, for all we know. Maybe in the whole universe. I think that could be fun." As he said this, an amused glint was apparent in his eye.

"Yes, yes, mhwua ha ha, and all that," Connor droned as if bored.

"I see us older folks are going to have to keep an eye on you youngsters," Liam laughed.

"Yeah," Faith added, "Make sure you don't destroy the Solar system or something."

Nicole just shook her head worriedly.

Once each person had decided what they were going to do, the group separated. Aiken and Connor spent the rest of the afternoon tracking down those people who'd had contact with Faith and had the potential for letting the cat out of the bag. Connor would stand watch while Aiken would overwrite their memories with the story they'd concocted. Meanwhile, Ethan, Liam and Nicole got Faith out of the infirmary under the suddenly not-so-watchful eyes of the nursing staff, thanks to some mental prowess on Nicole's part. Once they'd seen her safely home, they went their separate ways.

Aiken and Connor finished their task a little later. "That was the last one," Aiken said.

"Good, 'cause I'm hungry," Connor replied.

"I'm so shocked," Aiken teased.

"Laugh all you want," Connor answered, "but it takes energy to use these mental talents, and I need to stock back up."

They agreed to meet in the morning to practice their abilities and each went back to their family's apartment.

Chapter Thirteen

6:00pm Tuesday, May 19th, 2139

When Aiken sat down to dinner that evening with his parents, he paid less attention than usual to their conversation. He was startled, then, to realize they were both looking at him expectantly.

"I... sorry, what?"

His mother chuckled. "Must have been a busy day, even with no school. You've been off somewhere else all meal."

His father looked askance at her. "He found out his teacher died, Moira. Of course his mind is elsewhere."

"No dad, it's not that. Well, it's partly that," Aiken amended. "It's also…" He paused. How to explain without giving anything away?

"What if I found out a way of knowing people's secrets? The ones they thought were completely private and inaccessible. When would it be okay to get that information?"

His parents both just stared at him for a second, then looked at each other, as if for support. Aiken realized that he could peer into their minds to see what they were thinking, but doing so while asking them under what circumstances that would be acceptable seemed a little like cheating on an ethics test.

His mother started, "Are you talking about hacking someone's communicator?"

"No, mom. It's not anything illegal. Just suppose I came across the information, or knew of a way I could get it without anyone knowing."

"Well, being legal doesn't always make something right," his father rumbled. "If you were going to use the information against that person, to compel them to do something they'd ordinarily be against, that would be blackmail no matter how you came across the information in the first place. Even if you just wanted to embarrass them, it would still be wrong."

"But what if nothing bad would happen

to that person?" Aiken persisted. "Or what if they were helped because I had the information?"

"Well," his mother answered. "If you found someone was doing something dangerous and they didn't want people to know about it, then it might be okay to use that information to get them help."

"But we let people do things that are bad for themselves all the time," Aiken argued.

"Well, when people are old enough to judge for themselves whether or not they want to be responsible for the outcome of whatever they're doing, we generally just let people learn from their mistakes, unless their mistake is going to hurt other people."

When Aiken looked confused, his father took pity and explained further. "Look at drunk driving. Generally, we don't put limits on alcohol for people of legal age, but when they endanger another person by driving, we have a law in place to prevent that."

"So, if someone was going to harm someone else, then it would be okay to get information from them that wouldn't normally be available?"

"I suppose so," his father said.

"But how can you tell ahead of time whether you need that information or not?"

Aiken persisted. "If you have to have the information to know whether or not a person is going to hurt someone else, but the way to get that information is… problematic, when do you choose whether to get the information in the first place?"

"Aiken, that's a problem that governments have been wrestling with for years. Most democracies have generally favoured individual freedom over governmental access to information."

"What?"

"What your father is trying to say is that in an ideal world, we'd be able to prevent crimes by knowing ahead of time who was going to commit them, but the way of gathering that information would be so invasive that most people are only okay with trying to find that information after something's happened."

Aiken sighed in frustration. This wasn't really addressing the problem of whether or not it was okay to use his abilities. Well, more specifically his ability to read minds. Most of the other talents didn't have the same privacy issues, but being able to access, not to mention overwrite, people's thoughts seemed like a potential minefield.

It seemed like his parents might not necessarily agree with the uses to which he'd put his abilities that day, despite the fact that everything he'd done had been to protect himself and the rest of the class. He might need to be a little more choosey about using his abilities for less than noble purposes.

He thought of the other telepaths in the group. Olivia and Nicole had already shown that they were uncomfortable using their powers broadly, and he was positive that Diana would only want to use her powers unselfishly. That left himself and Ethan. Given the conversation they'd had that morning, he was pretty sure Ethan could be counted on not to go indiscriminately rummaging around in people's heads.

The topic of conversation turned to more mundane subjects and he spent the rest of the meal answering his parents with only half his attention as questions swirled through his mind.

That night, Aiken Drum dreamt not only of rainbow-hued lights, but also of a strange man illuminated by flame and sparks and smelling of smoke and death who walked toward him with arms outstretched. He awoke bolt upright in a tangle of sweaty sheets. Even as he tried to recall the dream, its tattered tendrils faded to the back of his unconscious mind where thought could not follow. Sleepy once more, he fell back into his bed and was asleep in seconds. He dreamt no more that night.

Chapter Fourteen

7:00am Wednesday, May 20th, 2139

The next day dawned bright and sunny, like every day (and, well, every night) in the Peary Dome. Aiken awoke slowly, savouring the feeling of all his senses waking as well. A new world of experience was open to him in a way it had not been the day before. His telepathic sense quested out and found the comforting presences of his mother and father seated, as usual, across from each other at the breakfast table. As he lay comfortably in bed, Aiken let his mind wander, free to explore as it would. He could almost feel his boundaries expanding as he tried to take in a view of the universe. Past the walls of the apartment he went, out of the dome he travelled, larger now than the moon, encompassing the whole solar system. He let his mind drift on the currents of interstellar dust ejected by the solar system and carried away on the invisible wind from the Sun. As his field of view magnified yet again, he felt himself joining with the universe. No longer sure where he ended and otherness began, he felt at one with everything. As he returned to himself, for the moment when his mind encompassed the whole of Peary Dome, he experienced a moment where he was connected to every living person in the dome. Some were just waking up, as he was. Some were at work. Some were going through some part of their daily routine. Aiken saw them all and, for a fractional part of an instant, joined with them all. He came back to himself, sat up and started his day.

The day passed moderately quickly, with Aiken meeting up with Connor in the morning and practicing their abilities. Aiken found that, having observed Faith using her talent the previous day, he was able to use the mental sight ability that had been in him all along.

Once school restarted the day after, the time seemed to pass more quickly. The students adapted quickly to the new realities of their

124

existence. The teacher who replaced Mr. Bertram arrived from Tranquility Station, and given that he'd had no previous experience with the classes, he wasn't aware that the tone of the course was different. The telepaths had to resist the temptation to get the answers directly from the sub's mind, just as the teleports and telekinetics had to resist the temptation to play jokes on the classmates with disappearing styluses and chairs that moved out from under them. As it turned out, the people that it was hardest to keep from discovering the secret were the students who weren't watching the drive test. Out of a school of around a thousand students (from the primary grades up through high school), only fifteen had ended up with special abilities. This could have led to some serious problems between the gifted and the non-gifted, but since the students who'd gained abilities were still, for the most part, convinced that keeping them hidden was all that stood between them and a lifetime as a lab rat, they managed to keep them under wraps for the most part.

The students who did discover the secret could be redacted back into naiveté, but Aiken was uncomfortable overwriting memories wholesale. It turned out to be much easier to talk them into believing that they had witnessed a display of some advanced physics experiment (all the gifted students were, after all, in either of the two classes involved in the physics course), and so this is what he had settled on.

The physics class had packed the first couple of pews at the funeral for Mr. Bertram, some looking genuinely distraught. After his enlunement, life returned more of less to routine, if not exactly normal.

The gifted group had taken to meeting a couple times a week in the Park to share stories and give and ask advice on the use of their abilities. It was during one of these meetings, about a week and a half after the drive test that Kaira discovered what her ability was. She had been scanned both by Faith and by the mechanical imaging device to confirm that she had indeed been altered in a fashion similar to the other students (they discovered through comparing their scans to the ones on file that no two students had been affected in the exact same fashion), but nothing had manifested itself.

Gwen was practicing her telekinetic ability on other students, picking them up and moving them around, or using her ability to place them in ridiculous poses. Nicole had heard about Connor's reconnaissance teleport trick, where he imagined himself to the top of the park, looked around while he fell, then popped himself back to safety. She thought that it might be modified for use with a telekinetic and anyone else, so she asked Gwen to lift her up high in the air over the Park (after making certain that no one was watching) to try. Gwen was willing and everything was going well until Nicole realised just how high she'd gotten, the ceiling in the Park, like all ceilings on the Moon, being quite a bit higher than Earth-normal. She panicked and somehow blocked Gwen's telekinetic ability. Gwen was no longer able to hang on to her, and Nicole fell. Aiken and Liam, the only other two who would have been able to help, were distracted discussing something that seemed important, and by the time they were in a position to do anything, it was too late. Nicole had hit the ground – hard.

Everyone rushed to the spot where Nicole lay, arms and legs bent unnaturally underneath her. It looked like she'd remembered her own telekinetic abilities just before hitting the ground and had slowed herself somewhat, but not enough to avoid injury.

Faith and Aiken used their mental sight to look at Nicole, who had a series of fractures in her extremities and internal bleeding in her torso. They were just deciding who would teleport her to the infirmary when Kaira spoke softly, "Wait."

Aiken assessed the situation quickly. Something in Kaira seemed to be pulling her towards Nicole's broken body. As Kaira approached the fallen form, Aiken could feel the energy build-up that seemed to be radiating from all of Kaira's somatic nerve cells. Kaira knelt beside Nicole and straightened her limbs. She set to work with her hands, instinctively moving her hands in a flowing pattern over the prostrate girl. Aiken looked on mentally and saw what was happening on a molecular level. He was astonished. Kaira seemed to be reaching into Nicole's cells and repairing them. Bones knit, blood flowed back into wounds which then sealed themselves up. Traumas vanished as if they had never been.

Kaira soon sat back on her heels as Nicole stirred. She opened her eyes and looked up at Kaira. "Thanks," she whispered. The rest of the students stood there in awed silence. Even with people who could make themselves appear and disappear at will, even with friends who could speak directly into their minds, the group had never had it hit home so strongly the power that they all possessed as in that moment.

Connor was the first to break the silence. "Whoa," he started, then stopped. Even his usual quips seemed to have abandoned him.

Aiken thought to Kaira, *See, I told you that*

you would have some amazing ability. At this, Kaira lowered her face into her hands and began to cry, the energy leaving her now that the crisis was over.

As if a spell had broken, the other students quickly moved to comfort Kaira and check on Nicole. Aiken hung back, still alert for undue attention from people outside the group. He thought he'd felt a curious interest from someone not part of the group, but the feeling dissipated almost as quickly as he'd felt it, so he swept it from his mind. He turned back to the group and saw that they were getting ready to disperse, the meeting time being just about over for the day.

As some of the students started to leave, Aiken walked over to talk to Nicole and Kaira about the experience. The two were still sitting on the moist soil where Nicole had fallen, talking earnestly. Seeing that they were otherwise occupied, Aiken turned to leave.

Nicole spoke behind him. "Aiken, don't worry, it's okay."

He turned back, "What?"

"It's okay that you didn't catch me. I can see that you blame yourself, and I'm telling you it's okay. It wasn't your fault."

Curiously, she was right. Aiken had been angry with himself, but only just realised it when Nicole mentioned it. He felt the tension he'd not known was there ease out of his back and he smiled gratefully at Nicole. "Thanks."

"No problem."

With a slightly lighter step, Aiken turned to go once more. As he headed back home, he felt a familiar presence following him. When he reached the corridor where his apartment was located, he stopped and waited expectantly. Soon enough, Diana came walking around the corner, slowing when she saw that Aiken was waiting for her.

"I sometimes forget how powerful your gifts are," she said offhandedly to him. "I guess they suit you."

"Thanks, I think," Aiken replied, nervous as always around Diana, despite the change in circumstances. Most of his classmates were beginning to see him as a collection of talents, no longer the "first moon baby." Aiken wasn't sure he was completely comfortable with the change.

"Anyway," Diana continued, "I was wondering if you'd mind helping me out with my gift. I'm having a little trouble with my directionality." She paused. "It can actually be kind of embarrassing to send a thought to the wrong person."

Aiken's nervousness increased tenfold. Spend time alone with Diana? *I could do that,* he acknowledged her mentally. "Where and when would you like to practice?" he asked aloud.

Diana appeared to think for a moment. "How about you come over to my place tomorrow evening?" she offered. "My parents will be out, so we don't have to worry about them finding out." Diana said this without a hint of guile.

"Uh, sure, I guess... that will work," Aiken managed.

"Great!" Diana gushed. "See you then, Aiken," she said, letting her hand linger on his arm, then slide off.

Aiken floated the rest of the way home, his feet planted firmly on the ground.

Chapter Fifteen
Thursday, May 28th, 2139

The next evening couldn't come fast enough for Aiken. The prospect of spending time alone with Diana simultaneously thrilled and terrified him. *At least,* he consoled himself, *we're going to be doing something I'm moderately good at.* He thought up all the exercises he could for practicing the projective telepathic ability. He had a hard time thinking of many, partly because of his anxiety for the practice session, and partly because his abilities had come to him so naturally that he hadn't needed a lot of practice to become proficient at them.

The school day crawled along, though

there was a bit of a bright spot at lunch time while he, Connor and Nicole were eating lunch. Diana left her group of friends to come over and say hi. A little thrill went up Aiken's spine when she appeared at their table and stayed to converse for a couple of minutes. When she left, both of his friends teased him about it, but he didn't care – he was walking on air.

When supper with his parents was finished and the appointed hour drew near, Aiken thought about simply teleporting into Diana's residence. Deciding that would probably be rude, he walked over to the apartment suite she shared with her parents.

He knocked on the door and waited. Knocking again, he reached inside with his telepathic sense. He felt Diana draw near to the door and withdrew his mental probe. When she opened the door, he felt his jaw drop. Diana had done her hair up in an elegant knot that showed off her neck to good advantage. She wore a simple dress that, in the moon's reduced gravity, swished lightly every time she twisted from side to side. The neckline plunged rather precipitously, and he felt his eyes drawn downward. Realising he was staring, he snapped his eyes upwards, embarrassed.

"Wow," he managed. "I feel underdressed. I thought we were practicing telepathy."

"No need to look frumpy doing it," Diana responded. "And you look fine," she reassured him. "Come on in."

Aiken entered her family's apartment. He realised he'd never seen an apartment quite this large in Peary Dome before. Of course, since Diana's parents were administrators, they were allotted slightly more room than the average family. As he looked around, he realised that he'd never seen an apartment that had so many things, either. Apparently, the Lafontaines had a larger than usual cargo allotment as well. Sculptures stood on accent tables, paintings hung on the walls beneath soft accent lighting. The sofa appeared to be made with real wood, a luxury on the moon, where pressed regolith, or duracrete, formed the basis of most furniture. *That must have cost a small fortune to have sent up here*, he thought to himself.

As he glanced around, he noted other items that looked like they were fairly valuable. Diana went into the kitchen to get them something to drink while they practiced, so Aiken took the time to inspect some of the items up close. In one corner, a clock that Aiken recognised from photos as being a grandfather clock ticked merrily away. Aiken found the unfamiliar noise somewhat soothing. It was a reminder of the stability of things to him. As long as someone wound a clock like this, it would go on ticking, always at the same speed, always the same number of ticks in a minute, same number in an hour, every hour. *Constancy*, Aiken thought. A person could live with a clock like this to get a sense of permanence, of steadiness.

Diana returned with the drinks and Aiken soon forgot about the room's contents. They sat down together on the couch, turned towards one another, while Aiken explained to Diana the exercises he'd managed to come up with.

They went over some of the basic ones, but Aiken continued to be distracted when Diana's leg would bump into his. They were running a set of drills designed to focus the telepath's projection on the intended target. Aiken thought that Diana was probably better than she gave herself credit for, but found a couple of areas in her projections that needed some work. They went over these, until Diana was able to focus a telepathic hail on Aiken's receptive probe halfway across the entire Dome.

They were taking a break from the mental exercise when Diana said, "I want to practice my command skill as well. After that thing with Mason the first day, I've been a little afraid to try the command tone. Even when people have said it's okay."

Aiken readily agreed. Anything to spend some more time with Diana. They sat opposite each other on the couch, and Aiken showed her the difference between sending and commanding. "I'll let you practice on me," he said, "but I'm going to shield so I retain conscious thought and I can tell you how you're doing."

Diana nodded her comprehension. "Remember," Aiken continued, "the easiest way to get someone to do something is to let them think they came up with the idea on their own. Connor's let me try this out on him, and I've found that it might be faster just to blast the command at your subject, but it will be more convincing and last longer if you place it in certain parts of their brain and let it percolate to the surface on its own."

"Fair enough," Diana said. As Aiken was composing himself in preparation to shield himself from the coming mental onslaught, Diana struck. *Kiss me*, she ordered.

Aiken had no choice but to obey. He turned his head and brought his lips up to meet Diana's. When their lips first touched, Aiken felt the fulfilled compulsion falling away. He reached up with his hand, cupped the side of Diana's face and deepened their kiss.

When he finally pulled back, he gave her a long look. "Why did you do that?" he asked.

"Would you have otherwise?" she asked.

"Probably not," he admitted.

"Well, then," she said, tilting her head to the side. He reached for her again, and this time of his own volition, brushed his lips against hers.

Aiken left a little over half an hour later, his head spinning. He knew he had to get home quickly or his parents would worry, but he couldn't help taking a little detour. He went to the Park and floated himself up to the apex of the dome to send his mind out to the stars with nothing between them and him except a thin layer of mesoporous silica. He pressed his cheek against the cold of the dome and closed his eyes. Once again, he allowed his telepathic sense to expand to fill the whole of the dome. He felt once more the connection to every being below him. He lingered for minutes more, then brought himself back down to the sprinkler-slicked surface of the Park and went home.

Chapter Sixteen
Thursday, June 11th, 2139

The next two weeks passed in a similar manner. Aiken and Diana would meet every couple of nights for "study" sessions. Surprisingly, given their other activities, Diana was actually making progress with her projective ability, to the point where she could accurately project a thought clear across the dome to a ten centimetre margin of error.

"Pretty good," Aiken said to her, giving her a quick kiss. "I bet you could hit a target in Crisium Base, if you tried hard enough."

"I don't know," Diana said. "The farther away I try to go, the farther off the mark I get.

By the time I got that far away, I wouldn't be able to hit anything in the whole Mare, let alone the base."

"Wouldn't it be nice to show off a little to everyone at the next meeting?" Aiken persisted.

Diana smiled slyly, "You're the only one I really want to impress, and you know I can't do it."

"You don't need to impress me," Aiken replied smoothly. "Plus, I think you can do it."

Diana searched his face for any hint mockery. Finding none, she leaned over and kissed him, then said, "You believe in me so much that you make me think I really can do it." She sat back into the couch and closed her eyes, composing herself. "Ready when you are."

Aiken sent a tendril of thought out effortlessly to Crisium Base. "Okay," he said, "try hailing over there. I'm on the second level, in the north-west corner at the edge of the dome."

Diana screwed up her face in concentration, which Aiken found endearing. Soon enough, he felt the questing edge of her telepathic sense close to where he'd extended his mental listening. She was mere metres away from where his receptive probe lay waiting. Scooting closer to her on the couch, he took her hand in his and murmured encouragement to her. Her projective sense touched the edge of his receptive sense and a charge passed between the two of them where they were joined at the hand. Their respective telepathic senses snapped back to their physical location, still entwined.

"Whoa," Aiken said.

"Yeah, wow," Diana added. "That was a thrill." She reached out and caressed Aiken's cheek. "You know," she said, "I don't think I could have done that without your encouragement."

"That's what I'm here for," Aiken responded.

"Oh?" Diana asked, mock-haughtily. "Nothing else?"

Aiken grinned, "Well, when you put it that way, I can think of one or two other things I don't mind being here for."

Diana continued to tease, "Oh, you 'don't mind' them, do you? That's it?"

"Alright, you win," Aiken surrendered easily, pulling her to him.

"You know," he said a couple of minutes later, "We should have a contest at tomorrow's meeting. We've got at least a couple of people in every discipline. We could have distance teleporting contests, accuracy in telepathy contests, strength of telekinesis..." he trailed off.

"I think that's a good idea," Diana said

enthusiastically. "Except, you'll win in all the categories."

"Well, I was kind of thinking that since I *can* do all the skills, I could be the judge."

"That would work," she responded. "This will be great – we'll get to practice our abilities, and have a little fun, too. We'll just have to make sure no one spots people and things teleporting in and out of the Park."

"I've been wondering about that," Aiken confided. "I think there's probably a way of shielding the area we'll be in, either using something like Hugo's invisibility on a larger scale, or some form of projective telepathic suggestion. Either people just won't see us at all, or they'll be totally uninterested in anything they do see."

"Sounds like you've got everything covered," Diana said.

"I've been thinking about this for a while, now."

"Well, it'll certainly spice things up a little at the meeting. Maybe make people push their limits somewhat. Take their abilities more seriously."

"Well, not everyone's been pulling pranks," Aiken said. As the students had become more used to having their abilities, they'd been more and more tempted to use them in public, even only in subtle ways. A couple of them had taken things a little too far, in Aiken's opinion (and evidently in Diana's as well). Hugo had been using his ability to sneak up on people and spy on them, leading to Ethan, Nicole and Aiken being used as spotters occasionally. Olivia had, on a couple of occasions, slipped into using her projective telepathic sense to make other students do her bidding, but as she was normally fairly commanding anyway, most people didn't notice much change.

"It only takes one idiot to blow the lid off what we're capable of, and then, we'll all be research projects over in Aldrin Center," Diana stated pointedly.

"I know," Aiken tried to calm her, running his hand along her arm. "We'll just have to keep an eye on things so that they don't get out of hand."

"You know," Diana said thoughtfully, "I wonder if it would be possible to plant a suggestion in the dangerous ones that they shouldn't use their powers."

Aiken was aghast, "You mean, like, turn them off from the inside?"

"No, no, nothing that drastic," Diana reassured him. "Only, let people know quietly that we projectors will have a little mind-to-mind with them if they don't shape up."

"I don't know," Aiken said. "Don't you think it would be better to convince them of the argument not to interfere on its own merits, rather than forcing the issue?"

"Maybe," Diana countered, "but this way would be faster, and you'd still be convincing them, just with a little help."

"I'm just not sure I'm comfortable 'helping' with my friends. Particularly since we all agreed not to that first day."

"Fine," Diana said somewhat sulkily. "We'll try it your way first, then when that doesn't work, we can try it my way."

Aiken remained unconvinced, but he knew that Diana was just as committed to her strategy as he was hesitant. He felt like it would be an abuse of his abilities, though he didn't say this to Diana, aloud or mentally. He left her family's suite that evening frustrated over his inability to communicate exactly why he didn't think it was a good idea to mess around in his classmates' heads.

When he saw Diana again, it was at the meeting of what the students were now calling the "Lunatics" club, a name that they thought would sound more innocuous to outsiders, and a play on the word that the ancients used to ascribe to people's changed mental state caused by the Moon. Jillian had been the one to suggest the name, but it was enthusiastically endorsed by the whole group. Even Ethan, joking that he would always call the group "Brainiacs Anonymous," had come around. The only unintentionally funny moment had come when Isaac had discovered that there was a synchronized low-grav swimming team also called the Lunatics based in the Aitkens-South Pole Base. Students, meeting in the school hallway would ask about new bouts of "lunacy", and would check to see if there was a "lunatic fringe" meeting scheduled. Often enough, Liam, who was still in charge of the group, would tell one of the projecting telepaths when and where the next meeting was, and they would get the message out mentally. It was a system that worked well, given the constraints they operated under.

This day, the Lunatics were once more in the Park, coming together in twos and threes. Aiken and Connor arrived from class together, and Aiken looked around for Diana. Spotting her, he went over and made to sit down next to her. She looked up at him, then quickly looked away. *What?* Aiken silently queried her. When she didn't answer, he sat down beside her anyway.

"What is it?" he asked out loud.

She turned to him, "Have you managed to convince anyone not to use their abilities yet?"

Aiken recoiled from the tone of her voice. "No," he replied carefully, "but I haven't talked to anyone yet."

"Well, when that happens, let me know."

Aiken was baffled. What had happened since the evening before to turn what he had thought was a simple disagreement into a full-blown fight? He asked Diana this very question.

"I don't understand why you're unwilling to use your abilities to their full potential," she said by way of an answer.

"I guess I just don't see that as the first way to do things. Especially since we all said we wouldn't mess around in each other's heads without permission."

"I know," Diana said, suddenly softening. "It's one of the things I find endearing about you."

And just like that, they'd made up. When Aiken spoke up during the meeting, there was a general agreement to his idea. Liam proclaimed that the next meeting of the Lunatics would be the first contest of mental abilities. They left the meeting buzzing with excitement. Everyone was determined to best their friends. Most said that they would spend the next three days practicing their skills.

Aiken and Diana left together, discussing the upcoming contests. When he left Diana at her parents' doorstep, he checked mentally, then popped over to the apartment Connor shared with his parents and younger sister. Connor wasn't too surprised to see Aiken show up in this manner. They were by now used to the display of powers among the Lunatics, and most had given up being envious of other students' abilities.

"Hey," Aiken greeted him.

"Hey, yourself. Do you want anything to drink?"

"Sure, what do you have?"

"Well," Connor replied, "We just got some bottled water from Earth, but I bet my dad won't let us have it. I think they're saving it for a special occasion. Also, we have pop and dehydrated orange juice."

"Ugh," Aiken said in response to the last choice. "Pop it is, I guess."

Connor popped himself into the kitchen, then back with two bottles of pop. "Here you go."

"Thanks."

"So, nice speech you made there at the Lunatic fringe."

"Thanks – you going to compete?"

"I guess I'll have to," Connor replied

easily. "I can't let Nicole walk away with all the glory. She gets to compete six times."

Aiken smiled. "I'm thinking of suggesting some team challenges," he said. "Like teleports & telepaths could team up for accuracy 'porting. You know, you go as far away from the start as you want, then Liam has to teleport something to your exact location using Ethan's telepathic guidance."

"Sounds interesting," his friend responded. "'Course, they'll have to be demonstration events," he continued. "No one left to compete against."

"Yeah," said Aiken glumly. "I had considered that."

"Well, all we have to do is find another group of lunatics," his friend joked.

"Actually," Aiken brightened, "I've been meaning to ask you about that. Have you found any evidence that anyone else was affected by the drive test in the same way we were?"

"Nothing," replied Connor. "I've been sending out discreet web inquiries for weeks, now and not a hint of another group like us, no word on what went wrong with the test, not even a mention of the precise nature of the drive."

"Well, I wouldn't hold my breath for that one," Aiken said.

"Still, it'd be nice to know, wouldn't it?" Connor asked.

"Yeah," Aiken sighed. "I'm guessing that if other groups of people are out there, they're probably staying under the radar like us. You wouldn't find us mentioned on the nets, either."

"True enough," Connor conceded. They pondered this for a moment. "You know," Connor said slowly, "you could go find out. You're a teleport and a telepath. It wouldn't be too hard for you to 'port yourself to the L4 station and scan anyone there for information."

"Could you accurately hit the L4 station?" Aiken asked his friend.

"Well, no. But I don't have your amazing mental talents," Connor said, only half joking.

"I still think your web searches are probably more discreet."

"Well, I'll let you know if I find anything out."

The two friends continued talking about the contest of mental ability scheduled for the next week until it was time for Aiken to leave.

Chapter Seventeen

Tuesday, June 16th, 2139

The day of the contest, Aiken woke slowly and, as was his new habit, stretched out his senses to encompass the whole dome. His mind soared once again to join the pulse of the universe, flying away from himself and joining with everything that existed. As always, he came back to himself slowly, and touched all the people living in Peary Dome simultaneously for a moment. Today, he lingered over that touch and wondered if he could connect all those touches through himself. He always felt more connected after, and wondered if that feeling could be shared. In his mind, he pictured a hand gathering up fistfuls of threads on the one side of him, and the same on the other side. He mentally brought his hands together to join all the strands for a moment. A sensation not unlike an electric shock swept through him, and he could feel a startled amazement in the minds of all who had come together for an instant of perfect understanding of those living and working around them. Aiken relinquished his mental grasp on the strands after a moment and opened his eyes.

Well, he thought to himself, *that was different.*

He wasn't the only one to notice. At the breakfast table, the usually reserved conversation was warmer, somehow. The words spoken weren't that different from every other day, but there was meaning behind them that was usually absent. As Aiken made his way to morning class, he noticed more people stopping to chat with their neighbours, more people genuinely inquiring about the well-being of those they passed by every day.

His classmates at school seemed affected, and even the Lunatics apparently couldn't tell what was different this morning, other than they were excited for the contest later that day. Aiken felt the energy flowing between different groups of people all day, and when he sensed other people's energy, he felt a residual surge in his own energy level, as if he were still tied in somewhat to the connections between people.

They had that afternoon off school, which was ideal for the Lunatics' purpose. The group went their separate ways for lunch, with some going to do some last minute practicing, and others taking a nap or eating big lunches to restore their energy levels.

When they reconvened in the Park, there was a carnival-like atmosphere. Everyone was laughing and joking, eager to demonstrate their skills to their friends. When all fifteen had gathered, Liam stood and cleared his throat to get their attention.

"Welcome," he intoned gravely, "to the first Lunatics mental challenge day." Snickers of amusement greeted his overly-serious pronouncement. Liam grinned widely, "Try not to kill anyone." He sat down, motioning to Aiken.

Aiken stood, more confident now in front of his peers than he had been a month ago. He established what he termed a "mental dampening field" over the proceedings, which would make any observer acutely disinterested in what they saw there in the Park. "Here's how it's going to work," he said. "Since I can only watch one contest at a time, we're only going to run one at a time. This'll also allow all of you to see what everyone else has been up to with their abilities."

He consulted a piece of e-paper he was carrying. "First up, object teleports." Liam and Nicole rose to cheers from their friends. Aiken spoke again, "This is a two-part contest. Part one, teleport the most massive object you can manage. Part two, make it appear as close to these target circles as possible." As he said this, he used his telekinetic ability to turn over thin circles of grass to form two bulls-eyes on the lawn of the Park.

"Everyone ready?" he asked. When both contestants nodded, he said, "Go!"

Liam and Nicole both creased their foreheads in concentration. Nicole closed her eyes to better visualise the target she was reaching for. Liam stared straight ahead, eyes unfocused. Nicole sighed suddenly and a grey shipping pallet stacked with refrigeration units appeared dead-center over her target. As it settled into the grass, Liam raised one eyebrow, then clenched his fists. The area over his target started to scintillate and the outline of a form could be seen. When Liam's chosen object finally appeared, there were oohs and aahs from the gathered students. Liam had reached out and plucked a mining cart filled with ore and teleported it inside the dome.

Aiken did a fast check, then said, "Liam wins for the mass part, and Nicole takes the accuracy award." Indeed, Liam's Herculean teleport was off-center on the target by a good thrity centimetres. Aiken reached out mentally and put both objects back where the contestants had gotten them from without too much effort.

"I guess that's why you're the referee," Liam said ruefully. "I get the feeling that you could have put a stack of bullion from Fort Knox on the target to millimetre precision if you wanted."

"We'll never know," Aiken replied cheerfully. "Next up, we have projecting telepaths." Olivia and Diana stood up to join Nicole. Aiken smiled at Diana, sending a tendril of encouragement her way. Nicole begged off this contest, saying she wanted to rest before trying the telekinesis events.

"Here's the rules," Aiken explained to the two remaining contestants. "Part one is you have to send your hail out as far as possible. Part two is that it has to land precisely on this line." Aiken traced a straight line in the grass. "I'll be listening in on this trajectory to see how far you can send, and how precisely. Other receiving telepaths are invited to listen in as well," Aiken said, "in order to maintain the integrity of the judge." The group laughed at his self-deprecating joke.

"Ready?" he asked the pair. They both nodded. "Alright, send away."

This contest was over in two seconds. "Once again, we have a split win," Aiken announced. "Diana wins for distance, and Liv for precision." The Lunatics applauded both the contestants as they sat down.

"Okay," Aiken continued. "Now we're going to have one of our skill demonstrations. Since there are a few Lunatics with no peer to compete against, we're allowing anyone to challenge them to a demonstration in their skill area." He looked around to see if everyone was still with him. "First up is Faith."

The girl with the wandering eyes stood up and said, "I can see anything anywhere, but challenge me to see something you can verify so you'll know I'm not cheating."

Isaac called out, "What's the poster on the wall of my brother's bedroom?"

Faith closed those disturbing eyes for a moment, then reopened them and answered, "It's a vintage movie poster for, uh, 'A Clockwork Orange'. Is that right?" Isaac gave her the thumbs up. "Anyone else?"

Connor had been consulting his wrist communicator, and now spoke up, "What's the headline of today's paper edition of the New York Times?"

Once more, Faith closed her eyes. This time she kept them closed as she read aloud, "American Cities in Crisis." She opened her eyes, questioning Connor with a look.

"That's it," Connor confirmed. "Where'd you look to find out?"

"Well," Faith answered with a wry grin, "I considered looking at your wrist com, since you evidently called up the information there, but I decided I'd make it a challenge. I looked into their offices in New York." She paused. "C'mon guys, give me something harder."

Hugo stood up. "How many cavities do I have?" he asked playfully.

Faith looked at him studiously, and Aiken could see mentally that she was retuning her sight ability. "Five fillings," Faith answered Hugo, "but you should probably go see about the two cavities that you don't have filled."

Laughter rose from the assembled students. Faith asked if anyone else had a challenge. No one else could think of one, everyone having already personally experienced her vision ability when she'd scanned their brains to confirm the neural connectivity increase.

Aiken stood again. "Alright, next we're

going to do the receiving telepaths." Ethan and Olivia stood up. "So here's the deal. You're going to see if you can pluck one clear thought from a person as far away from here as possible. I'll listen in to each of you in turn to see how far you've gone." He looked at both students. "Have you decided which will go first?"

Ethan nodded at Olivia. "Ladies first."

"Whenever you're ready," Aiken told Olivia. He followed her tendril of thought as it quested out, out of the dome, over the cold dry surface, until it started to weaken. Still Olivia pressed on, until she found Tycho Station. There, she found a maintenance worker just inside the wall of the northernmost dome. Scanning his mind, she extracted a thought as Aiken looked on.

"Bravo," Aiken said to Olivia when their senses had returned to their bodies. "Tycho Station," he announced to the rest of the class. "About forty-two hundred kilometres. Well done."

Next, Aiken followed Ethan's thoughts as they shot out of the dome and into space. Confused, Aiken followed along gamely, trying to figure out where Ethan's thoughts were heading. Soon enough, he saw Ethan's intended target. *You've got guts, I'll give you that*, he sent to Ethan.

When they returned, he paused for a moment, then spoke. "Midway Station," he said matter-of-factly. A hush fell over the group.

"Are you serious?" Connor asked.

"Yep," Ethan answered.

"That's more than fifty thousand kilometres," Connor breathed.

"Yep," Ethan repeated. A smattering of applause built into an ovation. Ethan sketched a bow, then sat down.

Aiken got their attention once more, then announced that it was time for the self-telekinetics. Nicole stood again, and was joined by Jillian. They were to fly a series of aerial manoeuvres designed to test their reflexes and their precision. Just before the girls launched, Aiken sent a mental image of the route that they should be taking to all the other Lunatics, so they could see how closely the two were following along. When Aiken gave the signal, both launched themselves upward to the first marker. They dove, swooped, turned over and twisted. Some of their motions were too fast to follow, and at other times they seemed to hang suspended in the air for seconds. All too fast, the display was over. Nicole walked away with the awards for both speed and precision.

"Okay," Aiken announced, "it's time for another couple of demonstrations. Hugo and

Isaac have come up with a little something." He sat down and the two boys stood up. First, Hugo held up a large piece of duracrete. Isaac concentrated on it and it began to shimmer. He put his hand out and through the chunk of pressed rock, wiggling his finger on the other side. He removed his hand, then nodded at Hugo. Hugo concentrated for a moment, then disappeared. Isaac reached out to confirm where Hugo was, then concentrated in turn. An area in midair began to shimmer as Isaac's skill was used. He reached out with his hand once more, and gasps ensued as his hand disappeared, then reappeared twenty centimetres away. To the onlookers, it looked like a section of Isaac's arm was missing. As they started to figure out that the missing portion was inside an invisible and insubstantial Hugo, they began to applaud in appreciation. Isaac withdrew his hand, and Hugo returned himself to visibility. Both students smiled and waved, then sat down.

Aiken nodded at Penny, and she stood up. The students, remembering what she'd done with the fountain the day of the first meeting, fell silent in anticipation. Penny didn't keep them in suspense for long. A patch of ground in the area where Aiken had made the targets began to ripple. The group could see that something was happening, they just couldn't make out what it was. Aiken used his mental sight to see that Penny was extracting grains of sand from the soil underlying the grass. Soon enough, Penny had a sizeable pile of sand sitting atop the sod. The pile began to grow indistinct as Penny moved the grains of sand around to the configuration she desired. A scale model of Neuschwanstein Castle formed quickly. The turrets and walls rose and doorways and windows became evident. The entire structure lifted upwards as a mountainside formed below the castle. In quick succession, the roofs were applied, and the creation was finished. The group gathered around to marvel at Penny's handiwork. Different students pointed out the fact that the tiles of the roof could be distinguished individually, that the stained glass windows were translucent, that the mountain had tiny pine trees dotted on its slope. After a few minutes, Penny told them all to stand back. As the group went back the places that they had been sitting, Penny looked once more at her structure, then smiled slightly as she concentrated again. A shimmering could be seen in the air over the castle, about two metres above the topmost turret. The other Lunatics began to chuckle as they saw what Penny was fashioning out of air. When the gigantic boot was more solid, Penny sent it crashing down into the castle replica, squashing the entire structure and sending sand flying in every direction. She used her ability to put the grains of sand back into the soil, leaving no trace of her construction. She sat down amid enthusiastic applause from the other students.

"Okay," Aiken said as the applause died down. "Self-teleportation is going to work a little like high-jump. I'll place the contestants farther and farther away, and they'll have to teleport back to the target area. If either one gives up or fails at any distance, the other must successfully complete the 'port at that distance to be declared the winner. You disqualify yourself if you don't land at least in the outside ring of the bull's eye." The outer ring was approximately two metres in diameter.

Aiken nodded to the two contestants, Connor and Nicole. When they signalled their readiness, he teleported them both to the outer edge of the dome. Both made the jump back easily, landing in the center ring of the target. Aiken moved them to the Serenity Station, then Hadley Dome, and so on until finally he had placed them in Aitkens Base at the South Pole of the Moon. Each time, both Connor and Nicole made it back fine, though Connor had started to drift a little off the mark on the farthest teleports.

"Well," Aiken said, "we've reached the end of what we can do on the surface. Either of you feel up to coming back from Midway?" When they both looked at him like he was crazy, he laughed and declared a tie.

Aiken spoke to the entire group, "So, onto our last competitive event, then we have a couple more demonstrations." He motioned to Nicole and Gwen Gabriel to step forward. "Okay, here's the scoop. I'm going to teleport two identical objects to the top of the dome. Your task is to grab a hold of the object without causing any damage to it, and lower it to the target area."

Nicole and Gwen both manoeuvred themselves into position and nodded to Aiken that they were ready. Both gazed upwards expectantly. Aiken mentally searched out the two objects he'd prepared earlier for this test. Finding them, he pictured them at the top of the dome, and they appeared. A couple of students gasped in dismay as they perceived the challenge that Aiken had constructed. Two cubes, one metre to a side, made up entirely of thin, interconnected glass tubes plummeted toward the ground. The structures were both heavy and fragile, meaning the girls would have to act deftly and swiftly in order to walk away with the win.

Both contestants screwed up their faces in concentration, and the cubes slowed almost imperceptibly. Nicole's cube lurched in midair, and though it came to a near standstill, an audible crunch was heard by the observers. A couple of students winced in sympathy. Gwen's cube continued fall, neither slowing nor picking up speed. Nicole lowered her cube slowly through the air, beads of sweat appearing on her brow as she struggled with the delicate load. Gwen's cube was slowing somewhat, but the group could see that it wasn't enough – it was going to hit the ground. It crashed dead-center in the target zone, crumpling in on itself, and finally collapsing with a crash. Nicole struggled to lower her cube to the turf, and it finally settled on the outer ring of the target. Aiken split the win between the two of them.

"Our last demonstration," he announced after cleaning up the debris from the two cubes, "is courtesy Mason Gabriel."

The lanky teen stood up and said, "The first demonstration has actually already been completed. I established a stock portfolio for the Lunatics in my name, and I've been successfully predicting short-term gains and losses on the New York Stock Exchange for two weeks now. I've paid back the loan my dad fronted me, and we still have more than four times the money I started with." The group looked at each other in astonishment.

"Are we billionaires?" Hugo called out.

"No, nothing like that," Mason answered to their disappointment. "I've only made a couple hundred thousand. Maybe enough to buy a car or something, but nothing really drastic. Of course, given enough time, we will eventually be rich. If the money doubles every six months, before long we'll have more money than we know what to do with."

There were grins all around at this pronouncement. "Of course," Mason continued, "we'll have the same problem there as we've had hiding our abilities. If there are all of a sudden fifteen teenagers spending money like moguls, questions will be asked, and we'll be exposed." While some students sighed in resignation, recognising the truth of this, some whisperings were still going on.

"Alright," Mason said, "anyone have another challenge for me?"

Connor raised his hand. When Mason inclined his head in Connor's direction, he asked, "Can you tell me what my mom's serving for supper?" There was knowing laughter from all the students, Mason included.

He closed his eyes and Aiken, monitoring him mentally, saw a process similar to Faith's mental sight begin, except rather than focusing on distance, Mason focused in on a particular time. He recalled his conversation with Connor the day of the drive test with regards to this very same subject. It didn't take long for Mason to find the moment in question. "You're having meatloaf." Connor grimaced. "And it looks like you're sitting at the table, so evidently no one invited you away from it." More laughter.

Mason was then beset with requests for test results, jobs after graduation, and other individual requests. Instead of trying to answer all of these, Mason announced that he'd look at the group as a whole to find out what would come to pass for the Lunatics. Once more, he closed his eyes, and this time, Aiken could see that the effort he expended was enormous to keep all fifteen people in focus. His voice, when he spoke, came out strained and unnatural:

> *"The fiery man of battle comes*
> *The challenge will be brought*
> *One will turn*
> *Two will fall*
> *A leader will rise to fight*
> *And sacrifice all to win"*

As he collapsed and fell to the ground, a stunned silence filled the space where the students had gathered. No one wanted to break the sepulchral quiet that followed his announcement.

When a voice was finally raised, it was all the more stunning for being unknown. "Well, that was a neat trick," the stranger said. "I wonder if I could see a little more?"

Chapter Eighteen
Tuesday, June 16th, 2139

Pandemonium followed the interruption by the strange man in their midst. No one had ever discovered their secret in quite so startling a manner. The students scattered in every direction, with the exception of Aiken, Liam and of course Mason, who was still sprawled out on the grass where he'd fallen. Aiken, thinking quickly, reached out mentally and froze the stranger's mental processes. He made a cursory scan of the man's thoughts. Surprised, he released his hold on the man.

"He's no danger to us," he told Liam. Liam still looked warily at the stranger. He was dressed casually in jeans and a black sweater, drawing no attention to himself. His face also was devoid of noticeable characteristics, as if it blended together features that would commonly be found in many people into one non-descript person.

"Who are you?" Liam asked.

"My name is Quinn Donnelly. I work for the government." He paused, unsure of how to continue.

Aiken filled in for him, "Mr. Donnelly is following up threads from the drive test."

"Quinn, please," the man insisted. "And yes, some, shall we say 'interesting' net queries brought me here. To tell you the truth, I wasn't expecting to find anything." He smiled ruefully. "Least of all a group of teens with, um, enhanced faculties."

"You better start at the beginning," Liam said. "And pray that Aiken doesn't make you forget everything when you're done."

"Hang on a second, though," Aiken interrupted. "I'm going to call everyone back. Here's the explanation we've been waiting for since it happened. Oh, and someone should look at Mason." Liam walked over to where Mason had collapsed and checked on him, while Aiken sent out a mental hail letting everyone know the situation as it stood. Those students who had left the normal way started to head back, and those who were able teleported or flew themselves back.

When the students had gathered once more and made themselves comfortable on the turf, Quinn Donnelly introduced himself a second time. "I work with the NSA," he explained. "I do mostly signal intelligence, trolling the nets for suspicious messages. Last month I was assigned to track down any leads on the failed drive test, since at the time, sabotage was still suspected." He looked around at the group. "They've since ruled it out, but they wanted me to follow up on what I'd found regardless."

"Which is what, exactly?" Connor called out.

"I'm glad you asked, Mr. Jacobs, since it was your web queries that started this whole adventure."

"Damn it, Connor!" This was from Olivia.

"It's not really his fault," Donnelly spoke up. "I'm very good at what I do. There have been a fair number of you out on the nets looking for materials related to faster than light speed travel and physiological alterations as a result of exposure to radiation. We would have put two and two together eventually." This mollified the group not a bit. "Look," Donnelly started again, "I'm not here to arrest you or anything. We know you didn't have anything to do with the drive test failure. I just want to ask some questions."

"Well, we have some of our own," Hugo said.

"I bet," the agent answered. "Fire away."

"For starters," Connor barged in, "what the hell was the drive test all about anyway?"

"I'm no physicist," answered Donnelly, "but from what I've seen, it's basically a quantum tunnelling device."

"You want to run that by us again?" Olivia asked.

"Okay," the agent answered. "Say you have point A where you're starting, and point B where you want to be. What's the fastest way between them?"

"A straight line," answered Connor automatically.

"Right," Donnelly confirmed. "And that works great if point A is here and point B is over at the edge of the Park. It even works alright when point A is here on the moon and point B is on Earth. Takes a little longer, but it works out alright." He paused to make sure everyone was following. "However, what if your point A was on Earth, and point B was in the Orion Nebula, sixteen hundred light years from here. You've now got a problem. You want to travel to the nebula, but to do so, even in a straight line takes longer than you have to live. Since living forever isn't an option, you've got to find a shorter path."

The students started to look a little confused. "Bear with me," Donnelly asked. "Now, we can't make that straight line any shorter. At least in this universe." He received incredulous stares from most of the students. "Beside our universe, there are potentially infinite numbers of parallel universes with some features that are the same, and some that are wildly different. So what the drive does is tunnel through what's called quantum foam, which is what the universe is made up of on the tiniest level imaginable. The drive tunnels through this foam into a universe that is very, very small. So small that the ship the drive is in actually touches both point A and point B at the same time. So the drive then tunnels back out of the tiny universe at point B, since it's already touching it, and presto! Your ship has arrived at more or less the same moment it left point A."

"Yeah, right," muttered a few of the students.

"Why don't you believe me?" Donnelly asked. "You've already seen it for yourselves.

What do you think your teleporters, as you call them, are doing? It's exactly the same thing, only using the brain instead of a supercomputer to calculate the tunnel into existence."

"Except that the teleports here can only send things a couple thousand kilometres away, not sixteen hundred light years, and they're only moving light stuff, not spaceships," Isaac noted.

"Hey," Liam said, "that mine cart was heavy."

"Well, for one, your brains aren't powered by a matter-antimatter annihilation reaction," Donnelly explained.

"So what's your talent?" Hugo asked him.

"Me? Oh, nothing like yours, I'm afraid."

"How'd you get past Aiken's barrier, then?" Diana asked.

"Just stubborn I guess."

Aiken nodded to confirm Donnelly's hypothesis. "I set up the field so that casual interest would be deflected, and nothing would inspire particular curiosity. It didn't occur to me that someone might be looking for us specifically. The field wasn't designed to deflect that kind of direct inquiry, because I didn't see the need. Obviously, that's changed."

"Anyway," Donnelly continued, "the drive failed because the Casimir energy formed by the magnetic bottle and its real-world counterpart sent too much energy across the Wheeler boundary of the quantum foam tunnel they were trying to build."

"If you say so," laughed Liam.

"Basically, they tried to pump too much energy into the other universe as a result of a phenomenon they didn't take into account when building the drive, and it blew up in their faces."

"Wait," asked Aiken. "The drive or the universe?"

"Both. As a result of the blowback from the quantum foam tunnel, the magnetic bottle lost containment, and the antimatter annihilated the whole ship."

"You're saying they destroyed a universe on a test run of this drive system?"

"Essentially, yes."

"Wait, if the itty-bitty universe is gone," Ethan spoke up, "how can we still do everything we do?"

"Well, as I said, there are potentially infinite other universes, so you're probably just using one with properties similar to the one that was destroyed."

"Did anyone die?" asked Nicole.

"It didn't appear so initially. The ship containing the drive was a remote-piloted drone, and the explosion was far enough away from the L4 station that it wasn't hit by debris or anything." He paused.

"But?" prompted Connor.

"But all the observers on the L4 station who had witnessed the test visually died within twenty-four hours of the event as a result of cerebral haemorrhages." The students looked around at each other knowingly. "Yes," persisted Donnelly, "like your instructor. We were pretty surprised to see his autopsy results, given that he wasn't anywhere near the drive when it went off."

"Wait," said Connor. "You said those who'd witnessed the drive test visually. Does that mean that there were others who did survive?"

"Yes," Donnelly replied. "Anyone who viewed the test through the intermediary of an electronic device seems to be fine."

"What kind of radiation affects only people looking at it?" Connor asked, not really expecting an answer.

"Quantum radiation," Donnelly supplied. "Things break down on a quantum level. The physical laws of the universe don't apply all the time. You're aware of Schrödinger's cat?"

"You can't determine the state of a quantum particle until you observe it, and then the quantum wave function collapses to form a describable state. The cat is both dead and alive at the same time until an external observer collapses the quantum wave function into either of those single states."

"Yeah, well, it doesn't really work like that, but suffice it to say that physics gets really weird on those scales. So yes, the radiation that came out of the quantum foam tunnel had to be observed directly to have an effect."

"So you're saying that anyone who saw the test with their own eyes was affected."

"No, only people who saw the test fail. The quantum radiation didn't escape the tunnel until the Wheeler boundary collapsed from the universe exploding."

"But why did they all die and we all lived?" asked Jillian.

"We're not sure," answered Donnelly. "I'm hoping that some tests will reveal that information."

The students began murmuring amongst themselves at the mention of testing, and Donnelly tried to reassure them. "We're only talking about some MRIs. Nothing invasive."

"Oh," Aiken said, "we've done MRIs already."

"What? They're not on record." Donnelly was surprised.

"Well, not officially, no. But we know none of us is going to die, and that's about all we're interested in at the moment, until we know about you and what the NSA wants with us." The other Lunatics nodded in agreement.

"Fair enough," Donnelly responded. "I'm going to want to see those MRIs at some point."

"We'll see," Liam said. "Convince us that you're no threat, and we'll talk about it."

"You do realise that you're talking to an agent of the government of the United States of America."

Liam chuckled. "You must not have seen the whole show here this afternoon. There's not really anything that you could do that we wouldn't see coming and be able to stop."

"While that may be true, your buddy over there," Donnelly indicated Mason with his thumb, "just warned you about someone coming to do battle with you."

"How do we know that's not you?" Hugo asked menacingly.

"He's not a threat," Aiken answered him.

"How do we know? We've only got your word on that, and you let him in through your barrier. Maybe you're working with him."

"Why would I do that?"

"I dunno, maybe you don't like that other people can do some of the stuff you can."

"Guys, this is pointless," Connor interrupted. "Why are we fighting?"

"Because your buddy here may or may not be covering for a g-man who might want to turn us all in lab rats."

"That's a lot of 'mights' to be getting angry over," Aiken shot back.

"Aiken," Diana interrupted, "You know I believe you, but you can see how some others might be worried."

"No, I can't," he turned on her. "And I can't believe that you don't believe me."

Hurt, she stepped back. "That's not what I said," she tried to explain.

"Oh, I know – you believe me, but you see how people wouldn't... how is that different than saying you have doubts?"

"Oh, quit acting like such a child. You know exactly what I meant."

"Apparently, I don't."

"Apparently." Diana stormed off.

Aiken, unsure of exactly what had just transpired, turned back to Quinn Donnelly to see the agent attempting unsuccessfully to hide a smirk. "What?" he snapped.

"Oh, nothing," Donnelly said innocently, "I just figured if people could read each other's minds, these sorts of arguments wouldn't happen."

"Yeah, well, not everyone can read thoughts," Aiken refused to be baited.

"You can, though," Connor pointed out to him.

Aiken gave his friend a dirty look, then paused. Connor was right. There was no reason for him to have snapped at Diana like that. Suddenly, he felt very embarrassed. "Look," he said to the NSA agent, "we're not going to sort this out standing around here this afternoon. Let's pick a time and place to meet tomorrow and everyone can have the evening to consider what you've told us." He turned to Liam. "If that's okay with you."

"Sounds good."

Hugo wasn't satisfied, "How do we know he's not going to disappear and tell his bosses back Earthside all about us?"

"I can keep an eye on him if you want," Aiken offered.

"Not good enough," Hugo responded.

"Well, find telepaths to take shifts, then. You've got the pick of Nicole, Ethan and Liv if you don't think I can handle it."

Hugo was appeased by this solution, and the Lunatics worked out a schedule for the telepaths other than Aiken to keep watch on Quinn Donnelly. The group broke up in a quiet mood that evening.

Just before everyone left, Connor turned to Aiken, "If Hugo was okay with the other telepaths monitoring Mr. Donnelly for the night, how come we didn't just have them verify your story? Four of you all saying the same thing would have been fairly positive proof that you weren't consorting with the government to kill us all off."

"Given his mood, I wouldn't have been surprised if he accused all of us of being in on it," Aiken grumbled.

"Not with Ethan backing you up. He and Hugo were pretty good friends even before the Lunatics."

"Yeah, well..." Aiken trailed off.

"Didn't think of it, did you genius boy?"

"I did, actually," Aiken answered, "but I think Hugo wanted something to go his way today, and it was easier to give up something small than to have to give up something bigger further along."

"I guess I didn't see it that way," Connor stated.

"Well, bear in mind, I can read minds," Aiken teased. Connor rolled his eyes, and on that note, they parted for the evening.

Later, Aiken considered telepathically hailing Diana, but decided against it, since he didn't really know what he would say to her.

Chapter Nineteen

Wednesday, June 24th, 2139

Aiken was getting into the habit of joining all the minds in the dome together for an instant as part of his morning ritual. It always seemed to have a positive effect on the way people treated each other for the few hours after the joining, as if some sort of residual connection existed between the discrete minds. Aiken also felt extra energised by his time connected to each individual for a split-second. He was sure that this extra energy was pushing his talents to grow as well. He'd noticed that it took less and less effort to perform some of the tasks that he practiced.

It had been a week since Quinn Donnelly had discovered the Lunatics and in that time, the NSA agent had been everything he'd said. Aiken supposed that the man figured correctly that there was no point in lying, since the receptive telepaths among the students would ferret out any falsehood almost immediately.

Quinn, as they called him now, had been fascinated to see their longitudinal brain scans, even though they only had records for four weeks. He pointed out to those who were interested that there were ongoing minor changes in the structure of their brains. Seeing these structural differences, he has posited that the quantum radiation had physiologically modified their developing brains, whose capacities were elastic enough during adolescence to absorb and adapt to the changes. It followed that the people who had died as a result of exposure to the same radiation had brains that were too static to absorb the changes and as a result, when their physiology attempted to shift, it caused aneurysm and haemorrhage.

Aiken had asked during this conversation whether that meant that because their brains were still changing, and they'd eventually grow to be static, if all the Lunatics would suffer the same fate as the other observers. There had been no answer at the time, and Aiken was hoping that today would be the day they'd find out. This was, after all, a pressing question for the Lunatics.

Aiken headed for school, energised as usual by the contact he'd had with other minds earlier in the morning. When he got to the physics classroom, he found a tense atmosphere.

"What's up?" he asked.

"A group of miners are trapped in a collapsed tunnel outside Shenzhou Base. No one can get to them in time, but they're linked live into the communication system so this is all happening real-time," Connor informed him.

"We're tapped in," announced Kaira. The students gathered around the broadcast unit to listen to the plight of the miners. Aiken stood off to one side and stretched out with his mind. South, south he roamed until he found what he was looking for. On the eastern edge of Mare Nectaris, the location of Shenzhou Base, were the Montes Pyrenaeus, where the Chinese were mining. He soared mentally over the western base of the mountains, searching. Finding the mine tailings, he moved in to get a closer look. He trekked mentally down the mine shafts, looking for the collapse that trapped the miners. When he found it, he was profoundly dismayed. There had to be ten tonnes of rock fallen into the tunnel. He wrapped his mental arms around the pile and attempted to shift it. It didn't budge. He focused more particularly on one large rock and pushed on it mentally. While it shifted, the way the pile had fallen in the low gravity environment had somehow locked the rocks into a sort of matrix, making them nearly impossible to remove individually. He looked for a smaller rock near the top of the pile. Finding one, he lifted it easily away from the rest of the pile and tossed it out the mouth of the mine shaft. The rest of the rocks that had been pressed against the one he moved shifted and settled.

This is going to take forever, he thought to himself. Out loud, he said, "How much air do those miners have left?"

"They estimate around thirty minutes," Gwen answered him.

"I know that look," Connor said, glancing at Aiken. "What are you thinking?"

"I'm thinking if we all work together, we can get those taikonauts back to their base before the air runs out in their suits."

"How are we going to do that," Hugo asked pointedly. "Only you and Gwen and Nicole can move stuff around, and I'm pretty sure neither of them can reach that far."

Aiken paused for a second, then "I've been thinking of a way that we can combine our mental energies through a focus person to achieve something greater than any of could do individually."

"How's that?" Ethan asked, genuinely curious.

"I'm pretty sure if you all let me, I can use your mental energy, apart from your individual talents, to amplify my telekinetic ability to the point where we'll be able to move that pile of rock."

"Is it dangerous?" Isaac asked, concerned.

"I'm pretty sure it isn't, but we could have Kaira sit out in case someone had a bad reaction to the link."

The students started warming up to the idea. They'd been waiting for a chance to use their new-found abilities for more than pulling pranks and impressing each other. Pretty soon, almost the entire class was on board.

"No way," Hugo argued. "You're not turning me into a zombie. Forget it."

"Suit yourself," Aiken said, barely managing to hide the dislike he felt growing for the other student.

He turned to Nicole. "Any word from the other class?"

"Yeah, they're all on board. They're just waiting now."

"Okay," Aiken said. "Get ready." He closed his eyes and allowed his mind to expand to fill the classroom. He gathered up the strands from all the students present, with the exception of Hugo and Kaira, and then followed Nicole's mental thread to the older class and linked up with them as well. As he drew on each student's energy, he felt like he was filled with light. Once more, he stretched his mind out to Mare Nectaris, this time easily finding the mine shaft opening, and plunging right in. First, he cut the line from the receiver for the taikonauts' suit radios to the broadcast antenna on the outside of the mountain. What they would do next did not need to be observed. Reaching the pile of fallen rock, he called on the energy available to him from the other Lunatics and reached out with mental arms to shift the rock. This time, he could feel that he was up to the task. He sensed the other students urging him on and encouraging him. They were united in purpose and the bond between them thrummed with life. Aiken gathered up all the rubble and swept it from the tunnel like so much dust.

Finding the miners mentally, he grasped each individual gently and manoeuvred them to the mine shaft entrance where their buggy waited for them. Then he selectively redacted their memories and sent them on their way. Finally, he re-entered the tunnel and filled it with his mental presence. Using the power of thirteen minds, he shook the mountain to its very roots, creating a moon quake that would be credited with the miner's miraculous escape.

He brought his senses back to the classroom, then gently relinquished each strand of thought and sank back into his chair. He was physically exhausted, but mentally thrilled. The effort he'd put into maintaining the link between minds for that length of time and channelling them all into his abilities had drained him physically, but the experience of extended mental contact left a residual tingle in his enhanced faculties.

"That was... intense." Connor was the first to put voice to their shared mental experience.

"Yeah," Jillian chimed in. "That was amazing. It was incredible to experience a different ability from the inside."

"We caused a moonquake." Isaac was in awe. Turning to Hugo, he said, "You should've been there. Wow, just... wow."

Hugo looked on disdainfully. "I don't need to be a part of your mind-meld. You don't know what else might have happened instead of helping out."

"But we did help out," Nicole argued. "We saved those men's lives."

"Good for you," Hugo sneered. "You're

my heroes. You want a medal or something?"

"What's gotten into you," Isaac asked him.

"Nothing. I just don't think I want to end up as the boy wonder's bootlicker is all."

What?! Aiken thought to himself. "I'm not forcing anyone to do anything," he said.

"How does that make it any better?" asked Hugo. "It's somehow better that everyone is falling over themselves to be your best friend now that you're a superhero? I don't think so. So don't expect me to fawn over you like you're some kind of god, alright?"

Aiken was taken aback at the intensity of Hugo's emotions. Taken together with his physical tiredness, he didn't feel like he wanted to argue just now, so he let it drop. The other students were still buzzing with excitement when their instructor walked in the door to begin the day's lesson.

Chapter Twenty
Wednesday, June 24th, 2139

Lunch that day was an epic affair. All the Lunatics, with the exception of Hugo got together to talk about what had transpired that morning. Aiken sat with Connor and Nicole, off to the side of the main group. Somehow, Quinn Donnelly had gotten wind of the rescue and came to the Park where the group was seated to discuss the morning with them.

Diana came up to Aiken as soon as she arrived. "Wow, Aiken, that was amazing this morning."

Aiken recognised the peace offering and accepted it. In the last week, he'd tried talking to Diana a couple of times, but each time it had been an awkward affair, helped out not one bit by his telepathic gift. She had been furious with him for the way he'd turned on her at that last meeting, but forgiveness was apparently now his for the asking.

"Listen, Diana," he started.

"No Aiken, it's okay. It's in the past."

"Yeah, well. I still feel stupid."

"A little humility never hurt anybody," she said with a smile. She reached her hand to him and he took it, and pulled her down next to him. Suddenly, the day's event seemed even more spectacular.

Nicole, seated next to him, rolled her eyes and said, "Careful, you two... the rest of us are going to need fillings if you keep that up." Aiken stuck his tongue out at her, and she responded in kind.

Donnelly wandered up just then and asked to join them on the grass. Aiken indicated an open spot with his free hand, and the NSA agent sat down.

"A fairly impressive showing this morning," he said by way of greeting. "You must be pretty proud."

"We all worked together to get something important done," Aiken answered, "what's not to be proud about?"

"Oh, nothing," the older man said. "I just heard that it was your idea that made it possible."

"If it hadn't been me, it would have been someone else," Aiken responded modestly. "I'm not any better at this than anyone else."

"Okay, now that's a lie, and we all know it," Quinn smiled.

"I didn't mean ability-wise," Aiken clarified. "I was talking more about coming up with the idea."

Donnelly wasn't so sure on that count, either, but let the comment pass. "So, what now?"

Aiken responded thoughtfully, "Well, we'll have to have someone looking at the news about the rescue to make sure that everyone followed the moon quake lead."

"The what?"

Aiken quickly filled him in on the last part of the group's effort. Donnelly looked as shaken as the mountain that had trapped the miners. "You caused that quake on purpose?"

"Yeah, why?" Aiken was mystified.

"Well, I can tell you right off, most people are going to fall for it. No one's going to believe that anything other than that quake cause the shaft to reopen. You guys hit six point seven on the Richter scale. I just figured it was the result of moving all that rock out. I can't believe you did that on purpose." He trailed off.

"When we work together," Aiken explained, "it's almost like the whole is more than the sum of its parts. As if, for every person who joins the link, not only is their energy added, but everyone else adds a little more energy too."

"So if all of you are focused on a goal, there's not a lot that could stand in your way."

"Does that worry you?" Nicole asked impishly.

"Not really, having studied you and now having gotten to know you a little better." Donnelly paused. "I think the vast majority of you are the kind of responsible people who wouldn't use your talents to further yourselves personally."

"Still, though, your employers must be concerned," Connor pursued, "I mean, they can't be happy with the thought of teenagers who can shake mountains, right?"

"My employers aren't aware of the full situation here," Donnelly confessed.

"Oh?"

"Well, for starters, I'm pretty sure that if I told them the truth, they'd take me off the case and send me for psychiatric evaluation as soon as I got back to Earth. More importantly, though, I don't know the full details of everything yet, so I wouldn't be able to answer their inevitable questions. They gave me considerable latitude to investigate here, so I'm taking advantage of that to get a more complete picture for my report."

"Speaking of a more complete picture," Aiken interrupted.

"Smooth, Aiken, smooth," Connor laughed.

"Anyway, I was wondering if you'd managed to find anything more out about the radiation's effects on our brains." He addressed Donnelly.

"I don't have a definitive answer yet," Donnelly responded, "but from the preliminary comparative scans, it looks like most everyone's rate of change is decreasing."

"And that's a good thing, right?" Diana asked.

"Yes. It lowers your risk of aneurysm if the brain development eventually halts."

"Wait, you said 'most everyone'. Who isn't slowing down?" Aiken asked, dreading the answer.

"I think you know," Donnelly responded without looking at him.

A sense of dread permeated Aiken's body. "You mean, if my brain changes don't slow down before my body's ability to adapt does, I'm screwed."

"Well… yes, more or less," Donnelly said apologetically. "I'm sure that won't happen, though."

"How can you be sure?"

"Well, for starters, it's only been a little over a month, so long term guesses at this point are futile. Also, each person's mental development is unique, even under ordinary circumstances. Some people's cerebral pathways keep changing into their twenties, for instance, while others are more or less static at sixteen."

"Is there a way to tell that?" Aiken asked.

"Not really. Because the adaptation that goes on is not physical, but rather mental in nature, there's no way to really see it. If I could borrow an analogy from computers, during adolescence, most people are mucking around with their operating system, their mind. You folks have had a hardware upgrade, and your operating system has had to cope with the changes to the systems it's used to using. Your continued physiological change may present a unique challenge to your mind, but if your mind is nimble enough, by the time the physiological changes wind down, it will still be capable of rewriting the necessary software."

"Well, that's not reassuring at all," Aiken said half-joking.

"At this point there's not really anything that can be done about it, so you might as well just trust that your mind is up to the task."

"Well, I sure hope so. I just don't understand why it's only me."

"I had a thought on that," Connor interjected. "Of all of us Lunatics, you're the one that's spent the most time here on the moon. You're the oldest moon baby, and the students who are actually older than you all came here later."

"So?" Aiken prompted.

"So, do you remember talking about radiation back when the drive test happened?"

"Vaguely."

"I'm sure. You probably can recall each individual comment."

"Maybe. I've been a little distracted."

"Anyway, the moon has less radiation shielding than the Earth, remember? That's why there aren't any Earth Lunatics."

Aiken nodded silently.

"Well, what if your body was already primed to accept more radiation because you are used to it from living here longer?"

"If that's true," Aiken mused, "then we should have seen a progression of abilities from mine to whoever is newest here."

"But we did, don't you see," Connor insisted. "Faith is the most recent immigrant, and she was the one most harmed by the exposure to quantum radiation."

"Well, who would be the next longest living here after me?" Aiken asked.

"That would be me," Nicole answered.

"Don't you see," Connor pursued. "Nicky has the next most talents. I bet if we mapped it out somehow, there would be a noticeable pattern."

Donnelly was tapping away at his wrist communicator, "He's right. People with multiple talents have been here longer than people with only a single ability."

"Is there any correlation between which ability they have and their time here?" Connor asked.

"If there is, I can't see it," Donnelly responded.

"Well, this is great," Connor enthused. "Nicky's brain stopped changing at the same pace, and she's been here almost as long as you. So you probably just have to wait."

Aiken was somewhat reassured by this. If it was just a matter of time, he supposed he could wait a little while longer. "I'm going to want to keep an eye on those change updates," he told Donnelly. "I don't want to end up like those other observers."

"I understand completely."

The rest of the noon hour passed uneventfully, with the Lunatics still buzzing about what they'd accomplished that morning. When the signal came that it was time to return to class, they went back energized for their afternoon courses.

While their English composition teacher was droning on about some writer who'd died two hundred years ago, Aiken and Connor were carrying on a mental conversation.

We should have another contest day, Connor thought, where he knew Aiken would be able to pick it up.

After how well the last one turned out? Are you nuts? Aiken responded.

Other than Quinn showing up, what really went wrong? Connor asked.

Well, not to put down our new friend or anything, but there are still some hard feelings over the way that all happened.

You're not worried about what Hugo would think? Connor asked carefully.

We don't need to create any more bad feelings, Aiken responded.

Hugo's feelings are not the problem, Connor said. *He's acting like a jerk because he's jealous of your abilities.*

What, you've got some secret insight? Aiken asked sarcastically.

No, I've just heard talk is all, Connor answered.

What that talk was, Aiken wouldn't find out. At that moment, the teacher noticed that he and Connor weren't paying attention and called on them to answer questions for the rest of the period.

Chapter Twenty-One

Friday, July 17th, 2139

The weeks passed quickly for the Lunatics. Since the mine rescue, the students had gotten more practiced at joining together to accomplish a task. Even Hugo grudgingly joined them on occasion. They tried channelling themselves through different people's talents, but discovered that it took a full telepath to gather and use all the mental strands, which limited the ability to Aiken, Nicole and Olivia. All three of them took turns at the head of the mental pyramid, but since Olivia's talents were limited to telepathy, she soon decided that it would be better for her to join as part of the power source, rather than the focal lens.

"After all," she reasoned, "all I can do at the head is shout loud enough to be heard on Neptune."

With Aiken or Nicole at the head, the group's talents were much more diverse. When Nicole gathered up the strands of thought, the group could lift large loads into orbit, should they choose. They could teleport objects and people back and forth between the moon and Earth. Quinn Donnelly had volunteered himself as a test subject for these attempts, and been surprised when they worked so precisely.

"We've been practicing on piles of rocks," Nicole told him mischievously after his trip. "You're not that different."

Aiken found that he had to limit his output when he wasn't in charge of the pyramid, or his mental strand tended to overwhelm Nicole and Olivia. He reined it in, until he discovered that he could send tendrils out to the other members of the power source and balance the load that way. Soon, other students began to feel Aiken's power flowing through them as they linked up. The whole group walked away from these sessions feeling super-energized.

When Aiken was at the focal point, the group could do nearly anything it put its mind to. On one day, more or less on a whim, they'd sublimated water out of the air to make it snow under the dome. While the air in the dome became noticeably drier, the students enjoyed their half hour in the Park with snow, until it melted and evaporated back into the air.

Donnelly had submitted his report to the NSA, after having had it looked over by Aiken and a couple other students. He wasn't sure why he was letting high school students look at a classified government report, but Aiken knew. The Lunatics had decided that in order to control their own public exposure, they would have to limit what Donnelly reported on. Aiken and Nicole had been tasked with redacting the agent's memories so that his report showed evidence of altered physiology, but made no mention of enhanced mental abilities.

Aiken was sorry to have to change the man's mind, but the group had deemed it necessary, and Aiken wasn't sure he disagreed. They were certain that if any government were to discover what the Lunatics were capable of, they'd become subjects of that government's weapons research program. So the report the government man sent out mentioned nothing of the students' capabilities. In order to ensure that nothing else got out, they had Donnelly clean out all the files and all the backups pertaining to mental abilities and convinced him that the altered brain physiology had simply quickened their response time, and nothing else.

When the agent was recalled at the end of a month, the students weren't too surprised. He'd reported nothing substantive and the NSA needed him back to work on other projects. He'd left net addresses where he could be reached, in case they had more questions about brain physiology and had departed two days ago on the shuttle outbound for Midway Station.

The students had more or less settled into a routine. Mondays and Thursdays, they got together in the Park to practice their abilities. The unaffected students joked about the "Physics club" that couldn't seem to get enough of each other's company, but no one was suspicious that anything else was going on.

Today was the last day of classes before the three-week summer break, so the Lunatics had gathered at lunch in the Park. Some of the students were leaving on vacation to other parts of the moon, so this was the last time they'd all be together before class restarted in mid-August. The mood was somewhat subdued. Not since the drive test that had given them their abilities had the group been separated.

Several Lunatics were telling the teleports to drop in anytime, and the projective telepaths promised they'd keep their friends updated every day. Aiken was talking with Connor about their respective vacation plans when Diana walked over to him. He could tell she wanted to talk to him alone, so he excused himself and walked over to where Diana was standing. Even aside from his telepathic gift, he could tell something was up.

"What is it?" he asked.

"Well, my parents and I are going to visit Serenity Station for the break."

"Lucky you," Aiken interjected.

"Yeah, it's just that Serenity is far away and full of things to see and do. I think it's unfair of me to ask you to wait for me while I'm off having fun without you."

"Wait, what are you saying?"

"I'm saying that maybe we should take a break."

Aiken did a quick surface mind scan to confirm what he thought he heard. He knew this moment was coming. He'd felt it building for a week or so now, but he didn't want to be the one to act on it. Now, all he felt was resignation.

"You're breaking up with me?"

"Aiken, you're a great guy, but I think we're better as friends." As she turned to walk away, Aiken realized it was for the best. He'd held an ideal of Diana in mind for so long that it was impossible for the real Diana to measure up to the mental image he'd had of her. He found that he was okay with the idea of remaining friends. He turned and walked back to Connor.

"Got dumped?" his friend asked, having watched the interplay.

"Yeah."

"You okay?"

"Yeah." Aiken paused. "I think it's probably for the best."

"Wow," Connor was impressed. "You're more okay with this than I thought you'd be."

"What do you mean?"

"I mean, you've been wanting to get together with Diana almost since she moved here. You had your chance and blew it, and you're okay with that."

"I didn't really blow it, is the thing," Aiken answered. "I just realised that my expectations for the relationship were different than the reality. I think hers were, too. It's better this way, I guess."

"How very mature of you," Connor teased.

"Yeah well, I think we've all done some growing up in the last couple months." The two were quiet as they contemplated this.

"So you're not going anywhere, then?" Connor broke the silence to confirm.

"Yeah, mom's big mineralogy conference is scheduled right over the break, and Peary's hosting, so that means we're staying put."

"Too bad. We're heading to Tranquility to visit the family. Ugh – cousins. I might have to teleport back to avoid them."

"These are the ones that are all younger than you?"

"Yeah. My sister gets along fine with most of them, but imagine being immersed in a sea of nine and ten year olds with ADHD."

"Ouch," Aiken commiserated. "You could always set up a game of hide and seek, then teleport yourself somewhere else. Tell them the first one who finds you gets a chocolate bar or something."

"Yeah, I'll be unbeatable at kids' games. Super."

"Well, if you feel up to it, come on back – we'll do some non-little-kid stuff and you can cleanse your palate before diving back in."

"It's a deal. Don't be surprised if you see me two days from now."

Aiken laughed. "Your tolerance level is that low?"

"We'll see."

On that note, the two friends headed back for the last afternoon of classes before the break.

**Part Two
The Damage**

Chapter Twenty-Two
Tuesday, August 4th, 2139

AIKEN!!! He woke in a panic. Someone had called his name. He searched mentally in the immediate vicinity for who would have called out to him. There was no one else in the apartment. His parents were both out at his mother's geological conference on moon mineralogy. He tried to relax and expand his mind to fill the dome to find whoever it was that had called to him in such a panicky voice. He was too wound up. He relaxed himself by taking a couple of deep breaths. In through the nose, out through the mouth. In through the nose, out through the mouth. *That's better.*

Once again, he let him mind expand to fill each nook and cranny of the dome. No one in Peary Dome had called on him. Mentally, he ticked off where the sending telepaths were vacationing. Nicole had stayed here in Peary, and Olivia had just returned, so that left.... *Diana!*

He sent his mind questing off to Serenity Station to find Diana. Mentally reaching the collection of domes, he cocked his senses to listen for Diana's telepathic voice. There was nothing. An unfamiliar mental echo permeated all of Serenity, but of Diana's mind, there was no sign. Pulling back, he tried to think of what to do. He couldn't look through the whole collection of domes fast enough by himself. He drew his mind back to Peary and called out to his fellow Lunatics. *Diana's in trouble – those who want to help, say "Aye" where I can see it!*

He got responses from Faith, Isaac, Mason, Nicole and Olivia. *Join with me to help look through Serenity.* Quickly, the other students, most of whom he'd woken up with his powerful telepathic hail, set their minds ready for Aiken to draft their mental energies in his service. With the combined power of the five other Lunatics and himself, he sent his questing probe back to Serenity Station. Marshalling the power at his disposal, he quickly swept the domes with his mental vision, seeing everything at once. *There!* It was Olivia who spotted her.

Diana lay curled in a ball in an empty hallway in an under-used section of the station. Without consciously thinking about it, Aiken teleported the six of them to her side.

"Whoa," Isaac said, unready for the sudden shift.

Belatedly, Aiken realized that he'd moved most of them in their sleepwear. Only Faith looked like she'd already been up and about at the early hour. That concern was suddenly subsumed when they saw Diana's body. It looked like she'd been in the blast-wake of a rocket engine. Her once-blonde hair was crisped to nothingness. Her skin was blackened and cracked. There was soot on the parts of her body that weren't ravaged by fire.

"Quickly," Aiken demanded. "Where's Kaira?"

"Uh, I think she and Jill went to Hadley for some R and R," Isaac answered.

"Can you get her here?' he asked Nicole.

"Not by myself," she replied.

"Use them," he indicated the other four.

As Nicole set to gathering up their mental strands for the push to Hadley, Aiken went to Diana. Deep scanning her, he found her life force, clinging precariously by a thread. The physical damage to her body was compounded by deep scarring in her psyche. Aiken didn't have Kaira's touch when it came to the healing ability, but he reached out anyway and reinforced the life that was so tenuously hanging on. A flicker of recognition passed over Diana's battered mind, but that was all. Aiken wanted to touch her, but was afraid of further damaging her ruined body. He held his hand palm down over her scorched skin and channelled his healing ability down his arm and through his hand to Diana. He couldn't feel anything changing in the damaged flesh beneath his hand and hoped that Nicole could find Kaira quickly enough. He tuned out everything around him and concentrated all his will on repairing the horrible damage wrought on the body lying in front of him.

After what felt like an eternity, he felt hands pulling at his shoulders and realised that Kaira had arrived. She assessed the damage critically, then, shaking her head in despair, set to work. Aiken sat back on his haunches and watched her mentally. Admiring Kaira's skill, he felt hope slip away even as she repaired Diana's broken form. He could see that Kaira was fighting a rising tide. Injuries compiled, and the work that Kaira was doing was soon overwhelmed by the sheer magnitude of the task. Aiken could see she was going to fail. He put out his hand to stop her. Angrily, she batted it away. Shaking with grief, he reached out again and drew Kaira back.

"You can't do anything more," he said.

"I know." The dam burst and Kaira started sobbing. Faith and Nicole drew her awkwardly back from the body to try to comfort her.

Aiken set to soothing Diana's last few moments. He reached out mentally and cradled her dying spark with soft touches. As she faded, he spoke calming words to her. Her mind was as weak as a leaf. As the last of her life slipped away, she thought two words: *Mason knows*.

Aiken bowed his head as Diana died there in front of him. Not worrying about hurting her any further, he reached out and stroked her burnt cheek softly. He felt a tremor go through his body, then another. He began to shiver there, in the middle of the corridor. He was shaking uncontrollably and couldn't get a hold of himself. *People might see*, he thought ludicrously. *We have to leave*. He couldn't form any more thoughts just then as a single tear made its way down his face. Suddenly he began to sob, great wracking cries shaking his whole body. He felt the hands of his fellow students reach down to comfort him, but he pushed them away. He wanted to be alone, but realised that he couldn't abandon his friends here in this strange place. Made strong by the emotions running through him, he teleported everyone back to where they'd come from, and erased every sign of their presence there in the hallway. Not wanting Diana to stay there undiscovered, he found a nearby security guard and mentally tweaked him to come and check out the corridor. Then he vanished himself to a place where none could follow and, weak, fell into a lifeless slumber.

Chapter Twenty-Three
Tuesday, August 4th, 2139

Aiken? Dimly, at the edge of perception, he heard a voice calling him. *Aiken, where are you?* He opened his eyes to blackness. Wondering where he was, he called out. *Who is it?*

The answer came back weakly, *It's Nicole. Where are you?*

I'm not sure, he answered. *Where are you?*

We're back at Peary Dome, she answered.

Back? he asked.

Yes… Nicole responded slowly.

Suddenly, it came crashing back on him. The call for help, the search, Diana's death. He just wanted to stay in this hole, wherever it was, and not come out. Then he remembered Diana's dying message.

Hang on, he told Nicole. *Where are you specifically?*

On the northwest edge of the Park, came the reply.

Aiken thought himself to their location and appeared dishevelled among his classmates. He saw from the puffy cheeks and red eyes that he wasn't the only one having trouble coping with what had transpired.

"Where were you?" Nicole asked him again. "I didn't know where to call, so I just sent it out wide."

"I'm not actually sure," he answered truthfully. "What is everyone doing here?" he asked carefully. Looking around, he saw not only the five others who'd been there in the morning, but also Connor, Liam, Penny and Gwen. They were all looking at him strangely. He realised he hadn't ever changed out of his flannel sleepwear.

"We need your help to find out what happened… what happened to Diana," Liam said with a tremble in his voice. "All we can figure from what we've heard is that it was no accident."

Aiken nodded, then rounded on Mason.

"Diana told me at the end that you knew. So spill it."

The others were shocked momentarily by the venom in Aiken's tone, but turned as one to hear what Mason had to say.

"It was the man of battle, the fiery one I warned you about," Mason sighed.

Aiken flashed back to that afternoon when everything had seemed so innocent. What had Mason said?

> *"The fiery man of battle comes*
> *The challenge will be brought*
> *One will turn*
> *Two will fall*
> *A leader will rise to fight*
> *And sacrifice all to win"*

Aiken remembered all too well now. The original shock at hearing this had been subsumed by the interruption of Quinn Donnelly, but now, eight weeks later, the warning seemed much clearer. *Diana was one of the fallen*, he thought to himself. *That means another one of us will die before this is over.* He felt like he was standing on the edge of a precipice, over a drop of unimaginable depth. He sensed a pressure at his back and knew that whatever happened next, nothing would ever be the same for him, or for the group. *Something new has come into being here.*

"Okay," Liam was speaking. "First, we need to find this man, and then we need to turn him over to the authorities."

Aiken thought to himself that Liam wasn't thinking clearly. If Mason was to be believed, and Aiken had no reason to doubt his prediction, only one of the members of the group would defeat the man, and only by giving up everything.

He felt his resolve harden, and spoke up, "That's not going to cut it. Mason saw one of us taking this guy out, not the cops. Besides, if this guy's as big a challenge as Mason's prediction implies, the police aren't going to be able to handle him."

"What do you suggest?" Liam asked.

"When I scanned Serenity by myself this morning, there was an echo or something. I think that's the bastard who killed Diana. We just have to look for whoever caused the echo."

"Well, it's a place to start," agreed Liam. "But there are going to be a lot of minds to scan."

"It shouldn't be that hard to find someone who enjoys setting people on fire," Aiken shot back. "If we join together behind a receiving telepathic sense, we should be able to ferret him out quick enough."

"And then what?" asked Liam.

"I say we give him a taste of his own medicine," Isaac said with hatred edging his voice. "Teleport him into one of the incinerators or something."

"That would be fitting," Connor agreed.

Aiken thought privately that they were probably underestimating their adversary, given Mason's prediction. He kept these thoughts to himself, however. "We need to get everyone else back here," he said aloud.

"Good idea," Liam agreed. "The more we have, the easier this should be."

"You come up with a list and I can bring them here," Aiken said. "I just need a minute, so figure out where everyone is before I get back."

Aiken teleported himself to his room, changed into some clothes, and looked at himself in the mirror. The face that stared back at him had eyes ringed with red and dark circles below them. *I look like hell,* he thought.

He teleported himself back to the group and looked over the list they'd compiled. Without a word, he started contacting the other members of the group, letting them in on what had happened, and offering to teleport them to Peary to join in on the search. Each of the students made excuses to their families about having to leave, and made ready for the trip. When they'd all gathered, they outlined the plan as it stood, and prepared to join together to teleport to Serenity Station. Aiken gathered up the strands of the thirteen minds and jumped the group to Serenity.

Chapter Twenty-Four
Wednesday, August 5th, 2139

Eight frustrating hours later, he conceded that they had failed. He and the others had scanned every inch of each of the domes and found no sign of anyone who could possibly have done what was done to Diana.

At around midnight, he'd gone to the security station to see if they knew anything more about Diana's murder, but the law enforcement officers were clueless. There was no sign of any kind of accelerant on Diana's body or her clothes. A fire in a sealed environment like a habitat should have set off alarms through the whole station, but according to the internal sensors, no fire had occurred, despite the evidence of Diana's body.

Aiken was sitting with a female lab technician going over the sensor readings. If she thought it was odd that a teenager who'd just walked in off the street was allowed access to the secure area of the law enforcement building, she didn't say anything. "As I said, there are no surveillance cameras in the hallway where it happened."

"Well, what do the other sensors show?"

"No fire, if that's what you're asking."

"No, we established that already," Aiken said. He prodded her mentally. He felt a pang of conscience, but smothered it. This was important.

"Well, what we do have is a temperature spike in the area."

Go on, Aiken ordered her.

She brought up a map of the dome where Diana was found, and zoomed down to the corridor where the body was. Touching a few buttons made the display change colours. "See, here's the hallway just before the estimated time of death." It was muted blue with a couple of orange splotches. A time clock ticked off minutes every ten seconds in the bottom right hand corner of the screen.

A sudden flare of white in the middle of

the screen caught Aiken's attention. "What was that?"

"We have no idea," the tech answered, "but it's undoubtedly what killed your friend."

"Back that up again," he requested.

The technician obliged, and he watched Diana's murder in false-colour heat maps for the second time.

"Again," he repeated.

He noticed something just a little further up the corridor. "What's that?"

"I don't know," the technician replied. "I didn't notice it."

"Can you slow down the playback at all?"

"Sure."

This time he was sure. "See, there," he said, pointing. "There's a smaller heat bloom up the corridor right before, uh, the, uh, main event."

"You're right," the tech confirmed. Calling in her supervisor, she pointed out the early heat mark. Her supervisor called the detective in charge and passed on the location of the new heat source. Aiken watched the recording twice more before determining that there was nothing else to be seen on it.

He waited for a couple of minutes for the law enforcement officer on the scene to call back with a preliminary analysis of the new location.

When he found himself pacing, he knew it was time to go somewhere else. He redacted his presence out of the memories of the technician and the supervisor and teleported to the corridor where they'd found Diana that morning.

He rendered himself invisible using Hugo's technique and watched as the crime scene analysts checked the location further up the corridor. He was careful not to touch anything so there would be no physical evidence of his presence, to the point where he floated himself above the floor as he moved along.

"There's nothing here either," he heard one of the analysts say. "No residue, no prints, no nothing. Just a little discolouration in the ceiling."

Aiken used his mental sight to zoom in on the discolouration. He didn't really know what he was looking for. It just looked like a warped ceiling tile to him. Disappointed, he headed back to the rendezvous spot where the group was supposed to meet up in about fifteen minutes.

The next person to arrive was Ethan, who had been tasked with looking into records to see if any of this type of crime had occurred in Serenity Station. Aiken looked at him questioningly. Ethan shook his head slowly and lowered his eyes.

"Let's hope Nicole has some news, then." Nicole had been given the job of going to Immigration Control to see if any new arrivals had flagged any alarms.

One by one the group returned and reported no success. Even Nicole hadn't found anything suspicious. No one with a previous criminal record had entered or exited Serenity Station in the last couple of days. The students reasoned it was a local, or someone had somehow circumvented the entry and exit protocols.

Once the entire group had gathered, weary and heartsick, they tried to decide what to do next, but too many people had too many different ideas, and the discussion went nowhere. It was late, they were tired, and they'd all just suffered a devastating loss. Aiken teleported the eight who'd been outside Peary back to their families, then linked up with the remaining five and moved the group *en masse* back to the Park in the center of their home dome. Even the bright sunlight streaming through the glass at the top of the dome couldn't allay the guilt and anger and helplessness Aiken felt. *I have all this power available and I can't even find one man*, he thought bitterly. *I can't even save a friend.*

The five that were gathered around him

223

sat silently together for a few minutes. Faith and Olivia leaned on each other, both having been Diana's friends. Mason, who'd also been in her class, sat with his arm around Olivia. Olivia and Diana had been close, and she was particularly feeling the loss.

"C'mon," Mason said to the two girls. "I'll walk you home." The three classmates got up and left, leaving the three younger students sitting morosely on the damp grass. Isaac looked at his wrist communicator, and noticing that it was two in the morning, announced that he too was heading home. That left only Aiken and Nicole. Nicole scooted over to sit next to Aiken.

The two friends sat in silence a while longer, then Nicole put her hand on Aiken's knee and said, "It's not your fault this time, either."

"What?"

"Diana's death wasn't your fault. Just like the time when Gwen dropped me, it's not your fault. You did everything you could to save her. You thought quickly, you brought in the people who needed to be there and she still died. You must be thinking that there is something else that you could have done. There isn't. She didn't die because of you. She didn't..." Nicole trailed off.

"Maybe if we hadn't broken up, she..."

Aiken trailed away.

"Would that have made a difference?" Nicole's eyes were compassionate. "No, this wasn't your fault."

Tears sprang to Aiken's eyes. These were hard words to hear. He didn't want to absolve himself. He still wanted to blame himself for not having done something, anything to save Diana's life. Turning to Nicole, he clung to her as once more that day, he cried. She hugged him tightly and repeated that he couldn't have done anything more for Diana. When he had finished, he felt like someone had put him through the ringer. Aches and pains that he hadn't noticed came to the forefront of his mind. He was tired. Not just physically, but mentally as well. The stress that he'd put his abilities through that day seemed to suddenly pounce on him, wiping him right out.

He stood and pulled Nicole to her feet as well. He needed sleep, and he could tell his friend was on her last reserve as well. "Thanks Nicky," was all he managed.

"Well, someone has to tell you," she smiled at him. "You're so stubborn that you think everything should just happen the way you want it to, and when it doesn't, you think there's something wrong with you."

He chuckled a little at her insight. "When

did you get so smart?" he teased her.

"I've always been smarter than you," she teased back. "You just never realised it until now."

A thought occurred to Aiken. "Someone's going to have to tell Kaira the same thing. I bet she's blaming herself, too."

Nicole agreed. "There's someone who should be blamed for Diana's death, but it isn't anyone in the group. We'll find him, though. Mason said so."

Aiken felt his resolve strengthen. She was right. Mason's prediction had said that the man of flames would be defeated by a member of their group.

On that note, the two friends parted, and Aiken, for the first time that day, felt hope as he headed home.

Chapter Twenty-Five
Friday, August 14th, 2139

A fruitless week and a half later, and Aiken's hope was just about spent. After they'd resumed classes on Monday, they'd held a memorial service for Diana on Wednesday. It was a sombre affair - while deaths happened on the moon with about the same regularity as back on Earth, this was the first classmate that they'd lost, and to have her taken in such a manner was a shock to all of them. The students who knew Diana huddled together for comfort. Aiken sat apart from them, feeling numb and, despite Nicole's words, somewhat responsible. He'd been back to Serenity Station every day since that terrible day the week before and still there was nothing to show for the investigation. His mind went back to the scene in the corridor at the most inappropriate times, and he knew that he was spinning his wheels, but felt compelled to do something to try to alleviate his lingering guilt. As the service progressed, Aiken felt the empty part of himself where Diana had been fill with some unrecognisable emotion. He stopped paying attention to the words spoken from the front of the auditorium and focused inwards. A strange buzzing filled his ears and his eyes blurred once more. He swallowed past the lump in his throat and returned his attention to the eulogy, recognising the emotion filling him at last: vengeance.

The investigators at Serenity, who hadn't had much to go on to begin with, had hit a wall. No new leads had emerged from the scene, or from Diana's body. While the death was ruled as suspicious, there was no known cause, or motivation. It was a perplexing case, and frustrating to the investigators, who were being pressured because the deceased was the daughter of dome administrators. With no leads, the case remained open, but no one was actively working on it.

This angered Aiken, even as he understood the reasoning behind it. There were other crimes in Serenity Station for the law enforcement people to focus their time and energy on, and the mysterious death of one teenager, important though her parents might be, was no longer at the top of their priority list.

The Lunatics had done no better with their unofficial investigation. There was no one in authority they hadn't mind-scanned, no one on the investigative team they hadn't questioned extensively. Nothing was off-limits when it came to the investigation, they'd decided. But eventually, they had run out of things to look for. A couple of times during the first two or three days after Diana's death, Aiken had, either by himself or with a few others, done sweeping scans of the whole of Serenity Station in an attempt to find the perpetrator. Nothing had ever turned up.

It was the last class of the day on the last day of the week, and Aiken fully intended to return to Serenity when class was done to see if anything new had turned up. When the final bell rang, he headed out of the classroom and down the corridor to the Park, intending to teleport out from a screened off thicket of bushes he'd found earlier in the summer.

Just as he exited the corridor leading to the park, Connor caught up to him. "I've got something you're going to want to see," he said.

He brought his wrist communicator up and set if to project. On the wall, Aiken saw a sight that was etched forever onto his memory. Except it wasn't Diana's body that lay scorched in the middle of the corridor on Connor's projection.

"Where is this? When did it happen?" Aiken demanded.

"It just happened," Connor answered breathlessly. "Well," he amended, "the body was just found. I've got my com scanning the news for anything like this, in case our guy turned up again."

"Nice job," Aiken said. "Where did this happen?"

"You're not going to like it."

"Spit it out," Aiken insisted.

"Tranquility Station."

Aiken swore softly. "That's not going to help our chances of finding this guy. There are a million people there, and they're coming and going constantly. We're going to need everyone in on this, right now."

"I know."

Aiken sent out a quick mental hail, apprising the Lunatics of the situation. They all agreed on the need to move quickly so that the perpetrator would not give them the slip again. In ones and twos they started arriving in the Park where Aiken and Connor waited. Once all fourteen were there, Aiken used their combined power to teleport them to Tranquility Station, close to where the victim had been found. The students quickly broke up into the teams they had used a week earlier in Serenity Station and began scouring the base's domes for any sign of the man behind the two identical attacks.

They ran into the Tranquility security apparatus on more than a few occasions, as the security forces were also on alert following the death. Aiken decided to cut right to the chase and went in search of the law enforcement group's headquarters. Once more, he finagled himself into the processing area where the technicians were puzzling over the materials they'd recovered from the scene. He found himself sitting next to a tech on a video machine again, and had him cue up the corridor where the most recent crime had occurred with the heat map. Once again, the killer had picked a section of corridor with no actual video surveillance devices, so the investigators were having to rely on secondary recordings. The time code on the video playback approached the time when the crime was committed. Aiken saw the heat outlines of two people walking into the corridor section. "That's different," he said to the tech.

"Not really," the tech replied. "Our equipment has a lower sensing threshold than

Serenity Station's."

Onscreen, one of the outlines became brilliant and blurry and then was no more. Less of the body of the victim had been recovered this time. Only enough had remained to determine that it was a male, aged eighteen to thirty. No height or weight characteristics had been determined yet, and it was too soon for a missing persons report to have been filed. They didn't know who the victim was.

"Can you run that back for me again?" Aiken asked. Knowing what to look for, this time, he pointed out the heat glow in the murderer's body just prior to the victim being engulfed in flames. In this higher-resolution recording, Aiken could see that the glow started in the killer's head, and spread to the rest of his body before shifting to the victim.

It starts in his head, Aiken thought to himself. Not yet ready to share his thought with anyone, he excused himself from the tech's presence and exited the laboratory, redacting himself out of their memories as he did so.

Once he'd left the building, he called mentally for Nicole, Olivia and Ethan. Updating them with what he'd learned, he told them to be on the lookout for someone else with mental abilities. *That may be easier to scan for than memories of murder*, he said.

You're right, Ethan thought where they could all pick it up, *there's something about our modified minds that unaltered minds don't have.*

Well, Aiken said to the others, *I'd like to keep this to just the four of us for now, until we're sure we're looking for a modified mind.*

You think it could be a Lunatic? One of us? Olivia asked. *Who could have done it?*

No, no, Aiken assured them. *For one, we were all in class today, when this latest murder happened, so we're all off the hook.* He could feel their relief coming through the mental link that bound them.

Alright, Aiken continued, *be on the lookout for someone like us.* With that, he withdrew his mental presence and began scanning his immediate area for signs of someone with enhanced mental faculties.

As he walked through the crowded concourses of Tranquility's Dome 3, he let his mind roam, looking into the shops and restaurants that crowded the boulevards of the dome's ground level. Once or twice he thought he caught a flicker of something on the edge of his consciousness, but when he chased it down, invariably it was nothing, or the outer limit of one of the other Lunatics' scans.

The search was wending its way through the cluster of twenty domes that made up

Tranquility Station. The students had split the search between them, with a receiving telepath in each of the three large groups, and Aiken alone as the fourth group, since he didn't require linking up to produce sufficient power to scan the whole level of a dome.

He took lifts from level to level until he'd covered all fifteen levels of Dome 3. He moved through the causeway to the larger Dome 7, and started once more on the lowest level. Once more, he caught a sense of something niggling at the back of his perception, but when he scanned the area more intensely, he found nothing.

Curious, he let his mind drift as he wandered aimlessly past rows of offices and conference rooms on the main level of Dome 7. He was no longer doing a grid search, but allowing his instincts to guide him. He had a hunch that would prove more fortuitous than the search they'd been previously conducting. There was simply no way to separate out one mind from the tens of thousands of others that crowded each of the domes of Tranquility Station. Rather than scan each mind as he encountered it, his consciousness was studiously casual, a brush against a mind here, a light touch on another there. Dismissing each mind as soon as he'd encountered it, he progressed his way across the two kilometre radius of the dome, arriving at the central core. Here, a bank of lifts going to each of the levels above proved a good choice for assessing the ebb and flow of people to each level. Instead of spreading his listening ability out over a whole level, he focused vertically to catch people coming and going from the lifts on each of the twenty levels of the dome. He sat down on a bench which gave a view of a half dozen of the fifty-odd lifts in the dome's core. As the people flowed in and out of the lifts, he alighted briefly on each mind, experienced it for a fraction of a second, then moved on.

Aiken was growing tired with his inability to find the man they were looking for. He contacted each of the other groups to find out what they had turned up. So far, no one had found anything out of the ordinary. No minds in any of the areas carried the aura of alteration by quantum radiation. None of the people that they'd scanned were the murderer.

He was sitting dejectedly on the bench, considering what their next move might be, when a man walked up to him and extended his hand in introduction.

"My name," the man said cordially, "is Zacharias Warman. I see that you are looking for something very particular and wondered if I might be of assistance."

Aiken looked the man over. He didn't look like a vagabond. He was dressed respectably in a dark grey business suit. His wavy black hair was slicked back from his forehead. His intense brown eyes looked out from under sharply defined brows, lending a look of keen intelligence to his face. He seemed friendly enough, if obviously a little peculiar for having approached a lone teenager in a crowded embarkation and debarkation area. He waved off the stranger. "I don't think you can help me," he said.

"Oh, no? The frequencies you are scanning are very familiar to me."

Aiken's jaw dropped in amazement. He had no scanning equipment on him. The man could only mean the mental search that Aiken had ongoing. Immediately suspicious, he asked, "Who did you say you were again?"

"Zacharias Warman," the man replied with a flourish. He pulled a business card from the inside breast pocket of his jacket. Aiken looked at it cautiously. Beside the animated personal icon, it listed the man's name and gave his occupation as "professional psychic", and his professional affiliation as entertainment division.

Aiken looked up quickly and asked, "How do you know I'm scanning for something?"

"My dear boy," Warman replied, "You're disturbing the aether as only someone intent on finding something could."

"Aether?"

"You know, the aether," the man looked confused. "That which fills the spaces between all things which have mass."

Aiken laughed. "You're nuts," he said.

"On the contrary," the man insisted, "I am the one who is sane. All telepathy is propagated through the aether."

"If you say so," Aiken chuckled. Evidently, this poor soul had deluded himself into thinking that he was telepathic and constructed an explanation that made sense to him.

I do say so, Aiken Drum, the man thought at Aiken.

Aiken stopped laughing, and for the second time that afternoon, his jaw dropped in astonishment. A non-Lunatic telepath. *So there are others*, he thought to himself. Quickly, he sent his mental probe at the man's mind, hoping to unearth the source of the stranger's telepathy. As his probe reached the outer surface of the man's thoughts, however, it was deflected. Once more, he formed a mental probe and sent it arrowing towards the man's mind. Again, it was effortlessly deflected. Straining, now, Aiken pushed against the stranger's mental shields.

"Now, now," Warman chided, "that's quite rude."

Aiken was astonished. None of his classmates could block him at that level. His astonishment quickly turned to suspicion. A man of this talent could easily have eluded the Lunatics' search for the killer. He began to question the man.

"Where did you get your ability?"

"Where did you get yours?" the man responded enigmatically. "All abilities flow from the same source. Each receives according his readiness. I myself have a variety of talents, some of which are marketable." He indicated the business card in Aiken's hand.

Aiken would not be dissuaded. "When did you get your talents, then?"

"Aiken, I am like you. I was affected by the QT drive as you were."

"Wait, what?" Aiken was confused. "How did you know that about me?"

"It's there on the tip of your mind, as is the suspicion that I am a fireman." Warman chuckled. "Which I'm not."

Aiken thought to himself deep in his mind that it was fortunate the man hadn't seen any more than that. He raised the strongest mental shield he knew how to construct, a skill he'd been developing working with the other telepaths at the Lunatics meetings.

"So," the man continued affably, "can I help you find something?"

"I don't think so," Aiken responded, unable to rid himself of the sense that something about this man was very, very wrong.

The man's expression turned stony. "You are making a mistake, Mr. Drum."

"I'm sorry?"

"I can help you. I can help you look. Don't turn me away."

"I'm sorry," Aiken explained. "I don't know you, and what I'm looking for is very important."

"I guarantee that it is not as important as what I can do to help."

"I rather doubt that."

The man paused, then said conspiratorially, "I can teach you a method to boost your telepathy ten-fold. Your search will go much easier."

"I don't have time to learn any new tricks right now," Aiken said. "If I want to boost my power, I'll just link up with some of the others." As soon as he'd said this, he recognized from the sharp look on Warman's face that he'd made a drastic mistake.

"And how many of 'the others' are

239

around here right now?" the man questioned him.

"A couple," Aiken tried to limit the damage he knew in his gut that he'd caused.

"I shall see if any of them are more amenable to my offer," Warman said, then vanished with a pop Aiken knew was associated with teleportation.

Damn it, Aiken thought to himself. He was frustrated with his inability to pin down what it was about Warman that gave him bad vibes. *Better call everyone back before he gets around to them.*

Aiken began contacting the search parties. He did not speak of Zacharias Warman, instead inquiring about their progress and asking whether they were ready to call it a day. While none the students wanted to stop looking for Diana's killer, the sheer size of Tranquility Station had overwhelmed them. They recognised that they'd given it their best attempt. They'd had a better lead on the killer and still hadn't managed to apprehend him. They had some new information, though, and that might make it easier if the killer struck again.

Aiken linked up with the group and they teleported back to Peary Dome. When Aiken saw how exhausted they were, he decided against telling them of his encounter with Warman, knowing that it would provoke a long discussion that would, in all probability, take them nowhere. Instead, he indicated mentally to Connor, Nicole, and Liam that he had something to tell them. As the other students trudged homeward, the group Aiken had requested gathered around him.

Aiken dropped his bombshell, "I met another telepath today."

Shock and astonishment followed Aiken's announcement.

"What? Who? Where?" the questions poured forth. Aiken went back over the story, including his impressions of Zacharias Warman. The rest of the group were disturbed somewhat to hear that there were others out there with mental shields capable of deflecting the probes of the group.

"Wait," Connor said. "I'm not telepathic, but wouldn't the fact that someone's shielded be a dead giveaway that they're like us?"

"It didn't feel like a shield until I really pressed against it," Aiken answered. "It was like there just wasn't a mind there. One-on-one it would be pretty easy to tell, but in a crowd, there's no time to match minds to bodies. If there was someone walking by that I couldn't see mentally, he'd pass right below my radar."

Nicole nodded her assent. "If Aiken couldn't detect him, you can be sure I'd miss him, too."

"I wonder what his ability multiplier is?" Liam mused aloud.

"No idea," Aiken responded, "but I'm fairly sure it doesn't involve a group of like-minded Lunatics. He was distinctly surprised when I mentioned that we linked. Though not that there were more of us."

"You mean he's got a technique for amplifying himself without any help? Maybe you should have taken him up on his offer to teach you," Connor suggested.

"No way. The guy creeped me out. There was something about him that just wasn't... right."

"I wonder if we could use our government connections to find out more about him," Nicole suggested.

"What are you talking about?" Aiken asked.

"You remember that Quinn left us his net addresses? I bet he'd be interested in someone else who survived the drive experiment with physiological changes."

"You're right," Liam agreed. "And while we've got his interest piqued, we should have him send us anything the government's got on this Warman guy."

"So when do we let everyone else in on this?" Nicole asked.

"Good question." Aiken paused. "If we keep it to ourselves, we're going to be accused of hoarding the power he offered. On the other hand, once the cat's out of the bag, there's no going back."

"I say we call a meeting for tomorrow, uh, I mean today," Liam said, looking at his wrist communicator. "Sometime in the afternoon so we can sleep a little."

With a plan in place, the four split up and headed back to their homes.

Chapter Twenty-Six
Saturday, August 15th, 2139

Rising early, Aiken decided to get some investigating done before the meeting that afternoon. He knew that they wouldn't get much accomplished over the weekend, given the number of government offices closed, but he also knew he had to try, for Diana. One place he did visit again was Tranquility's security headquarters. Nothing new had turned up in the time since he'd last been there, but he watched the recording of the attack again, trying to identify the killer. It was useless – all he could see were coloured blobs shifting around on the screen.

He returned to Peary disappointed, but not surprised. This was the same thing that had happened in the days after Diana's death. The futility that had overwhelmed him then he managed to hold at bay now. They had a whole lot more information this time out, starting with the fact that the killer was probably someone with enhanced mental abilities. Topping the list of suspects was the telepath Zacharias Warman, charming and dangerous as he'd seemed the day before. Unless and until more people with abilities announced themselves, all of the class's efforts would focus on Warman.

He'd know more about Warman once he'd talked with Nicole. She'd taken the job of contacting Quinn Donnelly and getting other information about Warman. He headed over to her place now. She was still on the nets when he arrived, so he waited for a couple of minutes in her living room. He looked around while he passed the time. He hadn't spent much time here since he and Nicole were kids, when they used to build forts in this very room out of cushions from her parents' couch. That couch was long gone now but the memories remained. He looked at photos on the wall and saw places he recognised in most of them. The earlier photos showed a happy family of three and Aiken distinctly remembered going along on a couple of family picnics with the Spencers when he and Nicole had started grade school. It was only a couple of years after those outings that Nicole's father was diagnosed with a form of bone cancer, too late to do anything but watch him die. He was buried on the moon outside Peary Dome, and Nicole and her mother continued to live in the apartment that they'd all shared, but something had changed in Nicole and Aiken hadn't come over much after that.

Aiken turned away from the photos as Nicole walked in from the hallway. She looked troubled, so he indicated the couch by the coffee table in the middle of the room, and they both sat down.

"Aiken," she said. "Quinn's dead."

"What?"

"Yeah. He died in a vehicle crash on July 28th."

Aiken did some figuring in his head. "That's less than two weeks from when he was last here. Is there any indication it was related to us?"

"Not that I can tell. The cars were so badly burned that the bodies were unrecognisable. They had to be identified through DNA."

"Wait, burned?"

"Yeah, the fuel cores exploded on impact.

There was a recall issued on the car that Donnelly hit because the cells had a tendency to destabilise with enough force."

"Oh," Aiken said. "Well, you're right. It doesn't sound like it has anything to do with us."

"Yeah, it's just too bad he's gone. We could have really used his input on this."

"I'm sure an NSA agent has more important things to look after than one murder on the Moon."

"Maybe, but now that we know that some enhanced person did it, that might pique his interest," Nicole argued.

"He doesn't recall that there are people with enhanced abilities, remember?"

"Oh, right." She paused. "Well, since the memory process is an overlay of new memories, maybe it's possible to peel back the new ones so we could have gotten at his originals."

"Can you imagine how mad he would have been to be tricked by a bunch of kids, though?" Aiken thought about this for a minute, his discomfort with their original interference with Quinn's mind resurfacing. "Oh well, it's a moot point anyway."

"Yeah," she responded gloomily.

"Well," he asked after a minute, "what else did you find out about Mr. Warman?"

"Not a lot," she replied. "I've got entry and exit points for a couple places on the moon, a request filed and approved for lunar work status as an entertainer, and that's about it."

"Can you tell where he was when Diana was killed?"

"Yeah, during that time, he was at Farside Station, doing mind readings and hypnosis at one of their casinos."

"What, really?"

"Yeah, he was doing three shows a night at the MGM Grand."

"Do we have anything more precise for the time of Diana's attack?"

"No, as near as I can tell."

"Well, it could still be him, then."

"How?" Nicole asked.

"He can teleport," Aiken explained. "He did it right at the end of our little chat."

"Oh, right, you mentioned that last night." She paused. "Teleportation through the entire moon has got to be harder than just jumping around inside a dome, though. Do you know how far he went?"

"How could I track him? He's got that blasted strong shield – it was like he just blinked out of existence there in front of me."

Nicole shrugged. "We'll figure it out," she said.

Aiken was a little more frustrated, "We need to see if we can get a lead on this guy. If he killed Diana and that other guy, we're not doing anything to catch him."

"We're going to get him, Aiken," Nicole said earnestly. "You have to believe that. Mason said it would happen."

"Yeah, but he also said someone else would die and one of us will 'turn', whatever that means."

"Yeah," Nicole reflected. "I'm not so keen on that bit."

"Well, it seemed kind of a package deal – we either don't catch the guy, or those parts come true, too. And I'm not happy with the idea either, but I think we owe it to Diana to catch this guy."

"Right," Nicole agreed. The pair sat in silence for a few minutes before Nicole mentioned that her mother had put some leftovers in the fridge. She offered to split them with Aiken and the two ate a quiet lunch at the kitchen table before heading off to join the rest of the group and share the information about Zacharias Warman with them.

When they arrived at the usual meeting place in the Park, there was no one else there yet, so they sat on the grass and waited for the others to begin showing up. Aiken was mentally toying with some of the insects in the grass, picking them up with his mind and putting them down, as well as using his mental sight ability on them to see them close up and inside. His mind wandering, he suddenly felt his vision snap into focus. Around him, the Park burned. Trees were crisped and the ground was baked. The air was singed and scorched his throat when he breathed it in. The smell of smoke and death was in the air and there were cries coming from people lying in and around the Park. These people – he knew some of them. Some of these people worked with his parents, some were parents of friends. All were burned. He saw out of the corner of his eye Kaira moving from body to body, lending aid where she could, lending relief where she could not help. He looked down at himself. He was covered in ash. His clothes were filthy and his skin was red and blistered, though even before his eyes, his body had started to heal itself. He drifted over to the closest person and asked them what had happened. She lay there oblivious to his presence. He called out louder. No response. He stood up and shouted as loud as he could. No one paid him any attention. It was like he wasn't there. Just then, he saw a monstrous dark figure rise up on the other side of the dome. Looming outside the dome, the dark man taunted him without words. *You cannot stop me,* he seemed to say, though nothing was spoken.

And just as suddenly as it had come to him, the vision left, and he found himself once more seated on the grass in the middle of the Park across from Nicole, with trees green and alive all around them. He sat up straighter and, blinking, coughed the smoke out from his throat. *Wait, smoke?* he thought. *Wasn't it just a vision?*

Looking across at Nicole, she didn't seem to have seen anything amiss. He sniffed at his sleeve. Definitely a burned smell to it.

He held his arm up to Nicole, "Smell this." She wrinkled her nose in disgust at the odour emanating from his clothes.

"Did you go see the body of that young man in Tranquility?" she asked.

"No, I was just... I mean, I thought I was... I think I saw..." Aiken was somewhat distraught by his inability to piece together what had just happened.

"Just start from the beginning," Nicole urged.

"I was sitting here with you, and I let my mind wander a bit and I had a vision. Only it wasn't a vision, because of the smell..." he trailed off.

"Wait, what do you mean?"

"Did I leave?"

"What, here?" Nicole was confused.

"Yes, just now – did I go anywhere?"

"Well, I wasn't watching too closely," Nicole said, blushing somewhat, "but if you did, you weren't gone for that long. No more than a couple of seconds."

"It was definitely more than that – a few minutes at least."

"A few minutes of what?" A new voice joined in.

Both Aiken and Nicole swivelled around to see where the voice was coming from. They looked up and saw Connor standing over them.

"That's what we're trying to figure out," Aiken told him. "I was sitting here, and then I wasn't, though Nicole says it can't have been more than a couple of seconds and I say it can't have been less than a couple of minutes."

"Of what?" Connor asked.

"Being gone," Aiken replied.

"I'm still confused," Connor said.

"Me too, honestly," Nicole added.

"Okay, I was sitting here and then I had a vision, only it wasn't a vision because my clothes still smell." He held his arm up so Connor could take a whiff.

"Whoa," Connor said. "Where were you?"

"The future, I think, only I still can't

figure out how I was there for a couple of minutes in the space of a couple of seconds."

"Oh, that's easy enough," Connor answered. "You just came back from minutes away back to right after you left."

"Uh, right," Aiken said. "Anyways, in this future, we'd just lost a fight, as near as I can tell."

"What do you mean?" Nicole asked, concern evident in her voice.

Aiken pointed all around, "Everything was burned. The grass, the people, everything. And there was someone outside the dome who caused it all."

"Who?" Connor asked eagerly.

"I don't know," Aiken answered dejectedly. "I never saw him clearly, but he was the cause of everything, I know it."

The three considered this as the other students started to drift into the park. Aiken decided to keep his vision to this small group for the time being, so as not to cause more anxiety to everyone.

When they were all seated, Liam stood up. Nodding to Aiken, he started, "I know we're all tired and frustrated from yesterday, and the time before." He paused for a moment, searching for words. "Yesterday wasn't a total loss, as it turns out. We collected some very useful information." The students exchanged curious glances, as if to see who among them had found something out.

When Liam gestured, Aiken stood and began, "As you know, when I went to the security station on Serenity to see if they knew anything, all they had turned up was a hot spot up the corridor from where Diana was murdered." Several students flinched at his blunt choice of words, but Aiken ignored them and forged on. "Yesterday, I went to the Tranquility security station to see if they'd recorded them same thing. Because their equipment is better than Serenity's, they were able to give us more information." Aiken paused, knowing that what he said next would be a shock to most of the Lunatics. "The killer strikes with his mind."

A dead silence fell over the group. After a few seconds, Gwen asked hesitantly if Aiken was certain. "As sure as I can be," Aiken answered truthfully. He went on to explain about the heat images recorded by the Tranquility Station security service.

"But," interjected Penny, her eyebrows furrowed, "we were all in class when that one happened."

"Yes," Aiken responded, knowing he was about to shock them a second time in as many minutes. "It appears that there are other people with the same powers as us. I met one yesterday."

The mutterings that had started up in the wake of Penny's question now turned into a full-blown roar.

Quiet. Olivia's command tone had the desired effect, and all the Lunatics fell silent. Aiken nodded at her before continuing.

"His name is Zacharias Warman, and he is an entertainer. He also has the strongest mental shield I've encountered, making it impossible for me to see if he was the killer." Aiken quickly went over the conversation he'd had with Warman the day before, but was interrupted when he reached the part where Warman had offered to teach him a technique to boost his power.

"So he knows some way of making himself stronger without linking up with anyone else?" Hugo asked.

"He was distinctly surprised when I mentioned that there was a way of linking with enhanced people," Aiken answered honestly.

"Wait, what?" Hugo was waving his hand in the air agitatedly, "you told him about us?"

Aiken looked glum when he answered, "It slipped out before I really had thought about it." He paused, then looked around the group. "He said he might try to find some of you to see if you were interested. I thought I should let you know in case he does find you."

"What should we do?" asked Ethan. "I mean, if he's stronger than you, he's going to be stronger than any of us." There were murmurs of assent at this.

"I'm not convinced that he is stronger, just his mental shield makes it difficult to spot or track him. It might be possible for Liv, Nicole or me to crack it at the head of the group, but I don't think any of us by ourselves could do it." Aiken paused. "Warman's ability to camouflage himself and deceive telepaths puts him at the top of our list of suspects."

"Yeah, and it's lonely at the top," Connor chimed in. Everyone had a nervous little chuckle at that, realising, as Connor had, that Warman was really their only suspect at the moment.

"The question is," Liam said, retaking his place in front of the group while Aiken gratefully sat down, "what do we do about Warman now?"

"We need to find him right away," Ethan advised. "We can't do anything about him until we know where he is." Murmurs of agreement greeted this.

"That's all well and good," Hugo interjected sardonically, "but how are you going to find him when Aiken told us straight out that even he can't sense him?"

"We don't need to sense him to find him," Aiken spoke up.

"How's that?" Hugo shot back.

"He gave me his business card, and Nicky says he's been working the MGM Grand in Farside. We just have to check when he's got a show scheduled, and be there."

"Okay, but then what?" Liam pursued.

Aiken shrugged and looked around to the other students for inspiration. No one said anything for a bit, then Olivia spoke up.

"I don't know about the rest of you, but if this is the guy that killed Diana, I want to see him destroyed. Someone that can do the things he did to another human being doesn't deserve any leniency." She looked around to see affirmation in the eyes of her classmates.

"We already decided that the cops wouldn't be able to handle someone like this, given Mason's prediction," Aiken reminded the group. "We just need to know if it's Warman or not. I bet I can crack his shield if he isn't expecting it, and I've got the group behind me."

Liam smiled tightly. "Sounds like we have a plan."

Connor looked up from his wrist, where he'd been fiddling with his communicator. "He's got a show scheduled at eight this evening."

"Great," Liam said. "We can meet back here at seven-ish and teleport over there." After the group had signalled their approval, the meeting broke up as everyone headed off to get ready for the confrontation that evening.

Connor, Aiken and Nicole remained sitting on the grass of the Park. When the rest of the group had dispersed, Connor spoke up. "Do you think you'll have enough juice to crack Warman right after you've teleported us through the center of the moon?"

Aiken snorted lightly, "Caught that, did you?" Connor glanced over at his friend. "I sure hope so. I wonder if everyone isn't putting a little too much faith in my abilities."

"I think it's more a matter of you being their only hope at getting a shot at Warman," Nicole interjected.

"Yes, Obi Wan," Connor laughed.

"I don't get it," Aiken said flatly.

Connor sighed heavily and muttered "heathen" under his breath.

"Well, I'd better go rest up before the big push tonight," Aiken said as he picked himself up. Setting off in the direction of home, he heard the voices of his friends pick up behind him.

"I sure hope he's up to this," Nicole said anxiously.

"Me too," Connor replied.

Me too, Aiken echoed silently.

Chapter Twenty-Seven
Saturday, August 15th, 2139

The evening came much too quickly for Aiken, and judging by the looks on the faces of his classmates gathered around him, it had come just as suddenly upon most of them. Fortunately, Aiken was feeling quietly energised from a nap he'd taken and a big meal. His parents had been concerned at his subdued demeanour at the dinner table, but he'd managed to deflect their questions until it had been time to leave.

Now he was in the park, getting ready to move the class the width of the moon, in order to confront someone who might well be responsible for the death not only of one of their friends, but possibly others as well.

As each student nodded their readiness, Aiken reached out for the threads of thought he knew were waiting for his mental touch. Grasping them, shaping them, drawing on them, he propelled the group through the event horizon of the universe and out the other side.

He'd had Ethan scout ahead to make sure their chosen arrival spot was empty of tourists, so when the group appeared out of thin air, there was no one around to startle.

The group appeared in the middle of an empty dining room, the loud pop of their arrival muffled by heavy draperies cordoning off a stage to one side of the room. Evidently, this was some kind of entertainment venue, but not presently in use.

Some members of the group sat down on nearby chairs, taking in the fact that they were now two thousand kilometres from where they started, having gone through another universe to get there.

Aiken held his head between his palms for a minute, trying to get the headache that had just started to tickle his brain under control. Nicole and Connor gave each other a concerned glance over his bowed head, but he didn't notice.

Regaining control, he straightened and turned to Nicole, "Lead on, Macduff."

"What?"

"It's Shakespeare," Connor came to her rescue, "and it's 'Lay on, Macduff'. Not a good choice, really, considering what happens to Macbeth immediately afterward."

Aiken rolled his eyes at his friend. "Trust you to pull out the word nerdery right now." Turning to Nicole he gestured forward, "Can we just go?"

Nicole started towards one of the exits to the room that they'd appeared in. The group trailed behind her slowly, members looking around to make certain that there were no dangers lurking.

Fortunately, the room the group exited into was also empty, and they made their way quickly into the corridor that would take them to the venue where Warman was supposed to be performing.

"You know," Connor said thoughtfully to Aiken, "maybe Warman's on to something."

Aiken threw a strange look at his friend.

"With the telepathy thing, I mean," Connor clarified. "We could have some pretty awesome stage shows with the talents we've got."

"Sure," Aiken nodded, "if all we wanted

to do for the rest of our lives was bilk tourists."

Connor shrugged. "I don't see how it's a whole lot different than the stock trading that Mason's doing on our behalf. We'd just be using our abilities more directly."

Aiken had no answer for this, so he silently paced his friend, thinking. He turned the problem over in his mind. It seemed wrong to him, what Warman was doing. But Connor also had a point. So what was the difference?

"We're not personal about what we do," he finally spoke.

Connor seemed to know what he was trying to say, "That may be, but we're just spreading our influence over more people, rather than just one at a time."

"Well, that," conceded Aiken, "but also, we're not getting into people's lives and tricking them personally. Lots of people have systems for playing the market and everyone accepts the risk involved. No one goes to a stage show expecting the psychic to actually be able to tease out your innermost secrets. I'm sure we could get access to people's bank account information from their minds, if we really wanted, or we could make them just give us the money, but that would be wrong."

"More wrong than taking it in aggregate from a whole bunch of people at once?"

"I guess I see the worst possible abuses when our abilities get personal, but what's the worst that could happen if we make money in the stock market?"

"People start copying us and it doesn't work anymore?" Connor replied.

"Not really," Aiken replied. "Even then, we'd have the advantage because Mason would be able to predict even that happening."

The friends fell silent as they followed Nicole, who'd researched ahead of time the course to follow to arrive at the venue where Warman was performing.

Their plan was simple: arrive at the auditorium during the performance, and spread out enough to cover the exits while Aiken, who was the only one that Warman had seen before, attempted to crack Warman's shield using their combined powers.

While Aiken sensed that the others in the group were eager for, and sure of the outcome of the encounter, he was more apprehensive. Lately, Mason's prediction had being weighing heavily on his mind, particularly the pieces about one turning and another falling. He hoped they weren't biting off more than they could chew by confronting Warman.

Aiken had tried himself to look toward the future to see if he could determine any more details than what Mason had seen, but whether Mason was more gifted than he at perceiving the threads of chance, or whether certain eventualities could only be seen from particular junctures in time, Aiken had had no more luck at ferreting out what was coming than the group had already from Mason's vision. In fact, aside from the glimpse he'd gotten in the Park that morning, he'd not been able to see into his own future more than a couple of days, and even those had been hazy. Aiken thought it could be that things could change so much that nothing could be perceived clearly. Usually, if he focused on one person or thing, he could follow it forward in time fairly distinctly. Now though, any time he tried to focus his vision in time, everything he saw looked like wisps of smoke, indistinct and fluid. It was troubling.

If Connor noted his silence, he seemed to put it down to preparing himself for the coming altercation and let Aiken walk on in silence.

All too soon, they'd arrived at the theatre where Nicole said Warman was performing.

The group split up according to their plan and encircled the lobbies on the two floors of the theatre. Apparently, Warman was a successful enough entertainer that he had a medium-sized theatre to himself for his show. That did nothing to reassure Aiken. If Warman had developed his talents that much in the three months since the drive malfunction, that spoke to his raw power more clearly than any demonstration of mental shielding.

Unless, he thought, *Warman's bilking the facilities people as much as his audience.* He was somewhat reassured by the thought. There didn't necessarily need to be the worst possible scenario to explain everything related to Warman.

On the other hand, he reassessed as he opened the door to the theatre, *maybe he really that powerful.* The packed auditorium would seem to suggest Warman was more than smoke and mirrors. Evidently, people were intrigued by his act, which probably meant he was powerful enough to pull off the act he was advertising.

Aiken stood at the back of the large open space. There was probably seating for six or seven hundred in the curved rows of plushly-appointed seats. He guessed that of those, only a dozen or so were open. At three shows a night, that meant Warman was playing to somewhere around two thousand people a day. Evidently, he wasn't overselling himself to the management of the dome.

He turned his attention to the stage area. As they'd planned, the group had arrived near the end of the one-hour show, and Aiken could see that Warman was just wrapping up. The stage was simple, but seemed somehow luxurious. Maybe it was the heavy draperies that hung at the sides and back, making the stage seem more like a puppet theatre than a stage. A shiver ran through Aiken as he realised how appropriate that was.

He'd been unconsciously testing the mental atmosphere in the room since he'd entered, and he realised that the control emanating from the entertainment on stage was not just to control the "hypnotised" subject, but also so that Warman could play with the crowd.

Aiken was stunned by this revelation. He closed his eyes and looked mentally at what was going on in the room. He saw each person present as a glowing outline of themselves in various shades and various intensities.

Looking toward the stage, he saw an intensely bright line connecting the volunteer on stage to Warman. Warman wasn't glowing at all. He wasn't there at all, visible only as an absence of light. *His shield*, Aiken realised, *it's still up.* So much for trying to catch him off guard. That wasn't the most worrisome thing Aiken saw, though. Not only was the hypnotised volunteer on stage connected to Warman, but so was every person in the auditorium. The strands of light that represented these connections disappeared into the dark shadow that defined the space Warman occupied.

Aiken was concerned. If this was anything like when he was connected to the other Lunatics, that would mean Warman's power would be multiplied by hundreds. This did not bode well for their attempt to crack his shield. Maybe it would be better to wait until the auditorium had emptied.

Nicky, he called out, *take a look at this.* He felt her attention shift in his direction, then contract as she narrowed her focus.

Damn it, she replied, *any reason he wouldn't be able to draw on the energy of non-gifted people to boost his power?*

None that I can think of, Aiken replied. *Do we go or wait?*

I think we have to go, Nicole answered. *Our whole reason for doing this now was that we know where he is. If we let this opportunity by, no telling if we can find him again later when there aren't as many people around and he has that shield up.*

Nicole's points were well taken. *Do you think someone should try to cut him off from all these people so he can't draw on them?* Aiken asked.

Is that even possible?

I have no idea, Aiken answered honestly.

We've never even tried it at home.

Probably best to just try and get everyone in our group in on the attempt to have as much power behind it as possible.

Aiken could see that Warman had sent the volunteer back into the audience, but was still connected to him mentally. The connection wasn't as strong as when the young man had been on stage, but it was stronger than the ones with the rest of the audience.

Warman was making some final remarks and Aiken could tell he was getting ready to leave. The audience was coming out of the distracted state they'd been in and were preparing to rise to their feet to applaud the performance.

Now or never, Nicole sent.

Let's do it, then, Aiken responded. *Is everyone ready?* he sent more broadly. When he got the affirmative from everyone, he drew the threads of their consciousnesses to himself and sent a massive mental probe arrowing right toward Warman, who was just coming out of his bow.

Time seemed to slow. The audience was starting to applaud, some starting to rise to give Warman an ovation. Their hands seemed to freeze before a single clap was heard.

Warman raised his head and looked

directly at Aiken, locking eyes with him just as the probe hit the edge of his shield. The wave of mental energy seemed to stagger Warman, who fell to one knee as the blast hammered his shield.

Aiken took a step toward the stage, head leaning out in front, as if by sheer physical force, he could push through Warman's barrier. He could feel that they were making progress. The shield was weakening, becoming less solid.

Suddenly, Warman surged to his feet and his shield snapped back to full strength. Aiken continued pushing, adding power fuelled by anger and frustration over his inability to help Diana when she needed it most.

Warman's shield slipped again, but again, it found focus. Aiken, despairing that anything could crack the man's seemingly-impervious shield, reached more deeply into the group of friends than any time previously. Not content with the energy they were offering, he delved back along the connection and drew out energy that they didn't know they have, and sent it along the probe to Warman.

For the third time, he felt Warman's control over his shield falter and pressed with the last of his reserves, hoping to push through the impenetrable mental shield.

AIKEN! The anguished mental cry came, *Stop it! You're hurting us!*

Confused, Aiken let his probe slip for a fraction of a second, and he felt Warman once more solidify the shield.

His focus distracted at a crucial moment, the probe shattered on the freshly- reinforced shield and Aiken fell forwards, scattering the threads of thought that he'd gathered to make the push. He saw the carpeted floor of the aisle between the auditorium's seats rush up to meet him, but could do nothing to stop it but close his eyes.

When he reopened them a second later, he was no longer in the auditorium, but back in the small dining room where they'd teleported into Farside.

He turned his head to the left. His classmates were sprawled out all around him on chairs and even on the floor. An anxious face appeared from the side of his view, peering down at him. It took him a second to identify the worried face as Nicole.

He coughed weakly and rolled to his side, discovering that he was on the floor. He tried to sit up, but his arms were too rubbery to support his weight, and he felt hands lifting him into a sitting position.

He nodded gratefully to Connor, who was helping him up. "What happened?"

Nicole looked around nervously, the

frown on her lips deepening with news she didn't want to share. He'd seen her look like this before, right after her dad died. A nameless dread crept over him.

"Nicky, tell me," he insisted.

She set herself, "Warman disappeared."

"Damn it," Aiken said softly, but by the look on Nicole's face, he knew the worst of it was still coming. "What else?"

"Three more people are dead," she said in a rush.

Aiken felt his stomach drop. He felt even weaker than before. "Who?"

"No one we know," Connor assured him. "We all made it through, more or less intact."

"Then who?"

"Three people in the audience," Nicole answered miserably. "The last guy up on stage, and two others."

Aiken leaned forward and held his head in his hands. "That's where he was getting the power to hold up his shield. He drained other people."

"We think so, too," Connor stated. "They all went like Diana and the guy in Tranquility."

Aiken's stomach heaved, and he vomited all over the floor in front of him. Connor turned his head, but Nicole squatted next to him and rubbed his back while his stomach emptied itself onto the carpet.

When his stomach had stopped heaving, he turned to her and said, "We killed those people, Nicky." There were tears in his eyes.

Nicole's eyes matched his, wide and wet. "We did not. That animal Warman killed them for their energy."

"Yeah, but he wouldn't have had to if I hadn't been pushing so hard."

"You didn't know."

"And that makes it okay?" He was growing angry. "They're still just as dead."

"I know," she said and finally turned away, tears streaming down her face.

"Nicky," Aiken said, reaching a hand out to comfort. He let it drop before it reached her, though. What could he possibly say that would be any comfort?

He looked away and noticed the haggard looks on the others faces for the first time.

"What else happened?" he asked Connor.

"Nothing," his friend answered. "When Warman disappeared after the third audience member burned, we got the hell out of Dodge."

"Who 'ported us back here?"

"No one had any power left after the push to crack Warman," Connor said. "We walked."

"What?" Aiken was incredulous.

"You drained us all," Connor said, looking at his friend cautiously. "Didn't you hear Nicky yelling at you to stop?"

Aiken glanced back over at Nicole. "That was you?"

She turned her head back enough so that he could see her red eyes and tear-streaked face. "Yes," she whispered. "You were hurting all of us."

Aiken was stunned. "I..." he started. "But I..." He couldn't seem to form a coherent thought. "I didn't mean to," he finished lamely.

"We know," Connor put his hand on Aiken's shoulder. "Didn't matter though. We were all tapped out, so we had to walk back here. Isaac carried you."

"How long?" Aiken was still having trouble putting the pieces together.

"We've been here for about half an hour, and it was another half hour before that that all hell broke loose."

He'd been out for an hour. And before that, he'd pushed so hard that he'd hurt his friends, not to mention been responsible for the deaths of three innocent bystanders. He felt his stomach turn again, but there was not enough strength in his body even for that much.

He mopped his brow with the back of his hand as he tried to marshal his thoughts. The group was obviously in no shape to travel, and yet, he thought, they couldn't stay here. With three more deaths, security forces would be amped up and a group of teenagers in a closed-off dining room with no record of them having arrived in the dome was bound to arouse suspicion.

He reached out mentally, or at least tried to. No thoughts went out from him. He tried to sense those around him, but nothing was happening. He panicked momentarily, until a voice intruded in his thoughts. *Relax.* He couldn't have disobeyed if he wanted, and as his thoughts slowed, he belated recognised Nicole's mental tone.

"You wore yourself out," she continued verbally. "Truth be told, you wore us all out. Some of us are starting to get back some ability, but don't push it."

Connor nodded in agreement, "We all sensed how much of your own energy you put in the push. Don't try anything for a while."

Aiken, now more settled, asked the obvious question, "How do we get back now?"

Connor gave him a tight smile, "We were just discussing that when you woke up from your little nap." He nodded his head over to a little group sitting together on chairs. Ethan, Liam and Jillian looked back anxiously at him.

Seeing that Aiken was more alert, Liam started, "We have a couple of options. First, we can wait until you or Nicole gets enough energy back to jump us home." At this, he raised a curious eyebrow.

Both Aiken and Nicole shook their heads at the same time.

Liam frowned, but continued, "Second, we can turn ourselves in with some story about line jumping past security."

Ethan interrupted, "I still say that's an idiotic idea. Can you imagine how many questions that's going to raise?"

"Not to mention," Connor interjected. "The story falls apart as soon as they look past the security issue to transport. No one will have a record of transporting us here, which is going to be a whole other problem to explain."

Liam sighed heavily, "I know. Also, we would automatically be at the top of the list of people suspected of killing those three audience members at Warman's show."

At the reminder of their responsibility for those deaths, Aiken dropped his head and felt the tears gather once more. He felt a hand on his arm, and looked to see Nicole smiling at him through her own tears.

He turned to Liam again. "Any other options?"

Liam shook his head in frustration, "We were kind of hoping you'd be able to come up with something."

Aiken felt more than saw the gazes from his classmates. "I can't think of anything off the top of my head, but if I come up with something, I'll mention it."

At this, a disappointed sigh went around the room. Liam turned back to Ethan and Jillian.

Aiken clenched his jaw in frustrated anger. He should be able to do more. He felt a squeeze on his arm. He looked over at Nicole, who was still holding onto him.

"This is not your fault either."

"How do you figure," he said bitterly. "Three people are dead, we can't go home because I sucked everyone's powers out and, oh yeah, the guy we came to confront got away scot-free and we have nothing on him." Aiken's voice rose during his tirade so that he nearly shouted the last.

Nicole let go of his arm and backed off a pace.

"Don't be an ass," Connor's voice came from the other side. "It's not Nicky's fault you're pissed off. You're mad because you're not a super-hero. So what? None of the rest of us are either. Want to blame someone? How about Warman? He's obviously the one responsible for Diana and the guy in Tranquility, and if you don't believe me, ask the three dead people in the theatre we just came from."

Aiken flinched back from his friend's harsh tone. Everyone in the room had turned their way, and Aiken wanted to crawl into a hole.

Connor wasn't finished, though, "Yeah, Warman got away, but we know who he is now and he knows we're stronger than he is. That's gonna give him a reason to start looking over his shoulder. I hope he's good and scared, so next time we hit him, he'll be weakened from the inside, too."

"Next time?" Aiken asked weakly.

"You bet your ass," Connor hissed. Aiken could see nods from other students. "We know who killed Diana. We know how he did it. And we can stop him. We just have to figure out how."

Aiken pondered his friend's words. They resonated in him, and he found his resolve growing.

"All right." He turned to Nicole, "Sorry."

"Accepted," she said.

He turned back to Connor, "I might have an idea on how to get home without giving ourselves up or waiting to get our full powers back."

"This I gotta hear."

"We use Warman's own trick." Aiken's pronouncement was greeted with stunned silence. He scrambled to explain, "Obviously, not kill anyone, but we know it's possible to take energy from non-gifted people. As long as we only take a little from a whole bunch of people, it should have the same effect as taking a whole bunch from one person."

At this, the tension in the room drained. Aiken even saw a couple of tentative smiles on faces as some realised they might not be stuck here.

"All we need is one of the full telepaths to start taking little bits of energy from the people closest to this room, then as their ability returns, they can range further and further getting bits of energy, and pushing them back into the rest of us. When we have enough, we can jump back to Peary."

Olivia stood up from where she'd been sitting with Faith and Penny. "I'm feeling okay," she said. "I can get started, if Aiken and Nicole aren't quite up to it yet."

Aiken smiled gratefully at her. "I don't know about Nicky, but I'll need a little more time."

He felt Nicole drift back to sit beside him, her relief at not being called on immediately also evident.

Hey, he thought, *I'm starting to get some ability back.* But when he turned his attention to Connor on his other side, he still couldn't sense his friend. Only Nicole appeared to his senses, like she and he were the only two in the room.

She put her head on his shoulder, and he wondered at this as he drifted into a light sleep.

Chapter Twenty-Eight
Sunday, August 16th, 2139

It had taken them a couple of hours to get the energy necessary to teleport back to Peary Dome. They'd all staggered off in various directions, promising to regroup the next afternoon to go over what had happened.

Aiken woke and panicked for a moment when he realised he wasn't in his own room. He turned his head to the side and the room swam into focus.

The dark was making things difficult to see, but Aiken tweaked his vision to allow more light to be seen. Evidently his abilities were back. Glancing around, he recognised from the photos on the wall that he was in Nicole's apartment.

He sat up on the couch where he'd apparently spent the night and immediately felt a wave of nausea pass over him. He groaned and heard an answering groan from behind him. Turning, he saw Nicole emerge from the hallway leading to the bedrooms, rubbing her eyes with one hand and stretching her other above her head, fingers splayed wide. Apparently she was feeling the same way he was.

"You look how I feel," she said, frowning drowsily at him.

"I don't know if I should be insulted by that," he said.

"Definitely," she replied.

"Well, then," he said, "I think it's completely unfair that you don't look as miserable as I feel."

"How sweet," she smiled. "Are you feeling better than yesterday at least?"

"Moderately, though I feel like I could eat a horse."

"Picking up some of Connor's appetite, are you?" Nicole teased.

"Maybe. You want to do breakfast, or should I head back to my place?"

"No fear," Nicole answered. "I don't think we have any horses, but I'm sure we can find something. Your parents will be okay with you coming in later?"

"Yeah, I told them yesterday I'd be out all night, so they're not expecting me back."

"Smart."

"I guess." Aiken paused. "It's not as if I was expecting something like what happened. Honestly, I thought we'd maybe crack him and then... well, I don't really know what I was thinking after that."

Nicole looked over at him questioningly.

"Okay, I thought we'd put the fear of God in him or something. I wasn't expecting this. I wasn't expecting more people to die." This last was barely more than a whisper.

"I know," Nicole said, moving to stand at the back of the couch and reaching over to put a hand on his shoulder. He reached up to grasp at her fingers, feeling despair overtake him once more.

"Maybe it's time we brought someone in authority in on this," he suggested wearily after a moment. "I know Mason's prediction said we'd be the ones to deal with this, but right now, I just want someone else to take care of Warman and not to have to think about those three people from last night."

Nicole squeezed his hand and moved around the end of the couch to sit next to him.

He turned to face her.

"I think that might be a good idea," she began, "but how do we even start to tell someone in a way so they'll believe us?"

"No idea," Aiken answered glumly. "Worst case, we could just go into their heads and make them arrest him. But that kind of compulsion usually doesn't last long."

"Yeah, that might not be such a good idea," Nicole agreed.

"We could just tell the truth, like we did with Quinn and temper the reaction in order to get the result we want."

"How long would that take?"

"No idea. Also, it could backfire and we'd end up at Aldrin with wires running into every pore on our bodies."

Nicole shivered at this, and Aiken decided that the downside to that option was probably too great to risk it. He recalled a similar conversation he'd had with Diana when they had been "practicing" her telepathy.

The best way to convince someone to do something, he thought, "is to convince them that it was their idea to begin with," he finished aloud.

"What?"

"If we plant enough suspicions in the minds of the investigators, they'll take the bait without us having to directly control their minds. We can lead them right to Warman."

Nicole pondered this for a second, tucking one leg up under her as she thought.

"The problem with that," she finally said slowly, "Is that even if they end up with Warman in custody, they're not going to be able to prove he did anything."

"Oh. Yeah." Aiken sat glumly silent for a moment. "Well, at least we'd know where he was, unless he wanted to explain how he vanished out of police custody. Unless he got impatient, his best bet would be to stay put, which gives us the advantage."

"What do you think the chances of that are?"

"Which, him staying put or getting impatient?"

"Either."

"I don't know. When I talked with him, he seemed fairly intelligent, but he's got to be running a little scared after yesterday. I mean, look how quickly he disappeared when our merge broke.

"I guess it depends on whether he's more worried about us, in which case he'd run, or about law enforcement, in which case he'd stay put."

Nicky thought about this for a moment,

"Yeah, tough call."

Aiken suddenly thought of something. "You said that there was an entry record for Warman coming to the moon?"

"Uh, I don't remember. I know that there were some for moving around between bases, but I can't remember if there was one for the moon herself."

"Can you find out?"

"Why?"

"Because," Aiken responded, "If he doesn't have an entry to the moon, either because he 'ported himself here or just from ducking through LEC, that would be the information we'd need to put the security investigators on his trail. And they'd have a legitimate reason to hold him."

"I'll check right away." Nicole unfolded herself from the couch and headed back towards her bedroom to get her wrist communicator. Aiken watched her go anxiously. If this panned out, they'd once again know when and where they could strike at Warman.

Before long, Nicole hurried back out of the hall, tapping away at the screen of her communicator. "I think you might be on to something," she said. "I can't find an entry record for him."

"Wouldn't they have noticed that when

he applied for an entertainment permit?"

"Apparently not," Nicole said with a tight smile, as she sat down again. "I think we've got the bastard."

Aiken was slightly shocked at hearing that kind of language coming from Nicole, who'd always been more reserved with her speech. He couldn't disagree with the sentiment, though. Warman was responsible for the death of at least five people on the moon, and one of them had meant a lot to Aiken. He couldn't wait to bring Warman down.

"So what now?" Nicole brought his thoughts back to the immediate situation.

"Well, I think we should let everyone else know, in case they have better ideas on how to proceed. So nothing until this afternoon." He thought for a second. "Is there anything on the newsnets about the theatre last night?"

"Are you kidding? It's all over every news site. No one knows what happened, but the theories are pretty wild. Some have made the connection to Diana and the guy in Tranquility, but others are saying micrometeorite shower, spontaneous combustion, heating unit malfunction, you name it."

Aiken shook his head. "Do you think it would be more worthwhile to go to the press with the bit about Warman's lack of entry record, or straight to the security office?"

"If we're planting the idea in someone else's head to check entry records, it might be easier to get a reporter on the story, since they'll all be looking for angles anyway."

"All right, so we have a plan. Now, you said something about breakfast?"

Nicole laughed. "Do all boys think with their stomachs?"

"No, just me and Connor," Aiken answered, smiling.

Nicole got up and headed into the kitchen, Aiken following behind. She rummaged through the fridge as he took one of the two spots at the table.

The two friends ate breakfast in companionable silence, then Aiken headed home, promising stop by for Nicole before the meeting that afternoon.

Chapter Twenty-Nine
Monday, August 17th, 2139

Aiken woke to the sound of his buzzer and, in a ritual he'd not done since Diana's death, reached for the threads of all the minds in Peary Dome to join them in a moment of shared consciousness. This morning, however, there was a strange taint to the flavour of the contact, as if some oil had spread over the surface of the usually tranquil pool of mentalities that made up the population of Peary. Confused, Aiken withdrew into himself. He woke fully, troubled by what he sensed in the minds of those closest to him.

If anyone else was aware of the change in

atmosphere, they didn't show it. His parents were their usual selves at breakfast, chatting about inconsequentials.

Aiken's ears perked up when he heard Warman's name mentioned.

"What was that, dad?"

His dad seemed startled that Aiken had taken notice of what he'd been talking about and just gaped at him for a second.

His mother came to his rescue, "They caught a guy they think might be connected to the deaths in Farside the other night."

"Oh yeah?" Aiken asked carefully, trying not to arouse suspicion with his interest.

"Yeah, some joker who'd stowed away to get here, then conned someone at Farside to give him an entertainer's license," his father picked up the thread. "It was during his show that those three people died. Actually, I wouldn't be surprised if he wasn't responsible for Di- oof!"

At that moment, Aiken's mother had elbowed her husband in the side, hard. He looked back at her for a second in hurt confusion, then a light seemed to click on.

"Anyway, they locked him up in Farside's security center until they figure out what to do with him."

"What's he being charged with?"

"Entry control evasion for now," his

father answered carefully. At that point, his parents changed the subject, and Aiken learned no more from them on the issue.

When he arrived at school later in the morning, the hurriedly finished conversations and furtive looks told him that his classmates had been discussing him just before he entered the room.

While it would have been possible for him to eavesdrop mentally on the conversation, the Lunatics had agreed not to use their abilities on each other without permission, so he refrained.

Instead, taking his seat next to Connor for the beginning of class, he leaned over and asked, "What's up?"

"Nothing," Connor answered.

"Oh, come on. I don't have to be psychic to know something's going on."

"It really is nothing," Connor insisted. "We were just talking about Warman getting arrested." His lie was unconvincing, even without using telepathy.

Aiken decided to refrain from probing his friend's mind for the time being. For one, he was still pretty exhausted from the incident in the theatre and any probe would be clumsy and likely ineffective. Also, he knew that if Connor ever found out that he'd probed without asking, he would feel violated, and their friendship would be strained.

He was quiet for the rest of the hour, and when morning classes were done, while the rest of the Lunatics left in a group, Aiken wandered off on his own to find a spot to sit and think.

He found himself wandering the perimeter of the Park and reflected on the fact that for someone who hated its artifice so much, he certainly had spent a lot of time there since the incident back in May.

Amazed at the change in fate, he was suddenly struck with the idea that he and Connor had been discussing that day before the whole drive malfunction had sent all their lives tumbling in a different direction.

He remembered talking about people in the future looking back on the momentous day. Well, there was nothing stopping him from doing it now – if Mason's future sight worked like regular sight, he should be able to see backwards as well as forward.

Settling himself down on a fake-wood park bench, Aiken closed his eyes and concentrated his inner sight on himself. He found it easier to look through time if there was a focus point, and the more familiar he was with the focus, the easier it was for him to track that focus forward. Now, instead of pushing his vision forward into the murky future, he let it roam back into the crystal clarity of the past.

Perhaps it was because he was near the same location, or because his mind was already intent on the day in question, but his vision snapped onto the test day almost instantly.

Looking around, he saw the circle of students lazily sitting around waiting for the test to start.

Over there, he could see himself and Connor talking to each other about faster than light travel and time, and on the opposite side of the circle... he gasped... Diana.

It wasn't that he'd forgotten how she'd looked in the couple of weeks since her death, but seeing her now, vibrant and alive, tore at a piece of his heart.

If only he could walk over to her and warn her, or warn himself. Unfortunately, it was only a vision. Soon enough, the drive would start, then the malfunction would send them all down the path to Diana's death.

It was painful looking at her laughing with her friends, carefree and unknowing, when he knew that just a few short weeks later, her vitality would come to a brutal end at Warman's hand.

As if thinking about it drew his mind, his vision skipped forward to the day she died. He followed her with his mind's eye as she walked into the hallway where she would meet her end. Warman followed along behind her, once and for all putting to rest any doubt in Aiken's mind that he was responsible. Aiken tried to call out, to scream out a warning, to stop this terrible thing from happening. He watched in shocked horror as Diana realized something was wrong. As she tried to turn to see what was happening. She clutched her midriff, where the heat started spreading. Aiken could see the distress on her face, and tears streamed down his cheeks as he impotently watched her fall over in utter agony, curl up and cry out.

The strength of her mental cry seemed to startle Warman, who looked around himself quickly, then staggered off down the hallway, and disappeared right before reaching the end of it. A couple of minutes later, Aiken watched himself pop into existence with those he'd brought along on their unexpected trip. Not willing to watch Diana die a second time in front of him, Aiken ripped his consciousness away from that place and back to the present.

He found himself seated where he had been; nobody around him noticed anything out of the ordinary. He must not have been watching long, or maybe as Connor theorized, his mind came back to a point just after he left.

He unclenched the fists he realized were balled up in his lap and was surprised to see that his nails had dug into his palms hard enough that he had bloodied his hands. Using the little he'd learned from Kaira while watching her heal, he closed up his wounds and repaired the damage. If only he'd known as much then as he did now, perhaps he could have kept Diana alive, or worked with Kaira to help repair the damage Warman caused.

He had at least learned why the second victim, in Tranquility, had been more injured than Diana. Her cry had interrupted what Warman had been doing and he'd fled, fearing discovery. Since the man killed in Tranquility had been ordinary, Warman had been able to complete what he'd only started with Diana.

Aiken wondered about the three that had died in the theatre. Were they in the same shape as the poor unknown man, or had their probe managed to knock Warman off kilter while he was in the midst of the energy theft he'd been making. Aiken remembered the strength with which Warman's shield had recovered under their assault and feared that the people in the theatre would be unrecognizable, identified only because they had been in their seats, or because they'd been with other people.

At that thought, Aiken nearly retched

once more. He'd not even considered the damage caused to extended families. Nicky probably had, though, he thought. Having lost her own father, she'd be much more aware of what they'd done, of the families they'd destroyed.

He was even more determined to put an end to Warman. If only they could have stopped him before any of this had ever happened. As soon as he thought of it, he knew he would have to try. If they could spare the class and Diana's parents and the families of the dead theatre-goers, then he had to try, at least. When he leaped forward, he'd just been focusing his vision. That made sense. He could see forward and backward in time, as he'd just experienced. If he could travel forward in time, he should be able to go back as well.

He thought back to the conversation he and Connor had been having the day of the test, how time and space were simply different facets of the same thing. So if he saw a great distance, he was actually looking back in time, but he could also tune his vision to stay in the same place and just look in time instead of in space. Maybe he could jump himself forward or back the same way, by simply "moving" himself while staying in the same place.

This could have big consequences though.

It would probably be better to check with someone first before starting to mess with time travel. He sent out a telepathic hail to Connor. *Hey man, I want to run something by you.*

Connor asked where Aiken could see, *Where are you?*

Edge of the park. Aiken pushed an overhead image of the Park with his location highlighted into Connor's consciousness. No sooner had he done so, than Connor appeared beside him with the usual pop of teleportation.

"What's up?"

"I'm thinking about time travel."

"Yeah, no, it won't work," Connor stated emphatically.

"What? Yes it will - I've already travelled to what we think is the future."

"Right, but I mean you can't go back and stop Warman before he kills Diana."

"What? How did you... I mean, how do you know?"

"Because it violates causality."

"What?"

"Think it through. If you go back and stop Warman, then you will have no reason in that timeline to go back and stop Warman, meaning he will do it again because you didn't go back. Or, worse, if you go back and stop the drive test, you will take away your own ability to go back and stop the drive test, which means you didn't go back and stop it. Causality."

"That doesn't make any sense."

"Sure it does. If you stop the drive test, by extension, you will never get any powers, so you will never have been able to go back and stop the drive test, therefore you cannot go back and stop the drive test. If you back and stop Warman, you will have given yourself no reason to go back and stop him, so won't have and he will just do the same things. You can't influence your own past, or at least not the parts that led you to where you are now. You could probably go back and change the flavour of cake you had for your third birthday without changing anything drastic, but once you start messing around with causality, you will be prevented."

"Ooookay. That seems random and abstract. How would I be stopped?"

"No one really knows, because no one's ever had the opportunity to go time travelling before, but this is all quite logical."

"What about alternate universes? Quinn said there are an infinite number of alternate universes out there. What if I made one where Diana never died?"

"If there are infinite number of universes out there, then there's already one where that happened. There's also one where the drive test went off without a hitch and we never got powers in the first place, and one where the Chixulub meteor never hits the earth, and dinosaurs remain the dominant form of life on the planet. You and I are lizard people in that one."

"Be serious!"

"I am being serious. You can't go back and change things and then come back here. If you split off another universe and jump forward to the present there, everyone left here will still have all of the deaths, and we'd be left to deal with Warman without you, because you'd gone gallivanting back into the past to save your ex-girlfriend."

"Oh."

"Yeah, hadn't thought that one all the way through, had you?"

"Well, I thought if I changed it in the past, it would be better here."

"Well, it wouldn't be. If we're going to deal with Warman, it has to be in the here and now, not in the past. Besides, what makes you think you'd have any more luck against him back then than you had recently?"

"Well, there would be two of me."

Connor rolled his eyes. "Okay, suppose you had gone back into the past and somehow beaten Warman by teaming up with yourself and saved Diana and all those other people. Don't you think you'd remember that?"

"What? Why? I haven't done it yet."

"Yes, but you would have done it in your past as well as in your future."

"Oh. Yeah. I guess you're right. I hadn't thought about that."

"No worries. I'm just glad you didn't go rushing off into the past without talking to someone about it."

Aiken felt surprisingly more settled than he had a moment ago, even though a course of action had been removed from him. Maybe it was because he couldn't regret not having helped out in the past anymore, or maybe it was because Connor had shown him that he needed to focus his attention on the future to beat Warman. Wait, the future!

"Can I go forward in time to figure out how to beat him?"

At this Connor looked thoughtful, then asked, "Have you had any luck looking ahead?"

"Not really, no," Aiken had to admit. The future remained as murky as ever, not revealing anything.

"Might not be a good idea to jump into something you can't see clearly, then."

"Oh, yeah." Aiken looked down at his hands, no blood visible now.

"Don't worry. You'll think of something."

"I wish it wasn't just everyone relying on me to figure out what it is that we're going to do about him."

"It's not, really. We just all know that you're the best bet for taking him down, so we're trusting you to show us how."

"I don't know if I can," Aiken said hesitantly.

"Well, what about using that trick from the theatre?"

"Which?"

"Where you take a little bit of energy from a whole lot of people to help boost the link?"

"Right. You know, that might work!" Aiken was enthusiastic about this idea. "So, we just have to find an area that has no one in the immediate vicinity for Warman to draw from, and lots of people further away that we can use as a boost. Then we have Nicky or Olivia link up with all the normals and gather their energy and feed it through to me and use it to crack Warman."

"Why are we cracking him again? Aren't we sure he's the guy now?"

"Oh, right." Aiken pondered for a moment. "Well, honestly, I don't know what to do with him other than that."

Connor smiled, "Well, in the stories about this kind of thing, usually, you wipe the person's mind, or their memories, so they don't remember they have powers, or sometimes, you can take the powers away."

"There's stories about this kind of thing?"

"Of course!"

Aiken looked over at Connor. "And what generally happens in these stories?"

"Well, good usually wins out in the end," Connor hedged.

"Usually?"

"I'm sure we'll take Warman out."

"Yeah, but how much more collateral damage will we cause in the meantime?"

"You can't blame yourself for those people in the theatre. That was Warman's doing."

"You think he feels bad about it?" Aiken inquired acidly.

"No," Connor answered honestly. "But I'm not telling you not to feel bad. People died. People who probably wouldn't have died if we hadn't gone to confront Warman. But we are neither responsible for their deaths, nor wanting to cause any more, which is what separates us from Warman."

"Still," Aiken persisted.

"Still nothing," Connor answered. "We will take all reasonable precautions the next time we confront Warman, but we have to do it. Remember Mason's prediction."

"Yeah, that's what I'm afraid of," Aiken responded. "One more to fall, and one to turn, whatever that means."

"You know what it means," Connor responded gently. "It means, as much as we don't want it, someone is going to go over to Warman's side. Or at the very least, refuse to help us when we need it most."

"You don't know that," Aiken answered.

"Not exactly, but you have to figure that's what Mason meant."

"Mason." Aiken said vehemently.

"You can't blame him for seeing what he did any more than someone who spots an oncoming train."

"Yeah, but someone who sees a kid on the tracks in front of a train usually tries to help out."

"Mason was trying. That's what his prediction is."

"It would be nice if he could be more specific."

"You know, I asked him about that," Connor said.

Aiken shot a look at his friend.

"Well, you know. It wouldn't kill him to help just a bit more."

"So, what did he say?"

"Apparently, he can't see very far into the future at the moment."

"I'm getting some of that myself. I can see back fine, but forward is all murky."

"Have you tried looking past the next couple of weeks to see if there's anything in the farther future?"

"Yes and no," Aiken said. "I can't follow any individuals forward that way, but if I look at something like Peary itself, I can see it months and even years from now."

"Well, that's reassuring in a way, I guess," Connor said. "Whatever happens to us in the near future, at least there will be something left afterwards." He grinned lopsidedly at Aiken.

"Yes, very reassuring," Aiken said drily.

"Have you tried looking forward along Warman's timeline?"

Aiken turned slowly toward his friend, a dawning realization on his face. "No, but that's brilliant! Even if we can't see more than a couple of days ahead, we should be able to nail down where he'll be at any time in those next couple of days."

"Whoa, there. I thought he was in jail."

"Yes, but how long is he going to stay there, do you think? Even if the charges against him stand, which they may not if he's a telepath and can convince people what he's doing is perfectly all right, if they try and deport him, he can jump the width of the moon at least, so we'd have no sure way to know where he'd gone."

Aiken screwed his face up in concentration as he attempted to look along Warman's timeline. He looked back along his own activities to that dreadful night in the theatre on Saturday, then skipped his gaze over to Warman and tried to go forward. The only problem was, as soon as Warman vanished from sight, Aiken couldn't scan forward along his activities, either. He tried skipping backward, but ran into the same problem. Reluctantly, he returned his gaze to the present.

"No luck. That damned shield of his seems to block any kind of vision of him."

"Does he always have it up?"

"I don't know," Aiken said thoughtfully. "Every time we've encountered him he has."

"Yeah, well think about those times. First, he approached you and knew you were telepathic, so he would have shielded. Next was the theatre, and he was using his own talent, and you'd just told him there were other talented people on the moon. No chance he would have left it down in such a vulnerable situation."

"You think he has to maintain it?"

"Do you?"

"Well, yeah. I mostly don't bother."

"Right, but you're not a multiple murderer trying to hide with telepaths on your trail."

"Granted."

"You think he shields in his sleep?"

"Good question. Even if he didn't, it would be impossible to track him forward from that point because as soon as he woke up, he'd shield and you'd lose him."

"Well, what if you weren't going to track him," Connor said grimly.

Aiken looked up at his friend's tone. He thought about it for a second, then nodded. He focused his vision on the dome on the far side of the moon where they knew Warman was being held. He narrowed his focus down to the security center and looked for Warman. There weren't many holding rooms in the facility, a reflection on the rarity of crime in a place with complete access control. Well, complete until teleports had shown up. Aiken found no one in any of the cells in Farside station. He broadened the scope of his search, but if Warman was in the security station, he was well hidden. His shield didn't hide him visibly though, so Aiken guessed he'd left somehow. He returned his vision to the Park.

"He's skipped out!"

"What? When?" Connor was a little disturbed by the news.

"I don't know. Think I should pop over and take a look in person?"

"Not yet. Let me try finding anything in the news first." Connor fiddled with his wrist communicator for a couple of minutes while Aiken stared into space, literally, in this case. "Nothing on the nets about him being released, and nothing about an escape."

"So either they don't know he's gone yet, or he was let go quietly sometime recently."

"That about sums it up."

"I think one of us should go over and see."

"Why are you looking at me? You're the mastermind, and I do intend that pun."

Aiken laughed, then asked, "You want to come?"

"How much use would I be?"

"You could stand lookout, like back when we went around wiping people's memories of Faith's injury."

"You should take Nicky. She's almost as versatile as you and more powerful than I am. She'll definitely be more helpful." Aiken glanced at his friend, but Connor had an inscrutable look on his face.

"If you insist."

"I think it's a better idea."

"Oh, alright." Aiken sent a hail out to Nicole, and no sooner had he mentioned that he might need her help with something than she appeared between the pair on the bench. Connor smothered a smile behind Nicole's back, but she didn't appear to notice.

"What's the plan?"

"Warman's not in Farside Security's tender clutches anymore. I want to find out if he's skipped out or been let out." He paused for a moment. "I have something for you to do, too, Connor."

"I hear and obey, sahib," Connor replied.

"Boys are so weird," Nicole interjected.

"Anyway," Aiken went on. "Just because I can't spot Warman going forward doesn't mean someone can't. See if you can get Mason to look along Warman's timeline for an unshielded spot where we can be, in order to hammer him."

"That's actually not a bad idea."

"You don't have to sound so surprised," Aiken groused. "I have been known to have one once in a while."

"Yeah, I think you're about due your

weekly allotment," Connor joked.

"No," said Nicole, "Remember, he had one already earlier this week?"

"Oh, yeah, that's right."

"You two should take your act on the road," Aiken grumbled. He smiled inwardly. Things couldn't be too bad if his two best friends were still finding some humour in the situation.

"Okay, we meet back here in three hours."

"What, right now?" Nicole looked at the two. "You do remember we have classes this afternoon?"

"Yeah, but what's more important?" Connor asked wheedlingly.

"Easy enough for you to say," she responded. "You only have to find Mason before class starts to give him a message. We have to go halfway around the moon and try and track down a madman."

"What can I say?" Connor replied. "Perils of talent."

At this, Nicole snorted, but she didn't argue any further. All three got up, and Aiken and Nicole watched Connor pop out of existence on their side of the Park and appear closer to the other members of their class.

"Ready for this?" Aiken asked.

"Truly? No," Nicole responded. "But I

trust you to get us where we're going." With that, she took one of Aiken's hands in hers and opened her mind so he could use both of their power to boost them through the moon to Farside station.

Chapter Thirty

1:00pm Monday, August 17th, 2139

They arrived in the same out-of-the-way dining room that they'd used the first time, Aiken guessing correctly that in the middle of the day, it was unlikely to have a crowd inside. He immediately sensed the presence of someone else close by, though, and pulled Nicole down by her hand, which he was still grasping. She ducked down quickly, also sensing the other in the vicinity. They both relaxed at the same time when they realized it was just a custodian, going about her business in the hallway outside the room. Aiken extracted his hand from Nicole's grip, regretting it somewhat.

They clambered back to their feet, then set out, making sure to leave the room on the opposite side as the custodian. Aiken hoped Nicole still had the mental map of the dome in her mind from their last trip, as he'd neglected to look one up before jumping over. He could probably skim a location out of a passerby's mind, but if Nicole could tell the way without delving into someone else's thoughts, so much the better.

Nicole set off determinedly down the hallway, so Aiken assumed she knew which way they were going.

Fifteen minutes later, they were standing in front of the security services building, having only taken one wrong turn that led them out of their way.

"What's the plan?" Aiken asked.

"What? I thought you knew."

"I was figuring on the frontal assault. Just go up and ask if he's there and take it from there."

"That could work," Nicole said. "Or it could turn out disastrously."

"Well," Aiken said, "We can always wipe their memories and start again if it doesn't go the way we want the first time."

Nicole looked at him, appalled, then noticed that he was hiding a smile. She smacked his arm with the back of her hand. "Don't be getting ideas like that. We don't want to end up like Warman."

"Oh, what?" Aiken countered. "One day, covering up an awkward question, the next, multiple homicide?"

"Well, when you say it like that, it sounds dumb, but I'm betting Warman didn't set out to become a murderer either."

"Be that as it may, he's not going to stop unless someone else is there to put an end to it." With that, Aiken turned and walked up the steps into the building. Nicole quickly caught up and together, they walked into the lobby of the little security station.

They stopped at the front desk, and the officer behind the desk made them wait a couple of moments while he read, from what Aiken could see, a gossip column on the affairs of the rich and famous. Finally, looking up, he asked boredly, "What can I do for you?"

"Hi," said Aiken in a friendly tone. "Can you tell us if Zacharias Warman is still here?"

"Why do you want to know?"

Nicole had apparently been considering an appropriate answer for this, because she immediately stepped up. "We were at his show and he left too quickly after for us to get an autograph."

"Autograph? Are you crazy? They don't let just anyone go back into the holding area!" The officer shook his head in disbelief.

Aiken picked up where Nicole left off. "You mean he's back there?" He craned his neck as if to get a look.

The desk officer said coldly, "Look. You're not going to get an autograph. He's under arrest. You do understand what that means, right? It means no fans going in and out. This isn't the Hilton, it's a detention center. Now, if you don't want to find yourselves in a cell of your own, you'd better head out."

Aiken looked at Nicole, an unspoken question on his face. She shook her head no emphatically.

Aiken changed tacks. "You have monitors, right?" he asked the guard. "Can we at least see him?"

Apparently, sensing that giving in would be easier than explaining why not, the guard pointed a device at one of the walls opposite the desk, and it became a screen showing an empty cell.

"See for yourselves. There he is snug as a bug in a rug."

Aiken and Nicole exchanged astonished looks. The cell was obviously empty.

"Um," Nicole started. "Where is he? I

don't see him."

The guard looked up from his reading and glanced at the screen. Aiken expected an explosion when the officer saw that the screen was empty, but instead, he gestured brusquely, "Right there on the bed, can't you see?"

Aiken shot over to Nicole *Something's been done to his mind, obviously.*

Can you undo it?

I don't know, should I?

If Warman damaged it somehow, we're the only ones that can put it right, Nicole insisted.

Okay, let me take a look.

Aiken's thoughts delved into the mind of the officer. He saw immediately that a sloppy patchwork of memories had been slapped together overtop of the guards senses, telling him that whatever he saw in the cell, his mind should replace it with memories of the cell being occupied. Aiken saw that if he just pried away the layers of new memories, he would again expose the senses of the officer to the realities of the situation. He carefully removed the memories that Warman's mental instructions had told the guard to use in place of senses, then removed the instructions themselves. This took a matter of seconds, and when Aiken returned his senses to his own body, he could already see the dawning realization on the face of the officer.

"What? Where did he go? He was right there!"

Aiken and Nicole scooted off to the side while the officer used his wrist communicator to talk to the guard on duty at the cells themselves. "What do you mean he's still in his cell? I can see here on the monitor that he's not!" He listened briefly. "I don't know what the hell is going on down there, but I'm coming down to take a look. Stay put so we can figure this out." Without a glance at Aiken or Nicole, he stood up and stormed off toward a locked door at the side of the lobby. Aiken motioned to Nicole to follow, and made them both invisible before following.

The officer stomped down the short corridor to another locked door at the end. Aiken could sense another person just beyond that door and while they paused to unlock the door, he pushed into the guard's mind. There, he found the same sort of mental papering-over that had been done to the officer at the front door. He again removed the memory substitutes and the mental instructions to use them in place of senses when looking into the cell. It was easier for him this time, but he wondered how many security officers had been similarly affected, and how long ago these instructions had taken effect.

The front desk officer opened the door and, on seeing the guard waiting on the other side, simply pointed down the hall lined with cells. Aiken and Nicole hung back, watching. The two security officers stopped in front of the second cell on the right and the guard keyed in a sequence that opened the cell door. Both officers looked into the cell. The guard, paling, stammered out, "How could this be? I just saw him not twenty minutes ago when I did my rounds."

"I don't know, Tim, but I have a feeling we've been played. If those kids at the front desk hadn't wanted..." he trailed off. "Hold on! Those kids! They insisted I look."

Nicole and Aiken exchanged a glance and, without a word, teleported themselves back out into the lobby to where they'd been standing, in front of the desk. Aiken hastily removed their invisibility and they tried to look nonchalant.

Not thirty seconds later, the officer came storming back through the door. "Okay, spill it," he sputtered. "How did you know that Warman wasn't in his cell?"

"Why would you think we knew that?" Aiken asked.

"Don't give me that," the officer said in a low voice. "I've been doing this job for twenty years, here and elsewhere. I can tell when someone's lying to me."

Yeah, but not when your own eyes are, Nicole sent to Aiken.

"We came looking for an autograph," Aiken tried to muster up some sincerity. He didn't think the officer bought it.

"Like hell you did." The officer paused. "That last show was the one that ended in disaster. No way someone wants an autograph after that. What's really going on here."

Aiken started to panic, thinking they'd maybe have to wipe the officer's memory after all. Recalling Nicole's admonition, and what he'd just seen of Warman's handiwork, he wasn't especially eager to try it.

Nicole spoke up, "You caught us. We're actually more interested in what happened at the end of the show. You see, one of our friends died in a similar fashion and we thought we could figure out what happened if we could just speak with Mr. Warman."

Aiken gaped at her. She was telling the officer everything. Well, not everything. Actually, upon reflection, this might not be a bad idea. It wasn't exactly a lie, but it wasn't precisely the truth, either.

The officer caught on quickly enough, "You mean, Miss Lafontaine. Terrible tragedy, that. Unfortunately, Mr. Warman was already questioned about that, and witnesses can put him here on Farside within minutes of her death. There's no way he was involved."

Aiken tried to look crestfallen at this news, but all he could think was *if only you knew*. However, Nicole had managed to divert suspicion with their plausible story and so the officer sent them on their way without too much hassle.

They got to the bottom of the steps in front of the building, and Nicole made to continue back toward the room they'd jumped in to, but Aiken stayed put. She looked at him questioningly.

"I wonder how many other guards have had their brains mucked about with to cover Warman's escape?"

Nicole saw immediately what he was saying, and the two of them made their way over to a nearby bench to sit and await the arrivals they were sure were headed in.

They didn't have to wait long. The two officers at the security center must have hit the alarm pretty hard, because the first pair of officers to respond zipped up on a slick little electric cart, barely managing to avoid colliding with some of the landscaping on the pathway in front of the center. Aiken had spent the intervening time going over what he'd done to the two inside the building with Nicole for just such a situation. Nodding to the pair, he slipped his mental probe inside the officer on the left while Nicole took the one on the right. They both found much the same thing as previously and undid the damage that much faster this time around.

"Only three more," Nicole said, when they'd both returned their senses to their bodies.

"What?"

"I checked how many officers are assigned to this security center, and there are seven. So only three left to undo the damage."

Aiken blinked at Nicole. He hadn't even thought to pull up that bit of information while he was fixing the problems that Warman had caused. "Nice work!"

The next officer that showed up was a young blonde woman who looked like she was expecting someone to tear a strip off of her. "What do you think," Nicole asked Aiken. "First year on the job?"

"First week, maybe," he answered, laughing. He motioned toward the officer gallantly, then sat back and watched as Nicole deftly arrowed into the young woman's thoughts and fixed what was wrong. "Well?" he inquired.

"What, you think I just stroll around in their minds, taking a look at whatever I want?"

Aiken just sat in silence, looking at her.

"Oh, fine," she laughed. "Three weeks into the job."

"So close," Aiken said.

The last two showed up within a minute of each other, so Nicole handled the second one while Aiken was busy with the first. When they were both fixed, Aiken and Nicole sat back on the bench to rest for a bit before jumping back home to Peary.

"I wonder how long he's been free," Nicole pondered.

"Yeah, I couldn't tell from the patches." Aiken chimed in. "It seemed like they'd all been applied at different times."

"Well, that kind of makes sense, as guards came on and off shift. And it wouldn't matter if they were imagining seeing him in the cell when he was actually in there, either."

"No, I guess you're right," Aiken answered. He thought for a couple of moments, "Well, it doesn't really matter, does it?"

"No, I guess not," Nicole answered. "It would just be nice to know whether he's been out almost since his arrest, or just since this morning."

"Well, at most, it's what, two days?"

Nicole nodded.

"Well, there haven't been any more deaths in that time, so at least he's keeping quiet."

"One thing bothers me."

"Only one?" Aiken teased.

"Well, he had to know that his escape would be discovered eventually, right? I mean, those memory patches were terrible. No way they would have lasted more than to the end of this week. You could sense the officers' minds already fraying the edges, trying to repair themselves."

Aiken nodded in agreement. "So?"

"So, what was he expecting to happen? Now he's got an alert out with his name and photo for every security service on the moon to see."

"Maybe he isn't on the moon anymore?"

"Do you think he can jump all the way to Earth?"

"He doesn't really have to, though. He could just jump onto any outbound shuttle once it cleared the moon's gravity and fuel allotment wasn't an issue anymore. Maybe he's strong enough to jump to one of the Lagrange stations."

"Yeah, because that wouldn't be suspicious," Nicole retorted. "The stations aren't huge. Some new person showing up would definitely be noticed. Well, except maybe on Midway. Is he strong enough to jump to Midway?"

"I don't know," Aiken said. "I hope not, because if he can do that without the energy he gets from killing people, then he's going to be a hell of a lot harder to deal with than we thought."

"Maybe." Nicole trailed off. Aiken looked at her questioningly, but she just shook her head.

"Ready to head back?" He asked after a moment.

She nodded, but also looked around pointedly. Aiken took her unspoken message. This was far too public a place to simply disappear into thin air, particularly with the security centre right across the pathway full of officers primed to look suspiciously on any disappearance, no matter whose. Aiken and Nicole picked themselves up off the bench and meandered aimlessly toward a hallway leading off this main corridor of Farside. They found a secluded corner and once again pushed themselves through the universe and across the moon.

Chapter Thirty-One
3:00pm Monday, August 17th, 2139

Connor was beaming when he found them at their agreed-upon rendezvous. "Pay dirt," he exclaimed triumphantly. "Mason pinpointed him down to tomorrow night. You'll never guess where he's going to be."

A feeling of dread stole across Aiken's chest as he shook his head at his friend.

"Right here in Peary Dome," Connor continued. "Our home turf. We've got the bastard to rights."

Nicole and Aiken exchanged looks. "Are you sure," Aiken asked cautiously.

"Yep," Connor continued on obliviously.

"We won't have to jump anywhere to meet him so we can be recharged and ready to deal with him once and for all." All of a sudden, he noticed the mood of his two friends, "What's gotten in to you two?"

"Connor," Aiken said gently, "Don't you remember me telling you about what the future looked like here in Peary when I jumped forward?"

"I've been thinking about that," Connor interrupted. "I think what you saw was a potential future, but now that you know about it, it doesn't have to come out like that."

"What about causality?"

"Not a problem, you're going forward, not back."

"Was there another time or place after that?"

"Why would you ask?"

"In case something doesn't work out the way we plan tomorrow night, it would be nice to have a backup."

Connor smiled. "As it turns out, I did ask him that, but Mason says it gets cloudy right afterwards again, and he can't see anything past tomorrow at all. That's why I think we'll beat Warman tomorrow."

Aiken began to feel a ray of hope, then remembered the feel of his vision. It had felt real, solid, immutable. He hoped Connor was right and that they could prevent it from coming true, but he had a sickening feeling that he was rushing headlong into disaster. Still, now they had a time for it, they could prepare themselves as much as possible for Warman's arrival.

"So what did you two turn up?"

"Warman's definitely escaped," Aiken said. "He'd covered it up by making the guards see memories of him in the cell instead of what was right in front of them."

"Clever," Connor said.

"Sort of, I guess. It was really sloppy."

"What do you mean?"

Nicole broke in, "The false senses wouldn't have lasted more than a week, so whatever his next move is, it has to be happening this week."

"You don't think that tomorrow..." Connor trailed off, suddenly feeling the shock of his friends. "You think he's coming here for us?"

"Can you think of another reason for him to come to Peary?" Aiken asked quietly.

"Plentiful sunshine?"

Nicole smiled at Connor's attempt at levity, but a somber silence fell on all three of them.

"Well," Connor finally broke the silence,

"If he's going to be here, we have to let the others know."

"Are they going to listen to me?" Aiken asked.

"Of course," Nicole answered. Connor looked unsure, but didn't say anything. "Plus," Nicole continued, "It won't just be you. I can tell them about Farside, and Mason can tell them about tomorrow. That way, even if people have an issue with you, which they don't, but if they did, they can't say that tomorrow is only on you."

Aiken looked at Nicole questioningly, but it was Connor who broke in. "Look, no one's blaming you for Saturday."

"Thanks for the reassurance," Aiken replied.

"No, that's not what I meant. I mean, it is what I meant, but not in the way you think." Connor sighed, then started again. "You frightened some people on Saturday."

"What?"

"No one is blaming you for the deaths. I mean that. They don't think you had anything to do with that any more than any of the rest of us. You just... you really..." Connor looked helplessly at Nicole.

"You took energy from people that they weren't giving you," she said gently. "People weren't expecting that."

"So what? So they think I'm like Warman? That I'll just suck the energy out of anyone to get what I want?" Aiken was angry. Here he was, just trying to live up to the expectations the rest of the group had set for him, and now they were scared of him? For what? For trying too hard?

"Aiken, they got hurt, and hurt people don't make a lot of sense when they lash out," Nicole soothed. She looked down in her lap for a minute, composing herself. "Remember when we were little and we played together all the time?" Aiken nodded, silent. "Remember how we used to go on those dumb picnics? My folks would pack up a bag of whatever food we'd have around and I'd invite you over and we'd come here and we'd eat and play?"

Nicole stopped for a moment more. "You know, after my dad died, I stopped calling you to come over for picnics. It wasn't that I didn't like picnics anymore. I think I just thought it would be wrong to be out here having fun without him."

Aiken nodded in understanding. "I get that. I guess being the brunt of it isn't any fun."

"Well, as I said, you'll have some other people standing up for you to spread out the idea so it doesn't come only from you." Nicole patted him on the shoulder, then quickly, leaned in and kissed him on the cheek. He looked at her, startled. She flushed, and without warning, disappeared with a pop of teleportation.

Aiken swung his gaze around to Connor, who seemed to be having trouble holding in his laughter. "What?"

"Man, you sure are thick sometimes, aren't you?" Connor seemed quite amused, but changed the subject before Aiken could inquire further. "So, when do we get everyone together to tell them?"

"Well, school's out for the day, so anytime." Aiken thought a bit more. "Unless we don't want to tell them until tomorrow."

"No, that's a bad idea. Let them get used to the idea. Plus, if anyone found out you knew before and kept it from them, that would look bad."

Aiken considered his friend's advice and agreed with it. He sent out a telepathic message to everyone in the group to meet at the Park at eight that evening. He received general acknowledgements from everyone and some curious questions, which he deflected by saying he didn't want to have to repeat himself to everyone.

He told Connor when the meeting was, then excused himself and headed home for the questioning he knew would accompany the notice from the school that he'd skipped classes that afternoon.

Chapter Thirty-Two
8:00pm Monday, August 17th, 2139

That evening, the group met at their usual spot in the Park. Aiken put more effort than usual into the shield around their group, deflecting not only curiosity, but visual and mental probing as well. They were effectively invisible from any conceivable would-be watcher. When everyone had calmed down and found a spot of grass to sit on, he stood up. He steeled himself against the looks in his classmates' eyes and explained that he'd been interested in finding out Warman's location and had found some things that were of interest to the entire group. He motioned at Nicole. She stood and spoke quickly and succinctly about what she and Aiken had found at the Farside station security center. Shocked gasps greeted her announcement, though the students couldn't have been totally surprised that Warman had gotten loose. Since their visit that afternoon, Warman's face had been on all the news bulletins. He was a wanted fugitive everywhere on the moon.

When Nicole had finished, Aiken stood again. "We had suspected that Warman was at large even before we visited Farside, but we didn't know where. As you know, he has an extraordinary powerful shield that lets him hide from our mental probes. This makes it difficult to track him around using conventional means." Everyone chuckled when he said "conventional" and even Aiken had to admit that the thought that mental searches were becoming normal to them was a little funny. He waved to Mason, and sat back down.

Mason moved to where Aiken had been standing and cleared his throat before speaking. "As Aiken just mentioned, our usual way of finding someone proved inadequate in Mr. Warman's case. However, as you're aware, my gift is sight of an unconventional nature. Aiken asked if I could look forward on Mr. Warman's timeline to determine a place where he would be in the future, so we'd have some advance warning, now that he's not performing at regular intervals at Farside Station."

"Get on with it, Mason," Ethan urged from within the group.

"Right. So, looking at his timeline, it was apparent that his shield prevented our gifts from perceiving him while it was active. So I looked forward until it wasn't active. That allowed me to pin down a time to look around for him. So it turns out that the time he will have his shield down momentarily is tomorrow, and the place is here."

Shocked silence greeted this pronouncement, but Mason apparently took no notice and simply walked back to his spot on the ground and sat down. The students were looking around at each other with stunned fear in their eyes. Aiken felt that if he didn't bring this meeting back on point, people might start losing it completely, and they wouldn't have anything planned for tomorrow at all. He stood quickly and got everyone's attention focused back on him.

"The good news is that we know where he'll be and we can be ready for him," Aiken said in as calm a voice as he could manage. "We can prepare."

"How?" It was Ethan, looking somewhat

shell shocked.

"I think our best bet is to use a variation on the technique that we used to get back here after Saturday evening," Aiken said. "We gather energy from the normal people around here and use it to boost our link so that we have more than enough power to take Warman down." He looked around and saw that people were seeming to accept this. "However," he continued, once they'd had a moment or two to process, "we need to, at the same time, keep those civilians out of reach of Warman, so he can't use them up in the same way."

"How are we going to do that?" Liam asked, genuinely curious. "Don't we need both the people and Warman to be close by?"

"Here's what I'm thinking," Aiken said. "I will try and draw Warman out into the middle of the Park where we can keep innocent bystanders away. The rest of you will link up behind Liv in order to provide the primary boost of power, and Nicole will link as many civilians as she can into a wide net to give us even more power as a secondary source. Liv and Nicky will feed the power through me at Warman. That way, I won't be drawing back through you, and you won't get overwhelmed by the civilians' power coming through the same link. Sound like a plan?"

He saw heads starting to nod, then people starting to get a little enthusiastic. He saw, for the first time since the debacle on Saturday night, hope.

Chapter Thirty-Three
Tuesday, August 18th, 2139

The next day at school passed interminably slow. The Lunatics had agreed to meet in the Park at seven that evening, but the day seemed to stretch out before them like taffy. Aiken couldn't remember a duller day in class. Even his favourite subjects weren't holding his attention, and his mind kept going over the plan over and over again, turning it about, looking for flaws. The only thing he could spot was that if Warman didn't behave like they'd predicted. He wasn't too worried about that, however. In Warman's place, Aiken was sure that he would be the target, since he represented the biggest threat to Warman, and everyone knew it.

There was danger in underestimating your opponent, Aiken knew, but also in overestimating. If they went into the confrontation this evening thinking that they were facing down an unbeatable monster, well then, their defeat would be achieved without Warman even having to work at it. In this case, the mental game was the only game, and if they could go in thinking they had a shot, that was half the battle won right there.

Finally, the last class of the day let out and Aiken trudged home. His parents could sense that something was wrong, but his reticence to talk made them give up questioning him. He ate supper without a word, then headed back to his room, where he quietly (as much as he could control it) teleported over to the Park in order to get ready for the coming confrontation. If his parents checked on him, they would be curious as to where he'd sneaked off to, but not enough to really do anything about it.

He'd considered papering over their senses with memories like Warman had with the policemen, but the thought of becoming any more like Warman gave him the chills. Besides, he needed everyone in the dome to be at their best if Nicole's link had a chance of succeeding.

He appeared in the copse of bushes off to the side of the Park, where many of their Lunatic meetings had taken place in happier times. He was startled to see a couple other faces already there waiting. Jillian looked up from her spot next to Kaira and smiled weakly at him. Over on the other side of the clearing, Aiken could see Liam and Olivia deep in conversation, and Isaac talking with Faith. Hugo was off to one side, nervously checking his watch. In fact, he estimated that more than half of the group was there already, either talking quietly with other people, or silently sitting with their thoughts. He looked around for Connor and Nicole, but couldn't see either of them among those already here.

He sat down off to one side and watched the group talk and go silent and change partners. There was a subtle dance at work here, and Aiken was fascinated by the interplay. He opened up his senses to the group and saw the bright bands of light that indicated bonds between many of the members of the class, even those sitting quietly on their own. He looked down at himself and was surprised to see bands of light of varying thicknesses and brightnesses leading off to all the members of their small group. He'd never have considered a few short months ago that he would form such meaningful bonds of friendship and trust with so many different people. He watched the dance of conversations continue, now seeing the connections between people ebb and flow as they started talking and as they changed conversational partners.

Just as he glanced down at his own links, he was momentarily blinded as a new brilliance shone out from them. He shut off his mental senses and looked around. Connor and Nicole had arrived more or less at the same time, and both were making their way over to where he sat.

"Ready?" he asked Nicole when the two arrived.

"I guess so," she responded hesitantly.

"What's the problem?" Aiken probed gently.

"I don't know if I'm up to this," Nicole responded.

"No one better to do it, Aiken replied. At this, Nicole seemed to brighten for a second, then it faded again.

"Take a look at this," Aiken continued. He opened up his senses again, seeing the connections between people once more. This time, though, he showed Nicole what he was seeing. He moved his consciousness out overtop of the dome and looked down. The bright spot in the center of the dome must be the Lunatics, he thought, but he didn't concentrate on it, rather making the focus the dimmer strands to the outside of the park. He could see hundreds, thousands of dimmer strands connecting the souls of Peary Dome to one another. He showed these to Nicole. *Look, Nicky. These people are all joined one to another, just like we are, and see* he showed links leading from the dimmer outer structure to the bright heart at the center of the dome *they're already connected to us.*

He returned both of their sights to the ordinary and saw that Nicole was feeling much better about being the focus of such a large group of people.

"I'll let you in on a secret," Aiken murmured to her. "I've already done linking with a larger group of normal people. Back before this whole thing with Warman started, before Diana, I used to link everyone in the dome together when I first woke up in the morning, and you know what?"

"What?" Nicole whispered back to him.

"People like it. They like the feeling of connectedness that it gives them. I found people were nicer to each other during the day when they'd had a sense of connection earlier. It was as if in really being connected at such a basic level, they were better able to appreciate one another. That's all you have to do, Nicky, you just have to get people to link into something they already want to be a part of. People, generally, want to be connected to something bigger than themselves."

While he'd been talking to Nicole, the last of the group had showed up, all of them earlier than what they'd agreed on. They all looked sheepishly around at one another.

Aiken grinned at the group.

Someone laughed and the tension broke. Aiken started getting them organised. The plan was for them to spread out around the periphery of the park, so that they wouldn't be close enough together for Warman to come after them all together, but that they could come to each other's aid if it was necessary.

The students spread out to their designated spots when Mason gave them a twenty minute warning. Aiken kept Liv and Nicole back to go over the details of their links and how they would feed the energy they gathered through to him. Finally, they departed and Aiken was alone in the copse. He looked around at this Park that he had hated so long and could see, as if looking into the past, but only though his memories. He saw himself and Nicole as children, running through the Park, playing soccer or Frisbee while her parents watched.

He was determined that no other families would be ripped apart by Warman's murderous tendencies. They would stop him here tonight.

He walked resolutely out to the middle of the Park and calmed his mind as he waited for Warman to appear.

He didn't have to wait long. With a pop signifying a teleportation, Warman was suddenly in front of him, looking angry.

"Aiken, my boy, you've gone and opened a can of worms now," he said icily.

"Right," said Aiken, "We'll see about that."

Warman laughed at him, then a look of concentration crossed his face. Aiken could feel a warmth building inside him as Warman attempted to burn him down. Frantically, he shielded himself from Warman's mental energy, then thought desperately on how he could link up to the two networks headed by Olivia and Nicole if he'd cocooned himself against mental energies.

A thought stole across his mind, that maybe they weren't as prepared for Warman as they'd thought. He looked across to his opponent, who had a wild grin on his face, seeming to taunt Aiken with his invulnerability. Aiken felt his anger build, then had an inspiration. As if unzipping his shield at his back, he pushed his mental block away from himself and toward Warman. He wrapped Warman inside his mental block so that he would be free to contact Olivia and Nicole.

He began squeezing his mental shield down on Warman, crushing the man's abilities inside a wall of Aiken's construction. *Now, Liv* he called out. He felt a surge of strength as the combined power of all the group flowed through him, reinforcing the wall around Warman and closing it in tighter against him. Soon, they would be able to crush his mental powers out of existence, and he would be a threat to no one.

He saw a look of panic cross Warman's face as he realized what was about to happen. *Now, Nicky!* Aiken sent, then a surge of amazing power flowed through him as Nicole gathered up the mental energy of thousands of ordinary citizens of Peary Dome to use in the fight against this madman.

The wall around Warman's abilities closed tighter and tighter and Aiken was savouring their triumph. He could feel the end approaching. Without being able to reach out and take energy from others, Warman's abilities were weakening. They were winning.

All of a sudden, it was like a black hole

had opened up in the middle of the Lunatics' network. Energy that should have been going to Aiken wasn't getting there, and Aiken even felt some energy from the other link start bleeding away into the darkness in the middle of the group's energy. Startled, the wall around Warman began to falter.

"Fool," Warman spat out. "Didn't you think I'd have a contingency plan in place? Didn't you think I'd know you'd have something ready for me? I chose this time and this place, not you! Watch as your plan falls apart."

Stunned for a moment, Aiken nearly lost his grip on the wall around Warman's abilities. How was he doing this? He was cut off from everything, from everyone. A second shock followed on the heels of the first. Now there was a spreading ripple through Nicole's network, breaking the bonds between people and clearing away the pathways that had been established for her to gather together the energy from the people of Peary Dome.

What was going on?

Aiken felt an uncontrolled surge of energy crash over him, wild and uncontained. He could feel Nicole's grip on the energy she was sending him weaken, then let go completely. From Olivia, there was nothing.

Aiken stumbled, physically falling to his knees.

"See," hissed Warman. "All you are is not enough to take me on. Best to leave me alone, boy." Then Warman shook off the vestiges of Aiken's shield and Aiken could feel once more the heat beginning to grow inside of him. Weak, he re-established his shield, but it was only barely strong enough to ward off Warman's assault.

"You won't find me so easily next time," Warman spat, apparently giving up on him and stalking off through the Park. Around him, trees, bushes and park benches leapt into flames. Alarm klaxons began to ring throughout the dome as one of the worst fears of residents came true - fire. Aiken lost track of Warman through the smoke and fell to his side, curling into a ball with his arms wrapped around his stomach, trying to heal the pain inside.

After a time, he rose and looked around him. His clothes were filthy and smoke hung in a pall throughout the dome. He reached deep within himself to find some vestige of power to quench the blazes still going on around the Park. He sucked the oxygen out of the air around the fires and they sputtered and died. He dragged himself wearily to a nearby bench and sat for a moment, then realized that there were people on the ground around the Park. Residents who'd come to help fight the blazes had been attacked by Warman as he recharged his energy levels.

Aiken could see that most of them were still moving, despite some having burns to their bodies. Kaira was moving among them, laying a soothing hand here and there, helping heal. Where the damage was too great, she eased the passing. Medical teams had begun to flow into the Park and had some of the wounded on stretchers on their way to the infirmary. Aiken stood and walked through the area, helping as best he could, healing what he could, helping move people out of the area if they were able.

"Aiken," he heard someone calling his name. He turned and saw Jillian struggling towards him. He hurried over to where she was and saw, aghast, that her leg was bent at an unnatural angle. The only reason that she was moving at all was the she was carrying herself through telekinesis. He put his hand on her leg and sent power into her. Her leg straightened and he could see some of the pain in her face begin to fade. He kept his hand on the break until he was certain it was as healed as he could make it, then helped her over to a bench nearby.

"You're going to want Kaira to take another look at that when she's able," he said when they were both seated.

She nodded her understanding, then

asked, "What about you?" She pointed down at Aiken's arm, visible below the cuff of his shirt, and for the first time, he took a look at himself. He looked like he'd been steamed, with angry red flesh all over him. No sooner had he noticed it, though, and it began to fade, his body healing itself once he was aware of the injuries.

When his skin had returned to normal, he murmured his thanks, then asked, "What about the others?"

"I haven't seen all of them, but most of them seem better off than us. I didn't even get injured in the fight - I was trying to carry someone to safety and my concentration slipped."

"Did any of them run into Warman?" he asked urgently.

"I don't know," she said, "I lost sight of him in the smoke."

"Damn it," Aiken muttered under his breath. Then louder, "What happened back there?"

"No idea," Jillian answered. "I thought we had him. We could all see through you that he was just about done, then it was like all our power went somewhere else. Like someone else was taking it."

"Someone in our group," Aiken continued. "Mason told us this would happen."

"You don't think..."

"What else could it be?" Aiken was angry. "We need to get everyone back together now and sort this out."

"Aiken," Jillian broke in softly, "People are hurt. Their family might be hurt, too. We can't meet right now."

"But Warman is getting away!"

"He's already gone, and with his shield, there's no way we can see where." Jillian patted Aiken awkwardly on the shoulder, then walked back into the smoke to see where she could lend a hand with cleaning up the disaster.

Aiken sighed, wanting her to be wrong, but knowing already that she was right. Nothing to do now but deal with the mess that Warman left behind. Tracking Warman down and dealing with him once and for all would have to wait. He got up and started helping once more, coming across more people he knew, helping where he could. Soon the Park cleared of everyone who needed medical attention. There were far too many white sheets still on the ground around the Park though. People who would never be going home to their families. More people to hate and resent the Park and the happiness that it used to represent. Aiken thought of his own parents... his parents! How could he have been so thoughtless? What if they were here?   Quickly, without even thinking about it consciously, he reached out to them mentally and breathed a sigh of relief when he brushed against their consciousnesses and sensed that they were in no immediate danger. They'd been late responding to the fire alarm because their offices were so far away from the center of the dome. It may have saved their lives, but Aiken would never know. He could sense their worry for him and placed a reassuring thought in each of their minds that he was probably all right.

Next, he reached out to all the Lunatics, to make sure that everyone had come through all right. Just as he was making contact, a stab of grief through the link overwhelmed him and he dropped to his knees as tears sprang unbidden to his eyes. He tried to figure out where the feeling was coming from, but the sensation was too overwhelming to pinpoint it. He tried to disengage, but the strength of the unexpected emotion bound him to the sufferer all the closer. He flowed reassurance and caring back down the link at whomever it was that was experiencing such pain, and after a couple of minutes, it had deadened enough that he could disengage from the mental link. He looked up from where he was kneeling on the grass, but the pall of smoke was still hanging in the air and he couldn't see far enough through it to determine who it had been in such anguish.

He stood and walked wearily to the edge of the Park, then started to slowly walk the perimeter, hoping to find the other members of the group. He made it as far as finding Ethan, Isaac and Faith clustered in a group, talking quietly before the exhaustion that had been creeping up on him finally overwhelmed him and he collapsed in a boneless heap.

Chapter Thirty-Four
Wednesday, August 19th, 2139

"You think he's okay?"

Aiken could hear muffled voices, as if they were talking from a great distance away.

"Should be - I looked at him, and the only thing seems to be a profound tiredness."

Slowly, as consciousness returned to him, Aiken realized the voices were talking about him. He tried to say something, to get their attention, but what he came out with was only a vague grunting noise, barely audible to his own ears. He tried again.

"Mmphf."

"I think he's waking up," one of the voices said. He felt a hand on his arm, squeezing. His eyes refused to open for some reason, so he gathered his strength and looked through them. Or rather, tried to. He couldn't seem to get his thoughts organized enough to make any kind of effort at using his mental faculties.

"Don't, Aiken," another voice said, low. "Something they gave you scrambled your abilities for a bit. Just wait and they'll come back."

Aiken relaxed. Evidently someone from the class was nearby if they were talking about abilities. He realized he must be at the infirmary from the smell of disinfectant that wafted through the air. Another familiar, comforting smell of citrus and spice was tantalizingly close by, but he couldn't put his finger on what it was. He relaxed back into what he realized must be a hospital bed and his conscious mind wandered.

When he came back to himself, he was able to ratchet open his eyes to catch a glimpse of his surroundings. He could see a light sconce on the wall to his right, but only open space to his left. He turned his head in that direction and saw that his mother was sitting in one of the uncomfortable looking chairs that hospitals everywhere seemed to provide for the families of the ill. As if sensing his gaze, she looked up from her reading and, seeing that he was awake, scrambled out of the chair towards him. She took his hand and looked down at him, beaming.

"You're going to be just fine," she said soothingly.

"I know, mom," Aiken responded. "I feel better already."

"That's great, honey!"

Just then, Aiken's father came through the door and seeing that he was awake, came to stand at Aiken's other side. "You gave us a bit of a scare there, Aiken."

"Sorry, dad. Just trying to help out."

"We know, and for some reason, I knew you were going to be fine."

Aiken smiled to himself. The message he'd delivered into his parents' minds had apparently worked.

"What would possess you," his mother began, "to go out into the Park yesterday when it was on fire like that?"

"Actually," Aiken answered. "I was there when it started. People were coming in from all over to help and they were getting hurt, so I was trying to help them out."

"Yeah, we heard from some medics that you were talking with people, making them feel better."

If only you knew, Aiken thought in the depths of his mind. Aloud, he asked, "Did they figure out what caused the fire?"

"No," his father answered. "There was a big news conference this morning on it, but they said to give it at least a couple of days to go over all the sensor data to determine what went wrong."

"From where I was sitting, it looked like the trees just started on fire," Aiken said, hating lying to his parents, but knowing they'd never accept the truth.

"Some other witnesses say they saw the same thing," Aiken's mother confirmed. "Also, someone swears they saw that escaped entertainer, Zacharias Warman."

"Really?"

"Well, given what happened at his show, it wouldn't surprise me to learn that people thought they saw him."

At this point, a tall woman in a white lab coat walked into the room. She stopped short when she saw Aiken was awake, but wasted no time shooing his parents out of the way so she could read the hovering displays showing Aiken's vital signs. Aiken saw her nametag read Peters.

"Well, young man, what do you have to

say for yourself," she asked sternly.

"I'm sorry?"

"Well, that's certainly a start," Dr. Peters smiled down at him. "You were severely dehydrated when you arrived, but now that we've got you topped up, you'll be fine. Back to normal in no time," she proclaimed.

Not as normal as you'd think, Aiken thought quietly.

With his parents supporting him, Aiken made his way out of the infirmary and back to their apartment. He hadn't walked that long a distance in a while, preferring instead to teleport whenever it was convenient. He was almost out of energy again when they laid him back down in his own bed.

"A couple of your classmates stopped by while you were out," his mom said. "Once you're feeling better, we can let them know you're up to visitors. Shame about the Gabriels, though."

"What?" Aiken asked urgently.

"Oh, I suppose you probably hadn't heard." She sat on the edge of the bed and took one of Aiken's hands. "One of the people who died in the fire was Mason Gabriel."

A shock ran through Aiken's body. *That must have been what Warman meant about not finding him again so easily.* But if Mason had been targeted by Warman, that meant that Warman had been told how they found him in the first place, which meant that whoever it was in the class who'd betrayed them was responsible not only for the group not being able to contain Warman, but also responsible for Mason's death. He grew cold at the thought and his mother, sensing something was wrong, looked down sharply.

It wasn't hard to look shocked, but Aiken's mother had no idea what Mason's death really meant, no idea of the depth of the despair that began to gnaw at Aiken. Mason was the only one who'd been able to pin down Warman. And to top it all off, he'd been predicting his own death when he spoke of the second to fall. Aiken wondered if Mason had known he wouldn't survive the fight in the park. It would be just like Mason to not say anything so as to not plant any doubts in the group heading into the fight. Aiken felt tears form at the corners of his eyes.

Oh and Gwen, poor Gwen. That must have been who he'd sensed back in the Park when the grief was overwhelming.

First Diana, now Mason. The older class had been hit twice by Warman. They could either fold and decide not to fight any longer, or, Aiken rather suspected, be emboldened to take

Warman out. After all, now that two had fallen and one had turned - and who was that anyway? - most of the prediction that Mason had made had come true. Then he remembered the part at the end, about someone sacrificing all in order to defeat Warman. He wasn't sure what that entailed, but he was pretty sure it was him that the prediction was talking about.

All this flashed across his mind in the space of a second or two, but he was surprised to see his mother still standing by his bedside when he'd come to the end of his train of thought. "I'm just going to rest a little more," he told his mother. She patted the hand she was holding, then stood and left Aiken's room.

No sooner had she closed the door behind her than Aiken heard two pops of teleportation, following one right on the heels of the other. He glanced up, fearful that Warman had gained access to his space, had come for him personally, but was unsurprised to see that it was Connor and Nicole looking down at him with concern on their faces.

"You guys better not get caught in here," Aiken whispered. "You'd have a hard time explaining how you got in here past my parents."

"No worries, man, we could just jump right back out if we hear anyone coming,"

Connor smiled.

Nicole asked how Aiken was doing. Truthfully, he was tired and feeling a little run-down still, but he needed information about what had really happened in the Park, information that his parents were unlikely to have. Still, he was happy to see his friends. Nicole said that she and Faith had been by his hospital room earlier, and he surmised that was who had been there when he'd partly woken earlier.

"Who was it?" he asked urgently.

His friends exchanged a hesitant look. Nicole started to speak, then shook her head and looked imploringly at Connor. She turned away, tears in her eyes.

Connor spoke hesitantly, "We think it was Hugo. He's the only one who hasn't checked in yet."

Aiken thought about this for a minute. He was shocked that anyone from the class would betray them after seeing what Warman was capable of, but he also knew that, according to Mason's prediction, one of them would do precisely that.

"So Mason was right," he said grimly.

"Looks like," Connor agreed.

"Do you think," started Nicole. "Do you think maybe we pushed him to it?"

"What? No!" Connor was adamant. "It was destined."

"I don't believe that," Aiken said quietly. "I refuse to believe that the future is unchangeable."

"Why not?" Connor asked. "It's not like Mason was consulting an Oracle or something. He looked into the future and told us what he saw."

"Yes, but not all of the things that would happen," Nicole interjected. "He didn't tell us about the fight in the theatre, or the other people who would die, or the linking together, or the mine rescue."

"But all of the things he did tell us have come true," Connor said.

"Not yet, they haven't," Aiken said firmly. "We still have the little matter of defeating Warman, and Hugo, ahead of us."

"Right," Connor said, and Nicole nodded. They were back on the same page. Nicole was giving Aiken a strange look though.

"What?"

"Nothing," she responded. "Just, uh, just wondering if you'd come up with a way to take Warman out."

"Well, things were actually going pretty okay in the Park today," Aiken started.

"Yesterday," Connor interjected.

"Right, yesterday. Anyway, things were going fairly well with blanketing Warman's abilities until Hugo sabotaged the Lunatic link. And then," Aiken continued thoughtfully, "something happened to the other, link, too." He looked at Nicole questioningly.

"What?" she asked, startled.

"Well, you were the one operating as the focus for the secondary group. What did you see happen?"

"Honestly, I couldn't say," she responded slowly, sinking down to sit on the floor beside Aiken's bed. She put her head in her hands, and Aiken sat up on his bed and put his hand on her shoulder. "One minute," she continued, "things were going fine. I did just like you showed me and gathered up all the strands of relationship among all the people in the dome and fed some of their power through to you. Then it was like some of them weren't connected to me anymore and worse, not just disconnected, but disconnecting others, too. Like the connections were infected and it was spreading." She stopped. "After a while, there just weren't enough connections to hang on to anymore. I couldn't draw enough power from the ones that were left without hurting them, so I let them go."

"That was the right thing to do," Aiken

reassured her. "After the experience in the theatre, it was better to let go than to take more than they could give."

"Well," Connor said, "Now we know what Warman was up to for the two days after he escaped from jail."

"You think he set it up on purpose?" Aiken asked.

"Of course." Connor enumerated on his fingers, "First, he recruits Hugo. Hugo tells him how we are trying to track him and what the plan is to beat him, so Warman knows when and where to drop his shield, and Mason sees that so we get ready for him. The problem is it's a trap. He's already decided where and when the fight's going to be. Second, he spends the intervening time going around Peary somehow infecting people so that when we try to use them against him, it backfires. Last, once it's obvious we aren't beating him, he takes out Mason so we can't see the next time he'll be unshielded."

He looked at Nicole and Aiken. "We should have known that he wouldn't have unshielded himself in Peary without having a damn good way out planned if things didn't work out for him. We had him on the ropes for a minute there, and I think it scared him, but then Hugo did whatever he had to do and the sabotage Warman had done to the normals of the dome kicked in and we were finished. Then he just powered himself back up again on innocent people who came to see what all the ruckus was and he took off."

Aiken sat there, stunned. How had he been so wrong in the Park. He'd thought they were on the verge of stopping Warman once and for all, but all they'd done was inconvenience him, and show all of them who was really the more powerful opponent. Aiken felt his stomach drop.

"We killed Mason for nothing," he whispered.

"Aiken Drum, you listen to me!" Uncharacteristically, it was Nicole yelling at him. "We did not kill Mason. Just like we didn't kill those people in the theatre or the man in Tranquility or Diana. That was Warman. He did that, and we're going to stop him from doing it anymore. You did not do this. It wasn't your fault that Mason died."

"Yeah, but if I'd just..."

"If you'd just what, Aiken?" Nicole demanded. "Don't be an idiot. Warman wants us to fall apart now, to second guess ourselves and to think that he's unbeatable. I know that's not true, and I'd hope you know it too. We nearly had him beat today. Maybe we try again that way, maybe we try something else, but he is not invincible, and working together, we're stronger than he'll ever be, because he's selfish and egotistical and in it only for himself."

Connor and Aiken exchanged glances. "Wow, Nicky," Aiken breathed. "I didn't know you felt that way."

"Of course you didn't," she said.

Just then, the three heard footsteps in the hallway outside Aiken's room, and Connor and Nicole disappeared with twin pops just as Aiken's mother opened the door. "What's going on in here? I thought I heard someone yelling."

"Nothing mom," Aiken said. "I was trying to find something to listen to so I could fall asleep and had the entertainment system turned up too loud." Matching action to work, Aiken scanned through the dozens of channels available on his in-room entertainment system and selected a channel of Baroque music. The haunting strains of Bach's Cello Suite Number 5 were punctuated by his door closing once more and he rolled over and, exhaustion overtaking him once more, drifted off to sleep.

Chapter Thirty-Five
Friday, August 21st, 2139

The next couple of days were miserable for Aiken and all of the Lunatics. Mason dead, Gwen stayed at home with her parents. The older class drew away from the younger to commiserate together. Hugo had indeed disappeared and, despite frantic requests from his parents, none of the Lunatics could tell them what had happened to him. With all the scorched remains from the Park fires now identified, it looked like Hugo had simply vanished. Aiken's classmates avoided the subject as much as they could. The adults could sense that the class knew more than they were letting on, but in groups or individually, no one was willing to say what had transpired in the Park that night. The sensor logs were, as it turned out, useless for determining what had happened. Without any intervention on the Lunatics part, even. They were spaced out so widely and covered such a huge amount of ground each that none showed the beginnings of the conflagration. According to the sensor techs, it looked like the fires started all over at the exact same time, which, had they asked Aiken, he could have said was true. Warman had wanted as many people in the Park in as short a period as possible, and he made sure that they would come.

His pyrokinesis - Connor's word - had been as devastating to the plants in the Park as to the people, but Aiken suspected that he hadn't been after their energy, just their status as kindling. It didn't matter. The trees were as dead as any of the unfortunate people who'd met Warman on his way out of the dome. By Aiken's count, all of the eight people who'd died that night had done so at Warman's hand. None had died simply by being present and helping fight the fires. There were plenty of injuries from that, but no deaths. Eight more people in the Park, plus Mason just outside. Warman was amassing quite a butcher's bill, and that was without knowing how many more deaths off the moon he might be responsible for.

Aiken had been working on figuring out a way of tracking him, but just like every previous encounter, Warman seemed to have vanished completely the moment he'd gone out of sight. More troubling, neither Aiken nor Nicole had been able to find Hugo. They'd been hoping his whereabouts would lead them to where ever Warman had been hiding out, but either Warman had shielded him, they were both out of range, or Warman had gotten rid of Hugo now he'd served his purpose. The last thought was most troublesome, but Nicole thought least likely.

"He might have a use for him later." She'd explained. "He doesn't need Hugo's energy, not with just having taken nine more people, and Hugo's got talents that Warman doesn't."

Connor had argued, hopefully, that with the extra power the dead in the Park represented, Warman and Hugo had jumped off the Moon and would no longer bother the Lunatics.

"What's the likelihood of that?" Aiken asked.

"Well, it would explain why you can't find Hugo," Connor stated.

"There's probably a simpler explanation for why we can't find him," Nicole said.

"Or sinister-er," Connor rejoined.

"That's not even a word!" Nicole exclaimed.

"True, but you knew what I meant."

Aiken smiled slightly at the byplay between his two friends, but it lacked enthusiasm. He had a feeling they were mostly putting on a show for him, but he appreciated the effort in any event.

"I think he's still here," he interjected when his friends paused.

"What makes you think that?" Nicole asked.

"Because it's not over yet. With Hugo on his side, Warman's got to know we think we will beat him ultimately, so better for him to force the confrontation and choose the time and place again, than to run and always be wondering when we'll show up to finish him off."

Connor was nodding thoughtfully at this. "Makes sense. He did put on a pretty good ambush last time."

Nicole looked at him sharply and he subsided.

"What I don't get," Aiken said thoughtfully, "is what happened to the secondary link. How could he have sabotaged energy that ordinary people didn't even know they were giving?"

"I don't know Aiken, but the link felt different than when the Lunatics all link together," Nicole responded.

"Of course it did," Connor said. "They're normals, not superior beings like us." He smiled. "Even without the racist overtones, it does make sense. Wouldn't the energy necessarily be different from people without mental abilities?"

"Yes and no," Aiken said, thinking aloud. "The energy is different, but the connections are more or less the same, the relationship between people is the link that the energy travels over. If the relationships were fundamentally different, then maybe it would be different, but just like when we join together and we're more than the sum of each individual, when all of the relationships between the non-mentally gifted are gathered together, they form something that's more that you would expect from what you're actually taking in. Whatever Warman did made the relationships that form the links different. I think we need to go find out what he did. At the very least, we'll need to fix whatever it is. At best, we'll be able to make sure that he can't do it again, so if we do face him again, we can rely on getting some energy from the people of Peary. Though they don't know it, they have as much reason as we do to want Warman stopped."

"Did anyone make the connection between the fires and Warman?" Connor asked.

"I don't think so," Aiken replied. "They're still pretty certain they've got him bottled up at Farside, since the shuttles in and out are the one thing that's pretty easy for them to watch. Of course, the fact that the reason he got arrested for LEC evasion has to have them a little worried. Still, I think they're pretty sure they've got the outbound flights covered, so they don't even think that he could be over here."

"I can't decide if that's a good thing or not," Connor sighed.

"You're right. Well, we'll really be on our own when it comes time to stop him anyway. There was never any doubt of that even with Lunar security looking for him." Both Nicole and Connor nodded at this.

"Okay, Nicole, can you tell us where the problem in your link started? We should see if we can narrow down the damage that Warman caused so we're not all over the dome running around."

Nicole shrugged, then said, "To be honest, I was too busy trying to solve the problem to pinpoint where it started. It sure spread fast once it kicked off, but it did limit itself."

"What do you mean?"

"I mean, not all the connections were affected. Some continued on as strong as they started right until the end. It was like a, what was that thing we studied in Chem last year? Where something sparks a reaction, then it goes like wildfire, then it stops?"

"A catalyst?" Connor offered.

"Yeah, a catalyst. It was like there was something waiting in some of the links, and when it started, it spread like crazy, but then just stopped."

"Well, that's good," Aiken said.

"How do you figure?" Nicole asked. "It's still going to take half of forever to check everyone in the dome to see if they're affected."

"Maybe," Aiken allowed, "but on the plus side, we know that whatever it was that Warman did, he either has to do it individually, which limits the number of people he can affect, or there's some limits on his power to influence under duress, which means that if we can hit him hard enough next time, he wouldn't be able to do as much as this time."

"Okay, I can see that," Nicole said, "but it's still going to take this side of infinity to get around to every person in the dome to see if they're wearing patches on their brain."

"Might, unless they're noticeable. You said the link felt different. Was that from when you first linked up?"

"Yes."

"Then all we have to do is link everyone together again and see where the problem is."

"That might work," Nicole conceded.

"If we know what to look for, I think so," Aiken said. "May I?"

"May you what?"

"May I check your memories so that I know what we're looking for?"

"Uh." Nicole stuttered. "What?"

"Well, I think if I know what to look for, I'll be able to track it down if we link everyone together and see where the problems are."

"You can't do that just by linking and watching?"

"Oh, maybe, but if you've already felt what the link is like when it's not right, then it will be faster if I have your memory to work off."

"Okay, but I'll push it over to you," Nicole countered. "You don't need to go rummaging around in my head."

"Fine," Aiken said. Connor, beside him, was ducking his head trying not to laugh.

Aiken wasn't sure what the experience of

having a memory implanted would feel like, since most of the time he'd gone looking for them as one of the telepaths with both send and receive abilities. He watched Nicole screw up her face in concentration, then release. All of a sudden, he remembered what it had been like to have all the strands of connection throughout the dome held together in his mind. There was weird vibration to them, like an orchestra with some of the instruments tuned not quite correctly. He recalled the horror of hearing the tuning go further and further out from true, and watching the threads unravel in his hands until he couldn't even hold on to the ones that were unaffected. The instruments that were still in tune had ceased to play as they noticed their neighbours were off key. Soon, there was nothing left to hold onto and the entire fragile edifice fell apart.

"Wow," breather Aiken. "That was... intense." Nicole blushed. "It's interesting to see how we interpret these differing sensations, overlaying them overtop of the ones we're more familiar with. If I'm right, I've actually sensed the issue before the fight in the Park, but to me it came across as an unpleasant taste and associated colouring. For you, you seem to have mapped the sensation auditorially. The whole concept of sound is such a different way of looking at it." He trailed off as he realized both Connor and Nicole were staring at him. "Anyway, I know what to look for, or rather, listen for, now. Thanks!"

"When do you think we should do the search?"

"Whenever's convenient, I guess. If the work is as slap-dash as the job Warman did on the security officers, we won't have too much trouble removing it."

"You want to meet tomorrow morning in the Park? We'll have a whole day to hunt down the problem," Nicole asked.

"Sounds good," Aiken said. "You coming?"

"No," Connor said firmly. "I wouldn't even know what to look for. My gifts lie in a different area. You two handle this on your own."

Chapter Thirty-Six
Saturday, August 22nd, 2139

The next day, Aiken walked to the Park instead of teleporting to see if he'd recuperated his strength from the ordeal earlier in the week. He was glad to sense that he was back up to more or less full strength, particularly given that this day might be full of jumping all over the dome trying to pin down the damage that Warman had done to the population. He saw, when he arrived at the edge, that Nicole had arrived already. Uncharacteristically, she was wearing a dress. More used to seeing her in slacks and a t-shirt, Aiken was taken aback momentarily, but continued forward gamely to meet her by the section of the Park the Lunatics had claimed as their own.

Nicole jumped up from the bench on which she'd been sitting when she noticed that he'd arrived. "So, where to start?" she asked.

"Well," Aiken answered, "we'll need to get a bearing on the people who may have been damaged by Warman's manipulations before we get going, so I thought we'd start by joining all the strands again to see where we can spot the issue, now that we know what to look for."

Aiken sat down on the bench and Nicole regained her seat and folded her hands in her lap. Aiken raised one eyebrow, then reached over and grabbed one of her hands. Closing his eyes, he pictured himself floating over the center of Peary Dome and saw all the connections between all the people who lived and worked and led their lives here. There were a dozen bright spots scattered through the mix and Aiken suspected those were his classmates, going about their usual business as best they could. He stretched out his mental hands and began gathering up the strands of connection between all the people in the dome. Before he'd even got fairly started, he could sense that something was off. The same oily texture he'd noticed earlier in the week was still present. He tried shifting his perception to the auditory sense that he remembered Nicole using and could hear faint notes of discord among the rest of the chord being played by the mass of minds.

From his vantage point, he tried listening in closely to hear which of the strands were causing the discord and found his consciousness zooming along a strand connecting two people Aiken didn't know. He could see moments from their relationship cast in a harsh light, which he sensed wasn't usual for them. Each of the pair was struggling against some force making them see the worst in each other. Aiken zoomed back out to see the whole structure again, then listened for another note off true. Again, he zoomed along a strand that seemed to have been affected by making the people anchoring it relish harming the other, even though each of them was also fighting this compulsion.

Instinctively, Aiken closed in on one of the people at the end of the strand. It was a young man in his early twenties that Aiken had seen around, but wasn't particularly familiar with. He was having an argument with his girlfriend and, rather than admit where he'd been wrong, he was insisting that the fault lay with her and her alone. Aiken probed into his mind and saw not the rough patch job that he'd expected, given Warman's work on the security officers in Farside, but something that looked like an amoeba sitting atop the man's consciousness, drawing certain things out of it and devouring them, and feeding other things back in. The pseudopods of the thought-amoeba appeared to be intertwined with the man's thoughts to a high degree. Aiken zoomed in even further and was distressed to discover that the connections between the amoeba and the man's thoughts were more subtle than he'd expected. This amoeba could live indefinitely on the man's mind, poisoning any relationship he had and making certain that the energy coming from him would be tainted with selfishness.

Aiken backed off thoughtfully. He checked a couple of the other people who anchored strands that produced discordant tones and discovered the same type of construct attached to their minds. Whatever Warman had done to these people, it would take someone with great skill and patience to rid the people who were affected of their parasitic companions.

Aiken returned his thoughts to himself and opened his eyes. Though hardly any time had passed, he was gripping Nicole's hand hard enough to start a cramp in his own. He let her go and sat back on the bench, rubbing his eyes.

"What do we do?" Nicole whispered to him.

"I don't know," he answered honestly. "I

didn't expect that."

"No," Nicole answered. "I was thinking it would be more like what we encountered at Farside. This was something else, something worse."

"You know the worst part?" Aiken asked. "The urges are already mostly there. Did you see how that thing operated? It wasn't generating the bad thoughts on its own, it was simply removing the obstacles that most people put in place to putting their worst impulses into action. They're already thinking those things, and those constructs, those blobs, are just making certain that they act on them instead of filing them away in the recesses of their mind." He lapsed into silence.

"So how do you overcome the worst impulses that people have if they have no self-control?"

"I don't know," Aiken answered. The pair sat on the bench for a couple of minutes, quietly turning the problem over in their minds. Neither could think of a solution that was as simple as the constructs they'd run into previously. Either Warman had learned a new trick way too fast, or he'd deliberately left the damage sloppy at Farside in order to, well, what exactly? Their ability to deal with the officers at Farside hadn't prepared them for what they'd face back at Peary, but if they'd not gone to Farside, they'd have been equally unprepared for what Warman had done here.

The two sank lower, unconsciously synchronized. "What if..." Nicole started, but then shook her head.

"Well, if we..." Aiken said after a minute, then stopped again. He looked at Nicole, but her frown only deepened.

Suddenly, she sat upright. "What if we're looking at this wrong?"

"What do you mean?"

"How did Warman get around to all of these people to implant the construct on their minds?"

"What do you mean?"

"How much time did Warman have to go around to all of these people?"

"Maybe a day at most," Aiken said, mentally counting it off. "He was arrested on Sunday and we went Monday to see if he was still in jail, and he'd broken out. The fight in the Park was Tuesday evening. So, if he came right here after breaking out, and he'd have to have been in jail for, what did we figure, eight hours to get to all the officers, he'd have had maybe two days at the very most, and that's without sleeping or doing anything else."

"Did he look like someone running

without sleep for two days when you encountered him in the Park?"

"No, definitely not."

"So maybe a day."

"I'd agree with that."

"How long do you think it takes to put something like the construct we saw in place?"

"I have no idea. The most we've ever done is change Quinn's memories a little and distract some people at the clinic. That doesn't take much work at all, but this is a whole different level of complexity. At the same time, since it's not really doing anything the mind doesn't do already, perhaps it's simpler to put in place than we might think."

"So," Nicole said with a mischievous smile, "You have no idea."

"I thought that's what I said."

"Yeah, but then you took two minutes to explain why you said it."

Aiken looked at her strangely, but realized she was teasing him.

"I guess I deserved that."

"Well, having two PhD parents probably doesn't help," Nicole said. "I've heard them talk and they can go on for half an hour on how they don't know something."

Aiken laughed. "That's for sure! Anytime I have trouble getting to sleep, I just ask my mom to read her doctoral dissertation. Boom! Asleep in seconds."

"My point," Nicole persisted after they'd stopped laughing, "is that Warman probably didn't have time to go around to, what, a thousand people, individually."

"And so?"

"So there has to be a connection between all of the people infected."

"I don't see how that helps."

"Well, what if the construct isn't implemented individually? What if it's something that's more generic than that? What if Warman found a way to infect a whole bunch of people at once, then pushed the same thoughts out to all of them so they'd take root in similar ways?"

"I'm still not seeing where this is going," Aiken confessed.

"Think diseases," Nicole said. "We have cancers," she paused, swallowing audibly, "which are individualized because they're basically the body's systems attacking itself. We treat cancers individually, based on the patient's genetics and body chemistry, right?"

"Right," Aiken agreed.

"But what about something like an amoeba?" Nicole countered. "What about something in drinking water that infects a whole bunch of people at once?"

"I think for most of them, you give painkillers and lots of fluids and rest."

"Maybe," Nicole persisted. "But some of them are nasty enough to require treatment beyond waiting it out. Then, the doctors use an amoebicide."

"So?"

"So, if this is just a construct that Warman whipped up and then pushed out to a whole bunch of people at once, then we should be able to do the same thing to fix it."

"What do you mean? I thought we'd just pry it out the same way as we did with the block on the security officers' perception on Farside."

"How long would that take?"

"I don't know, a couple of minutes, maybe."

"Do you have a couple thousand minutes to get out to each person who has one of these and take it out? That's a day and a half straight of doing nothing but removing mental constructs. I know it's the weekend and all, but is that really how you want to spend your time?"

Aiken was silent.

"So instead, we take a couple of hours to figure out a way to remove these from a whole bunch of people at once, then we don't have to spend our whole weekend running around like chickens with their heads cut off."

"Okay, I'm game," Aiken said. "Where should we go? Who else should we get in on this?"

Nicole looked startled for second, but quickly recovered. "Maybe my place? My mom is gone for the day." She trailed off. "I don't know of anyone else who's going to be able to help, though. Olivia's the only other full telepath, but she doesn't have any experience with something like this."

"No one does," Aiken argued.

"Point. Well, we could invite her, but the upper class seems to be avoiding us recently." Nicole paused. "As for others, I don't know if anyone would even be able to see it. Ethan might, but he wouldn't be able to do anything about it. Faith... I don't know, Aiken. I think we're the only ones we can really count on."

"Hmm." Aiken thought for a minute, then shook his head. "I guess we're it," he finally said. Standing, he held his hand out to Nicole. "Shall we?" He helped her up off the bench and the two stood for a moment like that, each waiting for the other to make a move. Finally, Aiken quirked his mouth and teleported them both to Nicole's living room.

They arrived in front of her couch and both sank down into it, Nicole tucking her legs up demurely under her.

"So, how do we get rid of a thousand mental parasites all at once?"

"I don't know," Nicole answered. "That's what we're here to figure out."

"Well, how do they do it with actual amoebas?"

"Like I said, amoebicide."

"So, they poison the amoeba?"

"Uh, I don't recall. I did a study on this for Biology, but that was a while ago." Nicole thought for a moment. "I don't think it's an out-and-out poison. It does something to interfere with the amoeba. Hang on a sec." She jumped up and ran back around behind Aiken. He craned his neck around to see what she was doing, but she'd run off down the hallway. He fidgeted for a couple of minutes on the couch, resisting the temptation to either go back and find her, or look to see what she was doing. Finally, he got up and paced around the living room, restless energy not allowing him to sit still.

He was looking at the photos on the wall once more when Nicole walked back in. He turned and raised one eyebrow questioningly.

"I found the report I wrote. Amoebicides, the good ones, anyway, interfere with the cellular processes of the amoeba, not letting them send messages around inside. Eventually, they die because none of their parts are working properly." Nicole sat back down on the couch.

"Is that helpful?" Aiken walked behind the couch to regain his seat and as he did, he caught a faint smell of cinnamon and orange, and noticed, for the first time, that Nicole had done something different with her hair. It was pinned up around her head with little sparkling clips. Had she had her hair like this in the Park? Aiken couldn't remember. He shook the thought from his head as he sat down.

"I don't know. We don't know if those constructs require something to keep themselves going, or if, once in place, they just feed off the person's mind or thoughts."

"Well, we need to look closer at one, then," Aiken said. Nicole nodded her head in agreement and both closed their eyes and sent their thoughts sailing out over the dome. Once again, Aiken looked down on a sea of lights, all connected by glowing strands. He listened in as he retuned his senses and immediately picked out the sour notes from the harmony that was more common for the people of Peary Dome.

Indicating to Nicole to follow, he flew down to one of the anchors for the strand vibrating out of harmony and saw a father whose son did nothing but disappoint him.

Aiken peered closer and saw the expected parasite sitting atop the man's thoughts, leaching out notice of all the boy's accomplishments and feeding in anger and disdain instead. Aiken moved his presence as close to the sickly-looking construct as he dared and sent a mental probe at it to gauge its reaction. The reaction was immediate and startling. The amoeba jumped at Aiken. Aiken moved backward, but the creature chased him. Startled, he zoomed back out to the level of the whole dome, but the construct followed him even there. He was beginning to panic. He didn't want to return to his own body, and risk the mental construct following him back and attaching itself to him. He zipped to and fro over the dome, all the while being chased by Warman's mental construct, frantically trying to think of a way to get rid of the pest. Finally, he decided that a simple approach might be best, given Warman's lust for power.

He mentally planted his feet and hurled a visualized bolt of mental energy at the amoeba creature. Its destruction was immediate and spectacular. As it faded away, Aiken swore he could hear a ghostly echo of Warman's voice, laughing.

Well, if nothing else, that should convince us that we can't do this one at a time, Nicole said.

No kidding, Aiken replied. *We don't have the time and I don't have the energy to psychically destroy each construct individually.*

So, what now?

I don't know, Aiken responded. *Without being able to see them closer, we're just guessing at what might be animating them. Any action we take to get rid of them might be as harmful as helpful, or more so.*

Both of their consciousnesses swirled over the dome, looking down at the play of light between the citizens of Peary. Now that Aiken was attuned to the aural sense, he could also hear the harmony that the vibrating chords generated. He watched and listened in fascination as the light and harmonies swelled and faded as the relationships between the people below changed.

Can you starve an amoeba? he asked.

No idea. Nicole paused. *But since we don't know what they're feeding on, how would we do that anyway?*

I was thinking something drastic.

Do I want to know?

I was thinking, if the parasites do live on thoughts, what would happen to them if the people they were feeding on had no thoughts for a while?

You can't be serious!

It might work, Aiken said lamely. *Do you*

387

have a better idea?

Nicole stayed silent for a while. Aiken's consciousness floated over the dome next to hers. He had a feeling she was mulling over some idea, but didn't know how to articulate it. A couple of times, he was tempted to break into the silence, but he refrained. It stretched, but not uncomfortably. It seemed to Aiken like their silence was filled with meaning, though if someone had asked him what the meaning was, he wouldn't have been able to say.

Finally, when he was about to ask if he could help tease the idea out, she said, *What if we overload them?* Aiken waited expectantly. *What if, instead of starving them, we fill them with so many of the thoughts and feelings that they've been pulling out of people that they're overloaded? What would happen then?*

I have no idea. Aiken chewed this over for a moment, then, deciding this was a conversation better held face-to-face, returned his thoughts to his body. He opened his eyes and saw Nicole do the same.

"How could we do that?" he asked.

"Well, that's the easy part, I think," Nicole said. "We amplify the harmonic chord that the healthy strands are producing. The sympathetic vibration in the unhealthy strands will send positive reinforcement to either end of it and hopefully overload the creatures that are making people hate each other."

"Nicky," Aiken said slowly, "You know that the strands and the music are just a metaphor, right? Like the amoebas themselves, they don't actually exist."

"I know that, you twerp," she said, smacking him on the arm. "Okay, you want down-to-earth reality? Warman has altered the thinking patterns of nearly a thousand residents of Peary Dome so that their good relationship impulses are being suppressed, and the natural over ride on their worst impulses is being removed. So they're acting in ways that harm the relationships they're in, without being able to control it."

"Okay, following you so far. How does your harmonic chord work in the real world?"

"We need to simply amplify the healthy relationships that exist all around the unhealthy ones. We need to make people love, Aiken," she said plainly.

"What?!"

"Well, how do you think you beat hate and indifference? By making people care about one another."

"How would you even... how can you...." Aiken trailed off.

"The same way you did it every time you

gathered up the strands of thought and forged connections before," Nicole said. "The metaphor holds while on the mental plane. You can simply amplify the strands of connectedness that exist already and people will respond in the real world by loving more."

"Are you sure?"

"Of course I'm not sure," she replied. "But it's better than nothing, and probably safer than making everyone in the dome black out simultaneously."

"Point."

"So when we start amplifying, you think the unhealthy strands will vibrate sympathetically, like a guitar left next to an orchestra?"

"Yes. In the realm of reality," she shot an arch look at him, "the people will recognize the caring in the relationships around them and want the same thing for themselves, making their relationships go stronger."

"So then the parasites will leave? Or would they go dormant and then reactivate when we stopped amplifying the healthy strands?"

"Aiken, honestly, I don't know. I just have a feeling, a really strong feeling, that this will work." She looked at him. "And hey, if it doesn't, then we get to knock out everyone in

390

Peary simultaneously for as long as it takes to starve the creatures."

They both laughed a little at that.

"Okay, so when do we do this?" Aiken asked.

"Well, we have to decide if we'll need anyone else to help boost the harmonics."

"You know, I don't think we will. The kinds of energy we're looking to get going generally are self-reinforcing and self-amplifying. Like when the class joins together and we're more as a whole than you'd expect from adding us up individually. When I joined the people in the dome together in the mornings, I didn't need to add any energy to the relationships, it just flowed and rebounded with more energy than before." He was getting enthusiastic about this plan.

"Well, there's no reason we can't try right now, then," Nicole said.

"Right, so how do we amplify what we want?"

"Boys really are clueless about relationships, aren't they?" Nicole asked. "Even ones who can read minds."

"Hey, gimme a break. I haven't always been able to read minds."

"Well," she said, "I think we just look for a strand that has the kind of energy we're looking for and match it to another one and keep adding strands until they're producing the chord we want. Then we find strands that are vibrating along with the ones we're using and add them. Eventually, we'll have all of the healthy strands included and the unhealthy ones will be brought along for the ride."

"You make it sound so easy."

"We'll see."

Chapter Thirty-Seven
Saturday, August 22nd, 2139

Hours later, the two collapsed bonelessly on the couch, entangling limbs but not caring. A minute passed, then two.

Finally, "That was.... amazing!"

"I know, Aiken," Nicole answered softly, unspoken emotion in her voice. "And it worked!"

Both quietly exulted. Their plan had gone better than they'd dared hope and now the dome was rid of Warman's pesky little surprises. The harmonic chord which had come to a thundering conclusion minutes before was still ringing across the dome, seen in the new way that all the residents looked at each other. An unexpected benefit of the amplification of the chord they'd wanted, or in more plain terms, of making people care about each other more, was that even the unaffected relationships benefitted from a new insight into one another and a new desire to put the other people in their lives first. Husbands were more loving to their wives and kids, bosses were more understanding with their subordinates. Aiken and Nicole had watched the whole thing happen and had boosted the process where it had been required.

As Aiken had surmised, the energy was self-amplifying. Once one person in a relationship acted more caring towards the other, it was often reciprocated and the energy built that way. The parasites, not knowing what to do with the outpouring of positive emotion, had tried to block all of it and in so doing had doomed themselves. Nicole and Aiken had watched in the metaphorical plane as the parasites exploded, overwhelmed by the task that Warman had given them and that had been made infinitely more difficult.

Aiken stretched out on the couch, slipping his arm beneath Nicole and she curled up to his side, exhausted. While the energy output had amplified itself, the two had been dashing all over and were now exhausted. Aiken

394

felt like they were kids again, just tired after a day of playing. *Got more accomplished today, though*, he thought tiredly as he drifted off to sleep.

His mind was showing him turbulent scenes from the past few weeks, and through it all, images of smoke and fire came swirling across the dream landscapes. Even innocuous images like testing out their abilities with the other Lunatics were tinged with gray swirling smoke. His mind jumped from scene to scene, faster and faster, and always the smoke and fire were edging the scene. Was his mind trying to tell him that all of this could be erased by Warman.

"No, Aiken Drum. Your mind is replaying this all so that I may observe and find out more about you." The voice was familiar, oily and laden with purpose. Warman stepped out of the shadows in his mind, and Aiken saw that his mind was replaying images as on a screen, but the theatre that the screen was in was on fire. Warman had somehow co-opted his memories and was playing them back like a movie.

"What are you doing here?"

"Trying to understand how you and I ended up on such different paths," Warman responded. "Given that we started at the same place."

Suddenly, the memories playing on the screen weren't Aiken's any longer. The view from inside a space station, a room with panels of glass showing the Earth far below. Technicians line the room, each at their own computer screen, all monitoring fluctuating graphs and bars of colour, or scrolling lines of text. The view shifts to look outside as a brightness begins to shine, pulsating and, to Aiken, familiar. It was a pattern of light that he would remember for all time. He is watching the drive test, but from much closer than where they'd been on the moon.

The light pulsates and then, just as when Aiken had watched for the first time, stops and explodes. The technicians that had been watching all fall to the floor bonelessly and the scene ends there.

The memories open next on an infirmary bed, on a transport shuttle. Looks around, there were others strapped in to all the beds that the shuttle maintained. It's the emergency escape shuttle, heading back to Earth at maximum velocity.

Next memory - a hospital room in a nondescript building. Blinding pain, a headache that pounded audibly. He sees bright lights circling around him and knows that if only he could capture one of those lights, that the headache would ease.

Reaching out arms to catch one, he grasps the edge and tore it, leaving some behind. He brings the light to himself and the headache backs off momentarily. The sound of a crash comes from the hallway and surprised cries from people outside his room.

Next memory, the headache is back, worse than before. Looking around, he sees none of the lights in the immediate vicinity. He senses some further away and moves himself closer to them, reaches out and grasps one and brings it to himself and the headache backs off immediately. He goes back to where he'd been previously and closes his eyes in relief, the sound of an alarm blaring somewhere outside his room.

Next memory, he's discharged from the hospital and learns that he was the lucky one of those affected by the explosion. Oddly, some seemed not to have been affected at all. The government is looking into it. He goes back to his dingy apartment.

He wakes up with the distant pounding of the headache starting again. He looks around for more of the bright lights, but can't see any. Closing his eyes, they immediately jump to the forefront of his perception. He collects another one and the headache fades.

Questions. A man named Donnelly asks him about the drive test. Asks him about the people who'd died. Asks about the people who'd survived. Tries to figure out why.

Another day, another headache, another light collected.

Police stop by, asking if he knows anything about two neighbours who had both died of what was described as spontaneous human combustion. Never heard anything, he reports.

Back to work, but not on the station. He starts hearing things that people aren't saying. Realizes that he can read what people are thinking. Starts to see how useful this would be. Goes to the casino. Wins huge. Gets tossed out.

Back at his apartment, the headache looms even greater. He collects another light. Police come by the next day asking about another neighbour. The light begins to dawn. At first, he is horrified by the realization of what he's done. He tries to stop. After a week, the headache is so unbearable, it feels like it's splitting his head open to the sunlight. He gives in and collects another life, but not in his building. He looks around for someone that no one will miss. There's a bum staggering down an alleyway with a bottle of something in a paper bag in his hand. He watches as he collects the light and is startled to see the man burn. While his headache fades somewhat, he retches at the smell of roast meat coming from the man. He swears to not take another.

Another week goes by and the headache has returned even stronger than before. He gives in, takes another unfortunate. This time, it's a worn-out prostitute standing on a corner watching traffic go by with dull lifeless eyes. He watches from across the street as she doubles over when he pulls her light out. Before long, she is a smouldering pile of ash. Even on the busy street, no one seems to notice and he convinces himself that no one will.

The next day, there is a short note in the news, but it's buried between notices on upcoming police auctions and the news of the latest celebrity wedding. He realizes that he's gotten away with murder. Twice. Well, more than that. He's lost track, really.

This time, he doesn't wait for the headache to develop. He takes a light just as he's starting to feel the pain. He realizes about the same time that not only can he hear people's thoughts, he can make people hear his if he aims them right. He can actually force some people to do things, but not consistently.

He walks among the people on the street,

unnoticed and unfeared, but he relishes the idea that he is more than they are, that he is superior to them. He's at the top of the heap. Doesn't need to work anymore from the money he's gotten from the casino. Wouldn't need to anyway, if he could convince people to do things for him. He is homo superior, the next stage of human evolution. He can take what he wants from whoever he wants.

Donnelly is back, asking more questions. He delves into Donnelly's mind. What's this? Memories covered up. Memories uncovered. A group of teenagers on the moon with the same kinds of abilities that he has. Must go check this out.

Arrives on the moon, drained. Jumps the line and gets an entertainer's licence because it's something that will give him little bits of light without any deaths. Checks on the students, but it's summer break. Heads to the primo vacation spot to see if any are there.

Blazing light, blinding light. Brighter than any he's harvested before. He must collect this. It will hold the headache at bay indefinitely. He follows the light. Starts to collect it. The girl before him calls out with her mind. It's one of them. Oh, shit! Now what? Go, go somewhere else. Emergency teleport. Energy used. Collects some that night from his audience, but leaves unsatisfied. Needs more. Headache is tingling on the edge of his senses.

Heads to a busy place where no one will notice him. Harvests a light. Not bright like what he was looking for, but enough to stave off the headache. As he is absorbing the light, notices blinding lights starting to arrive. They are looking. Looking for him.

He sees the brightest among them, glowing like the heart of a sun. Approaches him to talk. Is rebuffed. Fine. Disappears.

"Now do we understand each other?"

Aiken was absorbing all the information he'd just seen. Warman, it seemed, had started killing inadvertently, but had somewhere along the line, started enjoying it.

"I understand that you're a murderer."

"Murderer?" Warman replied. "Is it murder to kill a cow to make a hamburger? Is it murder when a lion kills a gazelle to feed? Is it murder when a bird pulls an insect from its burrow and crushes it for food? No, that's not murder, it's life."

"So you're what? The lion? The bird? I don't think so. You're a man. A sick one, but nothing more than a man."

"That's where you're wrong," Warman snarled. "You and I, Aiken, we're different. We're better than those around us. And you,

you are better even than most of those who are enhanced."

"Oh, if we're so much better than everyone else, what difference would that make?"

"Evolution, dear boy. Please tell me they still teach that in schools. Every evolutionary change is a replacement. When modern humans came on the scene, they didn't just wait for their predecessors to die out. They outcompeted them, and when that wasn't moving things along fast enough, they made war on them. And they won. Where are the Neanderthals now?"

"You want the dozen of us to supplant the entire human race?"

"We don't have to be the only ones. The plans for the drive are locked up, but they're available to people like us. We could make more superior beings. We could make the whole moon like us."

"Like you, you mean. Anyone whose brain is done developing needs to keep taking in energy."

"Yes, but that energy also imparts other talents. I started with simple telepathy, and now I'm nearly as gifted as yourself."

"The price you pay for those talents is too high. What about people who decide that a human life is worth too much, who won't kill?

You'd condemn them to die from an aneurysm like Mr. Bertram."

"Sacrifices must be made. Can't you see? This is the way forward. This is the next level for humans. This is making us what we were meant to become."

"We don't even know if it's heritable," Aiken said, remembering something from his own Biology class.

"So then we expose people to the change younger and they'll grow up with the abilities and we'll use our new knowledge and power to ensure that each successive generation has more than their parents."

"This is your grand scheme? To set off another quantum explosion to force people to become something they may not even be ready for? To force people to have to kill to survive?"

"People already kill to survive. Open your eyes."

"People kill other people to survive? Not so much anymore."

"If you want to make an omelette, you have to break a few eggs."

"Retreating into platitudes doesn't change the fact that you're talking about mass murder on a scale not seen since the twentieth century. I won't be a part of that, and neither will any of my friends."

"You're forgetting, one of your friends has already chosen to be a part of it."

"Hugo's made his choice, but he's the only one."

"Ah, yes, your friend Mason's prediction. Well, I'm much more a believer that we make our own fates than in some nebulous prediction that may or may not be accurate."

"Be that as it may, we're still going to have to face off, you and I."

"No, we're not," Warman said, almost apologetically.

"What do you mean?"

"Why do you think I took this approach to meeting with you, while you're asleep and your shields are down?" Warman smiled, and the sight chilled Aiken. "You're never going to wake up from this little nap. Nice work on the parasites, by the way - I have to admit, you took me by surprise there. I had hoped they'd keep you occupied much, much longer. Well, whatever the method, you're in my hands now."

Aiken looked around in desperation. The theatre that they appeared to be seated in had no exits, and Aiken, though he knew he was dreaming, had no doubts that Warman would make good on his threat to finish him off.

He felt a burning pressure in his midsection, just like when he'd been attacked by

Warman in the Park. He tried to shield to block it, but he couldn't. He tried to wake himself up, but didn't even know how to do that.

Agony rippled through him as the heat began to build.

"If it makes you feel any better," Warman said, "I won't need to harvest the rest of your friends for quite a while with the energy I'll gain from you. You're saving them for the time being by allowing me to take you now."

Aiken was curled up on himself and couldn't speak through the pain. He could feel his insides aflame, it seemed.

Suddenly, the pain cut off. Warman looked around in confusion, then astonishment as a ray of light, bright as the sun, burst through the roof of the theatre to bathe Aiken in cool relief.

"Leave him alone!" It was Nicole. She floated down into the theatre of dreams on a pillar of light, hair swirling around her head crackling with energy, a look a righteous fury on her face. She aimed her hands palms out at Warman and shot a blast of pure mental energy so bright that it washed out Aiken's vision.

When he blinked his eyes to clear them, he was awake and laid out on the couch in Nicole's living room. She was standing over him with her eyes closed and her fists clenched by her side. Her hair had come out of the clips she'd had it pinned up in, and the strands were standing apart from each other, like a giant charge of static had raced through her. Between her eyelids, light leaked out and when she finally opened her eyes to look down at him, it was as if twin search beams shone down on him. She unclenched her fists and her body relaxed. Aiken realized she'd been standing on tiptoe and as she came down off her toes, her eyes closed once more and she slid bonelessly to the floor.

Aiken caught her with his mind and lowered her gently to the carpet covering the pressed moon dust floor. He tried to get up from the couch, but agony shot through his gut and he realized the attack in the theatre in his dream had been the metaphorical representation of Warman's attack on his real self. He waited a couple of minutes while his body healed itself.

When he felt able, he got up off the couch and picked Nicole up off the floor. She felt fragile in his arms and, looking down at her, he realized how much energy she must have expended shielding him from Warman and then attacking Warman's dream self. Feeling drained himself, he couldn't pour energy into her the way he wanted, so he just staggered back to the couch and laid her out flat on it.

Not wanting to go back to sleep and risk

being attacked again, he walked slowly to the kitchen and peered into the refrigerator to see if there was anything available. He saw a block of cheese and pulled it out and went hunting for some crackers. He found them, then sliced up a quick snack for himself and Nicole. Unwilling to disturb her slumber, he kept part of his mind in watchful guard over her, but the rest was simply in a holding pattern while he assimilated all the information Warman had given him.

He finished off his half of the snack and put the rest back in the fridge for when Nicole awoke. He sat back down in the living room with Nicole's feet in his lap and thought about what Warman had said, about what he'd offered.

Were Aiken and his friends really the next step in human evolution? What if they did pass their abilities on to their children? Would they have started a new evolutionary arms race? How would you raise a telepathic baby that could command you to do things for them?

As his mind wandered, he realized that not once had he even considered the idea of making his parents and all the others under the Dome like them. The thought of his parents committing murder to stay alive made Aiken's stomach turn. They would sooner die than become like Warman. He knew Nicole's mother would feel the same way and would be surprised if most of the people under the dome wouldn't make the same choice. But if Warman had his way, then everyone in Peary, maybe on the moon entire would be faced with that terrible choice. Even if they could limit the exposure to those young enough to absorb the changes, they'd be creating a whole new class of citizens without the same constraints that normal people had. His group had been lucky in that, of the fifteen of them originally exposed, only one had decided to follow Warman's idea of morality. If an even larger group became exposed, and Warman was there from the start, offering his view on the way things should be, then there was no telling the kind of damage that might be done by a group of people with powers like Aiken's.

The idea made him shudder. This had become about much more than simply stopping Warman now. With his abilities, and Hugo's, it wasn't a stretch to imagine them actually going through with a plan to steal or make another engine to cause another explosion. Warman was capable and, seemingly, willing to see more people go through what he did in order to get or maintain his powers.

Was it even possible to shut his powers down? It had looked like it might be in the Park last week, but he'd managed to slip that trap and had simply killed some unfortunate bystanders in order to get the power he needed to keep doing what it was that he wanted. Aiken would need to confront him somewhere were there weren't other people around to take energy from if he wanted to ensure that Warman couldn't regain his power.

Unfortunately, it was extremely unlikely that Warman would ever let Aiken find him in a position like that. But, what if they created that situation? What if they could find a spot that didn't have any other people in it and make Warman go there? Could Aiken take Warman on in a situation like that and win? He'd have to, or Warman would simply teleport to a place that did have people and kill again to keep his power up. The seeds of an idea began to form in Aiken's mind, but before he could follow his thread of thought through to the end, he felt Nicole stirring beside him.

She rolled on to her side and blinked her eyes open, weariness written across every feature.

"Hey," Aiken said. "You can go back to sleep if you're still tired."

"That's probably not a good idea," Nicole said.

"I'll stay awake and keep a lookout for

Warman attacking you." He paused. "Thank-you, by the way. You actually saved my life back there."

"You would have done the same."

"If I'd figured out what was going on, yes. But still, thanks. Now go back to sleep."

"Too late. You've woken me up now."

"Oh, have I?" Aiken had been tracing his finger unconsciously up and down Nicole's foot and she now yanked it out of his lap and swung her legs down off the couch. Standing, she smoothed down her dress and looked at him archly.

"Yes. You have."

"Well, I didn't spend my whole time awake tickling your feet. There's some crackers and cheese in the fridge if you're hungry."

"Starved actually. Thanks!" She walked slowly over to the kitchen and opened the fridge. She rummaged around inside for a minute, getting out not only the snack Aiken had left, but a pitcher of water. She floated a cup from the cupboard over to her outstretched hand and poured herself a glass of water, which she downed before sitting down at the kitchen table with her crackers and cheese. Aiken came over and sat down with her. The pair sat in silence until Nicole had finished, then Aiken stayed put while Nicole tidied up.

"How much of what happened did you hear?"

"How much of what? I felt like I was lying down next to a fire, and I woke up and you were smoking, so I knew Warman was around somewhere. I tried to wake you up, and when you wouldn't, I just shielded you then went into your mind to see what was going on. When I saw Warman there, I got rid of him, but that's the last thing I remember."

Aiken related everything he'd learned about Warman to her along with what he thought Warman's next move might be. Nicole was appalled.

"All those people dead. And he wants to make everyone on the moon just like him?"

"That's my guess. He thinks having powers makes him better than everyone else. And he wants to create a new human race. He can't do it on Earth because of the radiation shield thing that Connor was talking about way back, but the moon would be perfect."

Nicole shuddered in an unconscious mimicry of Aiken's thoughts on the subject earlier. "Our parents. Can you imagine? They'd never... they just wouldn't."

"No, I don't think they would, but then they'd die like Mr. Bertram and everyone else on the station who saw the explosion with their own eyes." He paused. "One other thing, Nicky. Warman's here because of me. When Quinn went back to earth, you remember we altered his memories so that he couldn't report on our abilities to his bosses? Well, it turns out he talked to Warman after that and Warman spotted the alteration. He was intrigued enough by it to come here and find out who did it. It's my fault he's here."

"Oh, and you don't think that if we'd decided - remember, we all decided - to leave Quinn's memories alone, he wouldn't have spotted that in Quinn's mind and come after us anyway, and with more knowledge than he had when he first got here?"

"Yeah, but if we'd send Quinn back with knowledge of enhanced mental abilities in people who survived seeing the explosion, he might have been more circumspect in going to question Warman a second time. He might still be alive."

"You think Warman killed Quinn, too?"

"You don't?"

Nicole shrugged, but Aiken could see she didn't really believe that Warman was innocent of Quinn Donnelly's death.

"So now what?" she asked.

Aiken explained his idea about finding or making a place with no other people in it and getting Warman to show up there.

"How do we make him do anything?" Nicole asked. "It's not like we can reach out and contact him."

"I don't know," Aiken admitted. "We need to make it irresistible for him so he's guaranteed to show up. And then when he gets there, we have to keep him there until we're done, because if he weasels his way out, he's just going to jump somewhere and kill again to get his powers back."

"I don't even know how to start going about making something like that work," Nicole admitted.

Aiken smiled lopsidedly. "And that's not even our biggest problem."

"Oh?"

"Warman can attack us in our sleep," Aiken said and Nicole immediately saw the implications.

"Oh, crap."

"Yeah."

"So what do we do?"

"We're going to have a watch rotation. For all the Lunatics. And we're going to have to deal with Warman fast."

"Who can shield more than just themselves?"

"You, me and Olivia," Aiken listed off.

"We're going to have to switch off between the three of us, but I don't think I can shield more than a couple of rooms, so the Lunatics are going to have to spend a whole bunch of time together in the next little while."

"You don't think our parents will get suspicious?"

"We're going to have to take care of that, too." Aiken grimaced. Messing with people's memories was not his favourite activity at the best of times, and these certainly did not qualify as the best of times. He and Nicole could overwrite all the memories of all the Lunatics family members, but after what they'd seen of the way Warman operated, they weren't going to want to go too far down that path.

"On the plus side," Nicole said, brightening, "all that time together will surely mean that we come up with a plan to deal with Warman between all of us."

Aiken thought about this and agreed she was probably right. "So, how do we let everyone know?"

Chapter Thirty-Eight
Tuesday, August 25th, 2139

"This sucks," Ethan complained for the dozenth time.

"I know," Isaac said, "but the sooner we deal with Warman, the sooner we can all get back to normal."

The two were in the middle of a cluster of the Lunatics, trying to get comfortable in their sleeping bags on the floor of the school's gym. Off to one side, there were a number of tables set up, covered in drawings, ideas, notes and assorted other detritus that marked three days of confinement and planning. The group looked worse for wear and a number of them were already asleep under Nicole's watchful eye. Aiken was wandering around the perimeter of the gym, checking the mental tripwires they'd rigged up to go off if any mentality tried crossing the boundaries of the gymnasium. All twelve edges of the gym were humming with mental energies that would trigger an alarm that would instantly wake all the students if an intruder was detected. The design was Connor's, but the implementation was Olivia's. She'd proven surprisingly adept in manipulating mental energy to perform notification tasks, and she'd also figured out a way to have the network be powered from the collective mental energy of the assembled students so that no one student had to take the burden on themselves. It was an ingenious idea, and it meant more rest for the three who stood watch.

Unfortunately, they'd made less progress in coming up with a plan to deal with Warman more permanently and some of the students were starting to get irritated away from the comforts of all they were used to. While the gym did have separate bathrooms - one of the main reasons for choosing it - it didn't have much in the way of creature comforts. This was starting to weigh on some of the members of the class.

"I don't get why Warman would want to

kill me, though," Ethan persisted.

"Because of your dashing good looks, I'm sure," responded Kaira. "Now shut up and let some of us sleep."

Aiken couldn't fault his friends for their frustration. Aside from bathroom breaks, they'd essentially spent the last three days in one room. A large room, granted, particularly with the elevated ceilings all moon structures needed to have in order to deal with the decreased gravity, but a single room nonetheless. Even confinement to a palace begins to grate after a while, and a school gymnasium is no palace. They'd teleported in food regularly and had managed to "convince" the school administrators that there was a problem with the air circulation system, so they'd not been disturbed in all that time, but there was a limit to what people would endure, even if they knew the purpose for it, and not everyone was convinced of the purpose behind this.

The best news they'd had so far was that Warman had not attempted any more attacks on them. Whether this was a result of their preparations, or because Nicole had knocked more out of him than he'd expected, or because he was off doing whatever needed doing to put his plan in motion, they couldn't tell, but they'd relaxed somewhat in the meantime, which Aiken thought might be a bad thing. Some of the students were beginning to complain that Warman wasn't really out for them at all, and everything that Nicole and Aiken said to the contrary did not convince those who just wanted to go home and sleep in their own bed or take a shower in their own bathroom.

Connor was sitting at the planning tables with Jillian and Faith, trying to figure out a way to get Warman's attention so they could lure him out in the open. Aiken walked over toward them once he'd completed his check of their mental tripwires.

"Honestly," Connor was saying, "the best way of luring Warman somewhere where we want him has got to be just sitting put and dropping all the shielding around here."

Faith laughed lightly, but Jillian's smile looked forced. "And then what would happen?" She asked.

"Well," Connor said darkly, "he'd probably pounce on us and take a couple of us down before we found where he was and took him out."

Aiken snorted. "So, hit him just after he's eaten? Why am I not surprised that plan came from you?"

The girls both smiled at this, and Connor's black mood lifted for a moment. He turned to his friend, "Well, honestly, aren't we the best bait?"

"Yes," Aiken answered. "But try and remember what happens to bait."

It was Connor's turn to snort, but then he looked thoughtful. "Could we convince Warman that we were all somewhere without us actually being there?"

"You mean like have people's thoughts there without them actually being there?"

"I guess it would have to be their thoughts, wouldn't it?"

"I think that's how he finds us - he's shown no ability to see like Faith."

Connor thought for a moment more. "Could you teleport a thought?"

"What?"

"I mean, if we had people at one place just thinking their usual thoughts, could you have the thoughts appear to be somewhere else?"

"How would I know?" Aiken goggled. "I don't even know how you would grab onto a thought to make it appear somewhere else." He paused. "Why, what were you thinking?"

"If we could make it look like we were, I don't know, headed out on a shuttle, we could make Warman attack the shuttle and show where he was, then we could jump on him and take care of him."

"That sounds alright, but we still haven't solved the problem of making sure he can't get at other people to take their energy."

"Right." Connor thought for a moment. "What if, instead of a shuttle, we could do it with an empty space station? The station might be too far away for Warman to hit it at a distance, so he'd have to be close to it, then when he took down his shield, we could take him out."

"Sounds like a good idea, though, as I said, I have no idea if it's even possible to transmit a thought through a teleport." Aiken scrunched up his eyes in thought. "Maybe, though, if we have someone who teleports and is a telepath, they could make it look like they were sending thoughts from one place at the end of their teleport, but they're really somewhere else, at the beginning of their teleport."

"What do you mean?"

"I mean a partial teleport. Open the gates at both ends, and keep them open, then stick your head through and start broadcasting telepathically, and as soon as Warman gets a bead, then pull your head back through and you're back safe and sound away from Warman."

"Uh, how would that be any different than being bait and teleporting away the moment Warman showed?"

"Oh, right." Aiken felt slightly foolish. "Smaller target?"

"Yeah, but a more important one. Anything happens to your head and the teleport closes with you stuck in the middle, I think bad news for you."

"Yeah, you're probably right."

"Well, if you can figure out how to teleport a thought, let me know, because I have a feeling that would be useful."

"Isn't that basically what telepathy is?" Aiken asked.

"Hey, not all of us are telepaths."

Aiken rolled his eyes. "Duh, but what I mean is that if we're already doing it somehow, we should be able to figure out a way of making it work more broadly, right?"

"I don't know, boy genius, that's for people like you that talk with your brains to figure out."

"Alright, I'll get together with Ethan and Nicole and Liv and see if we can come up with something." Aiken glanced down at his wrist communicator and saw the time. "Uh, tomorrow, maybe."

Connor laughed. "I should be getting off

to bed, too."

The two friends walked across the gym to where their sleeping bags were laid out. Before lying down, Aiken checked with Nicole to make sure she'd wake him for his shift at watching. She agreed, smiling tiredly at him. Olivia and Nicole had both agreed to take extra shifts watching so Aiken could help with the planning more. He lay down and stared up at the beams crossing the ceiling overhead. Thoughts and images swirled through his head. He pictured happier times with the group of students asleep on the floor around him, earlier memories of classes in this gym, times spent in the Park when he was young and didn't bear the responsibilities that now burdened him. He longed to return to a time of carefree youth and innocence, but knew that was long passed. His last thought before falling completely asleep was "I wonder how Warman sleeps with his shield on."

What seemed like minutes later, his shoulder was being shaken and he sat up, startled and anxious, but it was just Nicole. She held out a cup of coffee, and even though he wasn't overly fond of it, he took the warm beverage from her and stood. Careful not to spill any, he stretched and groaned as his muscles complained of the floor as an unsuitable sleeping space.

"Anything happen?" he asked Nicole after a couple of sips of the hot, bitter brew.

"Not a thing," she responded, then yawned.

Aiken laughed, "Well, go get some sleep. I'm on until noon now, so don't worry if you sleep in. You earned it."

Nicole smiled sleepily at him, then headed for the sleeping bag on the girls' side of the gym. Aiken saw that she fell asleep almost immediately. He smiled and walked around the outside of the gym, sipping the coffee and checking the status of the tripwire mechanisms. Everything seemed to be in order, so he went to the planning tables and sat down to look over what the group had come up with most recently. There were notes scribbled on every available surface, and he couldn't make heads or tails of some of the notations. He saw over and over again "No people" written as a reminder to the group that they didn't want to endanger any other people, no matter what else they did to stop Warman. Enough deaths could already be laid at their feet, although, as Nicky kept reminding him, they weren't responsible for what Warman did. Still, it was hard not to feel a sense of guilt when he thought of all those people in the Park that had died because he, in his arrogance, had thought he had Warman exactly where he wanted him.

Truth be told, Aiken was afraid they were going to make the same mistake again and the idea frightened him. Mason was dead as a direct result of a confrontation with Warman and Aiken was afraid that more of his friends might be added to the list, despite what Mason's prediction had said. As he'd had pointed out, while everything Mason had said had come true so far, there were also things that had happened outside of the prediction, and if Mason couldn't see any further forward than his own death, then maybe the ending to the prediction wasn't as set as the rest of it. He glanced over to where Gwen lay sleeping on the girls side of the gym. Of all the memory alterations they'd made to the parents of the Lunatics, that had felt the worst. Still reeling over the sudden loss of their son, Aiken had had to take away their daughter as well, without being able to tell them the real reason why.

He wondered why they'd bothered lying to their parents. If they'd come out and shown their powers and abilities, sure some parents might have freaked out, but when they understood what the stakes were, Aiken liked to think that they might have been okay with the kids sequestering themselves for their own safety and to come up with a way of dealing with the threat. Well, it was a nice thought anyhow. Aiken suspected it wouldn't have worked out quite as well as he fantasized. It was a lot to lay on their parents all at once. "Oh, by the way, mom, dad, I can fly and teleport and read minds and force people to do things. But there's also someone out there who wants to kill me and my friends because we can do these things, so we're going to leave for a while now and go take care of him. See you later." Yeah, that might not have worked out so well.

On the other hand, evidently they needed some outside advice on what to do with Warman now. Three days with nothing to do other than come up with a way to beat Warman - well, that and fool around with the gym equipment, though that had gotten old pretty quickly. Basketball was a whole new game when some of the players could control the motion of the ball with their minds and others could pass to themselves by teleporting. Soon, they'd have to find something else to do though, or they might go stir crazy.

There was a thought niggling at the back of Aiken's mind. Something about the gym games and Warman. He let his mind wander, not trying to pull the thought out. He knew if he concentrated too much on it, it would disappear.

He thought back to some of the games the group had tried to play with their new abilities. The telepaths had been able to predict the movements of their opponents, the teleports could move themselves around the court at will without giving any hint to the other team about where they were going to be next, and the telekinetics could take what looked like a sure shot or clean pass away in an instant. Eventually, they'd tried to play with no powers, but everyone agreed that it was much less interesting that way, even though the game was complete chaos when they let all their abilities fly free.

And there is was: the anarchy of free play. The group had been focused on a way of bringing Warman to them and then trying the same thing as they'd tried in the Park - shutting down his abilities by blanketing them with their own, through the focus of Aiken. But what if they didn't need to? The beauty of their diverse talents was that they could all be applied simultaneously, rather than through a single focus. It might be wild and crazy, but it would be just as crazy to be on the receiving end of things, and if Aiken was any judge of how the basketball game had gone earlier, the group would definitely be hard to keep track of if they were all using what abilities they had simultaneously.

But that wouldn't help them defeat Warman. It might keep him distracted for a while, but to what end? Unless they had a way of permanently removing his abilities, or permanently removing him, all the distraction on the moon wouldn't help them out. And he wasn't sure they could kill Warman if they wanted to. He'd just jump to somewhere where there were people to regain his power once he figured out what they were trying to do. Unless...

Aiken was still pondering this idea hours later when the other students began to stir. They groaned and got up in twos and threes, being careful to not make too much noise. They knew that some had stayed up late working on their project and didn't want to disturb those still sleeping, particularly Olivia and Nicole. Aiken and Connor teleported a selection of breakfast foods to some tables off to the side of the gym and the smell of fresh coffee and Danishes roused some more students.

As they ate, Aiken told Connor his idea about using all of their abilities simultaneously to distract Warman, but admitted that he'd come up short on the idea of what they would be distracting him from, exactly. Connor nodded as he listened, took some notes and walked back to the planning tables without saying more than was absolutely necessary. For the first time, Aiken started to wonder of the stress of the situation was starting to cause more problems than having them all together in one place solved. Well, he wouldn't want to be the one testing the theory that Warman wasn't interested in killing any of them individually, mostly because he knew that Warman would try again as soon as he spotted an opportunity to come after Aiken. Maybe they could use that to their advantage.

He started walking over to the planning tables when he was suddenly aware that a consciousness was trying to breach their perimeter. As was everyone else in the room. Apparently, not content with just alerting the three telepaths, Olivia had set the tripwires to send a mental hail to everyone in the room. Pandemonium broke out until Aiken mentally shouted for silence.

The consciousness was probing its way around the room, seeming to test for a way in. The mind - and no one in the room doubted it was Warman's - checked all the walls, floor and ceiling of the gym for weaknesses, but Connor's design held and he wasn't able to get in. The system had been set up to switch from alarm to shield when Olivia sensed an attack on the perimeter might be imminent, and apparently it had worked exactly as it was supposed to. The mind went away and the group in the gym breathed a collective sigh of relief. It was short-lived however, as one by one, the communicators at most of the students' wrists began pinging to get their attention. A couple of them looked around in confusion, but most looked to Aiken to see what to do.

He nodded grimly and they all punched the accept button more or less simultaneously. Warman's head floated above each wrist and his voice spoke from everywhere, it seemed.

"Well done, well done." He smiled genially at them all. "That barrier was well emplaced and my congratulations to Miss Kitt, if I am not mistaken." Olivia's head jerked up at this, and she looked around to see a few pairs of eyes staring at her. Warman continued on as if he hadn't noticed. "The memory alterations were skillfully done, Mr. Drum, much more so than even I would be capable of. It took me this long to find out where you were, but now that I know, this can only end one way."

The students began to mutter. "I'm not interested in causing any more of your deaths," Warman continued. "It is only your own obstinacy at this point that makes that outcome more likely."

"Yeah, right," a voice called out. "Tell that to Mason." It was Gwen, and she was angry. The older students nodded in agreement.

"Mr. Gabriel's death was unfortunate and very much not a desired outcome of the confrontation in the Park between Mr. Drum and myself. Your brother," he addressed Gwen directly, "was simply in the wrong place at the wrong time."

"Bull." Gwen had her face set in a scowl that her friends knew meant she wasn't going to back down.

"Believe what you wish, Miss Gabriel, but I assure you, no one else will have to suffer your brother's fate."

"Is that a threat?" It was Penny. She had her hand on Gwen's shoulder and was looking down at the image of Warman projected over Gwen's wrist by her communicator.

"Take it however you want, Miss Metcalf. I'm simply communicating with you all to clear up some misunderstandings that seem to have cropped up between us."

"Misunderstandings? Look, Aiken's told us what you did and why. I don't think any misunderstandings are possible at this point."

"Miss Metcalf, I speak not of the past, but of the future." Warman looked right through Penny and addressed the group as a whole. "If you will content yourselves with staying out of my way, we need have no further interaction at all. Mr. Drum has made it quite clear his own feelings on the matter of allowing other people to share in our talents, but I want to offer others the chance to become what you are all taking for granted. I pledge that this will only be done for people who request it. Another drive test could be set up somewhere where no one who doesn't want to be affected need be exposed, but those who would like to experience life as you now enjoy it will be given the opportunity to do so. Voluntarily." His tiny avatars looked around at the assembled students. "Don't tell me that some of your peers, given the opportunity, wouldn't want to become as you are, or even more!"

"Yeah, what could possibly go wrong?" Faith asked.

"Miss Stevens, did you not receive a gift greater than that which was taken from you? Are you not better off now than you were before that fateful day?"

Faith persisted, "How can you be sure that other people harmed by the radiation will not be worse off. Nobody in our group chose the abilities they got. I could have easily ended up blind, with the ability to fly. How would that have worked out?"

Warman was not dissuaded, "I have faith, ironically, Miss Stevens, that you seem to lack, despite your name. The abilities that were given to us have amplified tendencies we all have naturally and while they may have taken away on the one hand, they certainly have given back with the other."

"How do you explain your own condition, then?" Liam asked. "Unless you're going to tell us that the ability to murder people more efficiently is somehow a gift." Aiken could see classmates nodding in agreement.

"I've already said all I'm going to say on that subject, Mr. Hall."

"Yeah, we heard. You consider people without abilities like ours as prey. I think that says all I need to hear about your desire to uplift those poor souls so they can be like you," Liam spat. "You've killed two of my friends. Murdered. Do you know how many people go through life without ever having someone they know killed by another person? And all of us have had two people in our lives taken from us, violently, by your hand." Liam walked to the center of the group. "I don't know what you were hoping to do here, but convincing any more of us to join your demented idea of the master race is not going to happen. None of us are interested."

"Fine," Warman growled out, finally losing his composure," I'm not asking you to join me, just stay out of my way, or there will be more mourning for you. Remember," he looked at each of them, "you may be safe in there, but your friends and families are out here."

"You son of a bitch!" Liam yelled, but Warman had already cut the connection. Mutterings started to grow among the class.

Liam walked over to where Aiken and Connor were at the planning tables. "Whatever we're going to do, we need to do fast," he said. Looking around, the three of them could see that Warman's final pronouncement was having the effect he must have wanted. Several students had sunk down to the floor, heads in hands as they realized the import of what he'd threatened. Others were simply holding on to friends, trying to get some support from those they trusted.

"Aiken has part of an idea," Connor said, gesturing. Aiken explained his idea to Liam, and also the fact that aside from a distraction, they didn't really have anything designed to deal with Warman once and for all.

Liam paused for a moment, thinking exhaustedly, then thanked the two and walked over to where Penny, Faith and Olivia were sitting and sat down with them.

"He's right, Aiken," Connor said. "If we don't come up with something soon, no one is going to want to stay in here any longer. They're going to want to be out there," he waved his hand at the walls of the gym, "protecting their families."

"Yeah," Aiken said glumly. "And out there is where Warman wants us, so he can pick us off one by one to feed his abilities."

"Yeah. On the plus side, no more murders since the Park."

"Yeah," Aiken replied. "I was kind of thinking that after Nicky walloped him, he'd need to fill up again, but apparently he was still powered up from the people in the Park."

"He won't stay that way forever," Connor said quietly.

"Don't you think I know that?" Aiken turned to his friend. "Don't you think I realise that every minute we spend in here is another minute he has out there to plan and carry out whatever it is he's going to do next? Every day we spend here nice and safe is one day closer to him killing again to keep up his powers? I want to deal with him as badly as everyone else in here, but time is not on our side, and I have a bad feeling we're running out of it."

Connor's head snapped up. "What did you just say?"

"I said, I think the longer we spend in here, the more likely it is that Warman will murder someone else out there."

"No, after that." Connor was insistent

"I said I felt like time was against us."

"Time..." Connor trailed off. He got a faraway look in his eyes and started tapping a stylus on his lower lip, a mannerism Aiken recognized as his furiously thinking pose. Finally, after a minute or so, Connor turned to him and said, "I know how we're going to deal with Warman!"

Chapter Thirty-Nine
Thursday, August 27th, 2139

"You really think this is going to work?"

"Hey, we have to at least try, right?"

Aiken and Connor looked around at their final preparations and were as satisfied as they could be. They felt that they'd pulled off the impossible to get everything together as fast as they'd managed. It helped to have the particular talents of their group at their disposal.

They'd succeeded in stealing the march from Warman when it came to the drive. They'd managed to sneak the next most finished prototype drive out of the guarded and locked storage yard where it was being kept at the L4 station. With telepaths, telekinetics and teleports at their disposal, it had actually been a fairly straightforward exercise. Aiken had gotten the group to the L4 station unnoticed, then stood back and watched for Warman or others to notice that they were there. The others did the distasteful work of taking the location and combination out of the minds of the station personnel - reduced to a skeleton maintenance crew in the wake of the drive disaster - and actually stealing the drive. They'd all teleported back to the gymnasium with their prize, bursting with confidence at a job well done.

Now, though, the doubts were starting to creep in. Not only did they have to deal with Warman, they also had to make sure they didn't get caught with the stolen drive, admittedly easier because of their location.

They were set up in the center of the mine from which they'd rescued the taikonauts earlier that year. The Chinese had not yet managed to get the earth-moving equipment they needed in place to get back into the tunnels where they had been digging before the cave-in. The entrance was blocked, but further back in the mine was still wide open and Aiken and Faith had scouted out all the tunnels to make sure none of them opened back to the surface. Not that it mattered a great deal with Warman being a teleport, but it was nice to know that no innocent by stander would be walking into the middle of their confrontation.

The space the class had cleared out in the center of the mine rivalled the open center of the Peary Dome, thousands of kilometers to their north. There would be room to move around here. They'd placed the drive engine in the very center of the cleared space, and the repurposed mine lights now flooded the area around it with brightness. The kinetics had closed off all the tunnels leading away from the area, and with a nuclear-powered oxygen factory online around the clock, there was now enough air to breathe. Aiken had augmented the oxygen produced by their electrolysis machine with air he'd taken from the largest domes on the moon. He'd been careful to collect only a bit from each of the domes, but the whole moon was now involved in the effort to stop Warman, whether they knew it or not.

Now all they had to do was wait for Warman to show up. A few of the Lunatics were shielded so that a cursory glance at area by Warman would only reveal the presence of some of the Lunatics, but they could possibly keep some as a surprise. Having learned from their lesson with the wrist communicators, all of the students had left their wrist communicators back in the school gym, which was now reopened to the rest of the students as the "problem" with the air system had been "fixed". Aiken smiled at that. The grumbling from the class about cleaning up the gym after three days of living there around the clock made Aiken have some sympathy for parents everywhere. There would be no evidence, however, that they class had stayed there. There was still hope that the students might be able to return to their usual lives when this was over, and the less questions people raised about their activities, the better.

Aiken looked around the space inside the mountain and wondered for the umpteenth time if they'd managed to anticipate everything Warman might do to ruin their plan. Probably not, but unlike the last time, there wasn't any one thing that could go wrong to bring the whole plan crashing to a halt. They were flexible and prepared. They were ready. Only they were starting to get bored.

It was Faith that spotted Warman. She had her sight tuned broadly to the whole mountain, looking for the opening of a teleport window. Warman might be able to shield his thoughts, but even he couldn't hide his physical presence, so Connor's plan relied on Faith being able to give them warning of his approach.

Faith was, in turn, being monitored by

Olivia, so that if Warman attempted to mess with her ability to see him from outside of her radius of vision, Olivia would be able to spot it. She rebroadcast immediately to the whole group that Warman was in one of the minor tunnels on the south side of the mountain. Faith followed him visually as he approached. Aiken felt when Warman's scan swept over the group and it sent a shiver of anticipation down his spine. If they managed to make their plan work today, Warman would never again be in a position to threaten anyone.

Connor, on feeling Warman's scan, took another quick look around to see if everyone was ready. Several students were looking extremely nervous, but all appeared to be ready. Aiken hoped that their shielded friends had managed to elude Warman's scan. They'd left enough people out in the open that it was plausible that they were all that had decided to confront Warman. They were hoping that Warman would think his threat against their families and friends would have sent some of them back home to defend against him individually.

Not that their plan relied on hope. Aiken could see in the eyes of some of the others a desire for revenge. Warman had taken two of their friends from them - three, if you counted

Hugo - and in so doing, whether he realized it or not, had made enemies of some of the most powerful people on the moon. Their anger would fuel their desire to see Warman brought low.

Aiken resisted the urge to check on everyone one more time. He trusted his friends to do their part, and he had his own role to play in making sure Warman went down once and for all. He mustn't get distracted by emotion.

Still, he couldn't help sending two short, tightly held messages to his best friends. "Good luck, guys." Connor looked over and nodded. Aiken knew Nicole could not send back anything, since she was busy shielding the group that was hidden from Warman, but he knew she'd be wishing them luck, too.

After the long wait, knowing that Warman was in the same place as they were, but not right in front of them was almost unbearable. They were all on the edge of a knife of anticipation, wanting to get this over with and not able to do anything about it. It was infuriating.

And then, something happened. Or tried to, in any event. Connor had surmised that the engine would be Warman's first target, because if he tired getting that, he could jump away, kill and regain his powers, then come back and deal with the class later. The engine rocked on the ground, unseen forces at work battling over it. Penny's face was scrunched up in concentration as she created a barrier of air around the engine that made it impossible to move telekinetically. Warman had shown no aptitude for teleporting objects, which was good, since they hadn't managed to think of a way of blocking a teleport, but since people who could only teleport themselves needed to be in contact with the object they wanted to move, they could prevent that from happening with physical barriers.

Suddenly, Penny's head moved to the side and her eyes narrowed again. She was herself now being buffeted by some unseen force, but the barrier she'd built around herself was able to take all the telekinetic blows that Warman aimed at her. Olivia was responsible for her mental defence as well and was holding up well under whatever assault Warman was attempting to use on her mind.

Aiken was now watching with Faith as Warman, frustrated, teleported to another spot in the mountain to come up with another way to attack them. He could almost have laughed out loud, Warman was making mistakes. He'd not considered that even in the dark of the tunnels, he would be physically visible to one of Aiken's group.

Or maybe he had. Aiken could see he was still resting in the tunnel, but the engine was now rocking again, albeit much slower. Narrowing his eyes, Aiken scanned the area around the engine carefully, but he saw nothing. The engine kept moving, however.

Suddenly, Aiken understood. On one of his teleports, Warman must have, for a split second, materialized in the cave where the Lunatics were while carrying Hugo. He must have dropped Hugo off, then continued his jump so fast that it looked like he'd never stopped. Sneaky, Aiken realized.

"Hugo," he called out. "Drop the invisibility or Penny will have to crush you under a thousand kilos of air."

Several of the other students looked up in surprise, but catching on to what was happening, started to make their way toward the rocking engine. The rocking stopped abruptly and Aiken tried to follow where Hugo went, but his invisibility extended into every spectrum Aiken could see, and he'd either learned shielding from Warman or was using part of Warman's shield. Aiken would have to remember that he was here, or they risked him causing further complications.

Faith started to call out a warning, but

before she'd gotten much more than started, Warman was in their midst. A couple of students squeaked in surprise and moved away from the area he was standing in. Aiken stalked forward to meet him. He knew his part of the plan, and just had to hope that the others remembered theirs.

"What do you want, Warman?" he asked.

"You know bloody well what I'm here for, boy," Warman spat. "It's past time you acknowledged me as your better and got out of my way before someone else gets hurt."

"I'm not afraid of you," Aiken shouted.

"More fool you, then, Aiken Drum! I have been lenient so far, but my patience for your meddling is at an end. Now, give me the drive and I'll let you all die of old age instead of burning from the inside."

"Come and get it!"

Warman tried to walk toward the drive, but his feet appeared to be mired in some kind of invisible muck. He attempted to teleport away, but Aiken was blanketing his abilities again, and Warman couldn't muster the power he needed.

Suddenly, a mine cart filled with ore appeared in the air over Warman's head. Liam was struggling off to one side of the cave to move it into position immediately above

Warman, but Warman was using his own abilities to try and shove it aside.

"Now," Liam yelled, and the mine cart plummeted toward the ground and Warman below. Warman made a grasping motion, but seemed unable to get a hold of it. The students could see that the cart glittered faintly and knew that Isaac had rendered it insubstantial. A moment before it would crash into him, the cart stopped glittering and smashed into the physical shield Warman was forced to raise over himself.

Unfortunately, the mine cart and ore was enough mass to smash through Penny's grip on Warman's feet, and he surged forward toward the engine. Penny re-established the barrier around his feet, but he'd gained some distance. Distracted as she was, Penny didn't sense anything was amiss until her head snapped sideways, her eyes rolled up and she fell to the ground, unconscious.

Jill picked up Kaira and flew her to Penny's side, but it was too late - Warman had reached the engine. He rubbed his hands together in glee and reached out to place them on the engine, but at that moment, a hail of small stones flew from the wall of the cavern and peppered Warman's back. Gwen stood ramrod-straight with a glare on her face that Aiken even looked away from. Her fury lending her strength, she picked up larger and larger rocks and hurled them at Warman, never letting him catch his breath. Liam joined the fray and started teleporting all sorts of objects over Warman's head and dropping them.

Warman backed off from the engine so it wouldn't be damaged by the debris swirling in a maelstrom of Gwen's making. Warman fought back by igniting the rocks and flinging them back out towards the students, but Aiken was intercepting them before they could hit his friends. Kaira revived Penny, who, though somewhat groggy from Hugo hitting her across the head, managed to recreate the binding she'd put on Warman's feet earlier.

Aiken could feel Warman weakening and sent a narrowly directed message to Nicole *Anytime now.* He didn't get any acknowledgement, but didn't really expect any. Nicole was likely in the middle of the most dangerous part and at the same time the most outlandish part of the whole operation. To her was given the task that Connor had come with as their way of defeating Warman for good. She, Ethan and Connor were going to be the power source and guiding force for an ability they'd never tried, never really even imagined, except in flights of fantasy, before Connor came up with it. Aiken hoped they were well on their way to getting it ready.

Warman's wall of fire that was protecting him from the rocks and mining equipment that Gwen and Liam were pelting him with seemed to be thinning and Aiken hoped for a break-through soon. He needed to be ready.

All of a sudden, a scream started off to his right, coming from a patch of thin air about ten meters away from him. Smoke began pouring out of what looked like a hole in reality, and Aiken realized too late what was happening. Warman's strength rebounded just as the charred corpse of Hugo appeared on the ground on the spot Aiken had started towards. He turned his head with tears in his eyes. Hugo might have turned on them, but no one deserved to die like that.

And now Warman was stronger again. Aiken redoubled his efforts, but he was using only his own strength in this combat and it wasn't enough to overcome Warman's new energy. The wall of flame swirled around and over Warman and caught all the rocks Gwen was pelting him with, turning them to ash on the floor around him. Even the larger objects Liam was teleporting into place over Warman's head ended up as so much slag on the floor.

"Penny," he called out. "Can you make anything with the stuff that's piling up on the floor around him?"

"Maybe," she called back, "but I'm not sure if I can both hold him in place and make something else."

"How long do you need?"

"Maybe fifteen seconds."

"Get ready," Aiken said. He used his telekinesis to bend the air around Warman so that the flames he was creating guttered and flickered. As soon as Warman realized what Aiken was doing, he pushed his flame out further to bleed air out from the rest of the room. The flames swirled and roared and the heat from them was like a physical thing in and of itself. If they didn't deal with him soon, they were all going to drop from heat exhaustion or worse, oxygen deprivation as the flames sucked all the breathable atmosphere out of their enclosed space.

Aiken was just about at the end of his abilities, but he could see that whatever Penny had done was affecting Warman. The circle of flames closed in tighter, giving the students a little more breathing room, in both senses of the phrase. The wall of fire thinned again, and Aiken laughed as he saw through and realized what Penny had done. All the ash and molten rock that Warman had created by burning the debris that Gwen and Liam had sent his way was crawling up his form, creating a Warman statue with him at the heart of it.

For the first time, Aiken saw a look of fear flicker across Warman's face. Could this be it? Could they beat him without the need for drastic measures? The air behind Warman began to warp, sparkle and change. It was like something was forming a bubble out of the air, or perhaps a lens. Aiken could see the edges of a warped area of air right over Warman's shoulder. Warman couldn't see it, distracted as he was by the molten rock crawling up his body. The shape behind him solidified, as much as could be said for air, and now looked very much like a lens. On the surface closest to Warman, things were moving. Aiken could see cloudy shadows whisping across the surface of the object.

"Aiken, now!"

His time had come. Focusing all his mental energy on Warman, he called out to Penny, "Now!" She released all of her constructs at the same time. Warman staggered at the sudden release of pressure on his legs and looked like he was about to fall forward. Unfortunately, they wanted him to fall backwards, into the lens construct. Aiken unleashed his telekinesis and *pushed* Warman back. Warman was lifted off his feet and sent flying, but he'd looked over his shoulder just as

Aiken shoved and reached out for the edge of the statue base that Penny had made. His fingers scrabbled to grab on, but he was grasping at air. His face hardened and, in a split second, he drove his fist down into the rock of the floor, fire streaming out of his hand. He grabbed on to the handhold he'd just made and formed the rock back over his hand, giving him an anchor that held him in place. His body pointed straight out behind him, like a signpost pointing back at the lens.

The activity on the lens intensified. A brightness shone out of it that briefly illuminated the whole cavern with blinding light.

Warman strained to look up as Aiken walked towards him, leaning away from the swirling mass of air behind Warman.

"What have you done?" Warman cried out.

"We're making sure you can't ever hurt another person again," Aiken said calmly.

"You're going to kill me?" Warman smiled nastily. "Then you will become me."

"No, we're not going to kill you. We're just going to... limit your options somewhat." He was now shouting to be heard over the roar of wind being sucked into the vortex.

"Tell me what you've done!"

"We've created a tunnel to the past." Aiken smiled. "Just like you can see in space, and by refocusing, see in time, it turns out not only can you teleport in space, but if you set it up differently, it turns out you can teleport in time. Not that it's going to help you, mind you. We're sending you back a couple of million years. Before there were any people. No one to harvest, Warman. You're done."

Aiken was now mere feet away from Warman, and the air from the chamber was still rushing towards the time vortex that Nicky had created with her, Connor and Ethan powering it. The mental force of the vortex made using any of his powers around it impossible, a little trick they'd discovered when they'd experimented creating a time-jump the day before. The closer you were to it, the less you could use your abilities. They knew Warman couldn't teleport away even if he was at full power, since his feet were basically at the threshold of the construct, so he felt safe (moderately) coming closer. Unfortunately, the air in the chamber wouldn't last forever, and the other students didn't all have the ability to teleport to safety, so it was up to Aiken to make sure that Warman went through before they ran out of air.

He glanced back over his shoulder at the other students and saw that the ones who had been shielded previously were now out in the open, all watching the end of this man who'd caused them so much grief. Aiken knelt down by Warman's hand and, one by one, peeled Warman's fingers from his handhold. He could feel the class's eyes on him as he did.

"Goodbye, Mr. Warman," he said as he peeled the last one.

"Aiken!" he heard a girl's warning off to the side, and looked toward the source of the noise as Warman flew backwards toward the lens. Out of nowhere, Warman's other hand snaked out and grabbed Aiken by the wrist, hauling him forwards toward the vortex.

Aiken dug his heels in and leaned back, but he could feel himself sliding ever closer to the lip of the lens, past which there was no return. His fingers dug at Warman's, wrapped around his wrist like a vise, but to no avail. If Warman was going through, he was determined to take Aiken with him.

"So that's what the last part of Mason's prediction meant," he said to himself. A feeling of peace settled over him and Warman's shocked look of outrage told Aiken that he realized what Aiken was about to do, too.

Aiken stopped digging at Warman's fingers, stopped digging his heels into the floor and let himself be pulled forward. Knowing what was coming, he closed his eyes and smiled.

He saw nothing, but he heard a far off, drawn-out scream. He felt an icy chill pass over him as he crossed the event horizon of the time teleport and he could swear, just before the freezing sensation completely enveloped him, that there was a sudden band of pressure around his ankle. He felt Warman slip away in the time tunnel, heading back for their rendezvous a million years in the past. Then he felt nothing but an icy chill seeping into his pores as he lost consciousness, tumbling through time.

Part Three
The Aftermath

Chapter Forty
Wednesday, September 2nd, 2139

Connor sat morosely on the pressed duracrete bench. The gym was packed, but he felt utterly alone in the midst of the throng. The last week had been an exhausting whirlwind. After Aiken, and then Nicole, had disappeared through the time teleport, it had been up to him and Liam to try to salvage the rest of the group's chances. Damn Nicole for following Aiken anyways! He knew exactly why she'd done it, but when she grabbed Aiken's ankle and followed him through the portal, the last chance the group had of keeping the whole thing under wraps had disappeared when the portal snapped shut behind her. Since neither Liam nor he had the strength to either teleport the whole group, nor to get them individually all the way back to Peary, they had teleported the remaining Lunatics one by one to the closest base. Well, not the closest base; that was Shenzhou, and no one had wanted to add "international incident" to the troubles they had already. Ten teenagers showing up unannounced in Tranquility Base with a wild story about crazy mental powers, and a stolen drive prototype that was supposed to be under lock and key on a space station thousands of kilometres away would be enough of a sensation as it was.

They'd hustled to the security station, intent on telling their story to someone with a bit of authority, but they hadn't counted on the fact that there'd been a lunar stringer in the station interviewing the security personnel about the possible connections between all the people who'd died from "spontaneous combustion" on the moon recently.

Somehow, she'd managed to hear enough of their story to connect the dots and had quickly filed the story of her career. Within a day, the security personnel had been fending off a small army of freelancers all intent on snagging an interview with the "super teens".

The Lunatics had been quietly shipped back to Peary under armed escort. The drive prototype had, of course, been taken into custody by dour-faced men who promised that they would be getting to the bottom of this immediately.

Parents and siblings, initially skeptical, were quickly convinced with a demonstration of various abilities and quietly took their wayward offspring back home, furtive glances passing back and forth constantly.

The telepaths found this enormously funny, of course, the parents, security personnel, reporters and various hangers-on not having thought through the entire implications of having mind-readers among those who they were now regarding with wary admiration (well, not all; inevitably, there had been some hostile to the whole idea).

Olivia, as the sole remaining send-and-receive telepath, became a sort of clearinghouse for all the stories, reactions, rumours and downright goofiness that the Lunatics experienced as a result of being thrust into the public eye. Since she and Ethan could also listen in to conversations that others were having about the group, and she could rebroadcast as necessary, the group was never caught unprepared for the next media assault or round of government questioning.

Still, it had been a long week. Today, finally, they were setting aside time to grieve their missing friends, Aiken, Nicole and Hugo. No one had had the heart to tell Hugo's parents about his betrayal, and besides, up to that point, he'd been a good friend to many.

The funerals were just now wrapping up, with people standing around, sharing memories of the missing. Soon, the gym, the only room in Peary big enough to hold all the families (aside from the Park, which was still damaged from the fight with Warman), would be reconfigured as a banquet hall for a luncheon.

Connor felt a hand on his shoulder and looked up to see Liam smiling gently down at him.

"That could have gone worse," Liam said.

"Yeah," Connor said morosely.

"Cheer up," Liam said, still smiling. "They might still be alive. The whole point of the plan was so that we weren't killing Warman, so Aiken and Nicole probably made it too."

"If they ended up a million years in the past, with no way of getting back, then by definition, they can't still be alive."

"Way to see the up side," Liam said replied.

"I'm trying, I really am," Connor

responded. "But you have to think that if they'd survived, they'd have found a way to leave a message of some sort. You know, a cave painting in a place they knew would get discovered saying 'Hi, we're from the future – let our friends know we're okay.'"

Liam snorted. "Maybe they just don't think as logically as you."

"Yeah, I'd believe that if it was just Aiken, but Nicole's smart enough to figure that out."

This time, they both smiled.

"How are things at your place?" Liam asked.

"Not bad, considering. My parents keep joking that this is going to save them a bundle on shuttle costs, but I think they're just trying to hide how freaked out they are. To be fair, remember how we were when we first found out?"

Liam smiled in remembrance. "Yeah. We were kind of idiots about it."

"Well, we might still have been without Warman. Without Diana."

Liam nodded thoughtfully.

"How about your folks?"

"Kind of like yours, I guess. They keep joking that I'll be FedEx's undoing, but I think they're hoping it will just go away."

"Man, I didn't even think through all the

ways we could make money off of this," Connor said.

"Yeah, somehow I don't believe that."

"Okay, maybe I've thought of one or two, but I didn't even consider parcel delivery."

Connor looked up and noticed that a number of other Lunatics had gathered around while he and Liam had been talking.

He smiled tentatively at them and received the same in return. By common consensus, they all sat together as the adults in the crowd rearranged the benches from an auditorium-style arrangement to something resembling a dining area.

Maybe it was because they were so engrossed in their conversation, or maybe because they were so used to the extraordinary happening every day, but it was one of the non-powered people attending who first noticed the wavering patch of wall.

The exclamations brought the attention of the Lunatics to the phenomenon and they stood as one to go investigate.

Connor murmured to Isaac as they walked over, "Is that you?"

"No, it's something else."

By that time, they were all standing around the patch of wall in a rough semicircle, the rest of the mourners having backed off a few paces.

The edge of the glowing patch shaped itself into an oval, and the wall at the center began to waver and glitter. Shapes began to move in front of the section of wall.

Startled, Connor spoke for all of them, "You don't think?"

"I don't know," Ethan answered, "but if it is, we're going to want to back off a bit."

The group moved back as one, and their apparent apprehension set off a mild panic in the rest of the guests until Olivia calmed them with a mental command.

The disc solidified and then shone an incredible brightness out into the room. In the afterimage, Connor could see distinct shapes in what was now a lens bulging out into the room.

The group backed off another step as air began to rush out of the shape and into the gym. The smell of pines filled the air of the room and the slight overpressure made everyone's ears pop.

A curious and now calmer crowd began to gather behind the Lunatics, waiting in anticipation for something to happen.

A leather boot appeared, then a leg, then Aiken Drum himself, tanned and fitter than Connor had ever seen him, leaned out of the swirling vortex, finally standing a bit off to the side of it. A look of concentration came across his face and the vortex intensified, and then Nicole came tumbling out into Aiken's arms.

The vortex snapped closed behind her, leaving a bright image suspended on the wall.

The pair straightened and turned to the assembled crowd.

"Hi," Aiken said lamely. "We're back."

Chapter Forty-One
Wednesday, September 2nd, 2139

"So it turns out you can hold open a teleport tunnel from either end," Nicole was explaining. Once the pandemonium of their arrival had died down, Nicole and Aiken were treated like visiting royalty, and now were seated at the center of a large group of eager listeners, powered and non-powered alike.

"Yeah, as long as you're not caught in its wake," Aiken chimed in.

"Right," Nicole continued, her fingers entwined with Aiken's. "So we've been jumping our way back forwards until now."

"You couldn't have come back any

sooner?" Connor asked.

"Given that our first few jumps were ten thousand years each, we're lucky to have landed in your lifetimes at all," Aiken chuckled.

His parents looked at him aghast.

"He's just kidding," Nicole reassured them. "As we got closer, we took smaller jumps. It also uses less energy, so we didn't have to rest as long between them."

"Yeah, I think our last one was what, just over a decade?"

"About that," Nicole agreed.

"You pinpointed a ten-year jump down to the week?" Connor asked. "Now I am impressed."

"We try," Aiken laughed.

"Any sign of Warman?" Liam finally broached the subject that all the Lunatics had wanted to know, but none had dared ask.

"Not a thing," Aiken answered. "We ended up more or less where we wanted on Earth, but our estimate of how far back we went is a little sketchy. Warman could have landed a year further in the past or a thousand."

"He's definitely in the past, though?" This time it was Connor.

"Yes," Nicole answered. "Aiken and I left the teleport tunnel out the side when it destabilized too much."

"Because you were in it, and you'd been powering it," Connor surmised.

"That's what we think, too," Nicole answered. "But I distinctly saw Warman still heading down the middle of it when we left."

"Crashed, you mean." Aiken said, smiling warmly at her.

"Yeah, that's one way of putting it," she replied. "We just ended up in a heap on some hillside. It was probably half a day before either of us could even sit up, and Aiken was not well suited to the gravity."

"Fortunately, I have other strengths," he responded.

"So then," Nicole continued, "I flew up high enough to see we'd landed in South America, like we planned."

"We thought we'd be spending the rest of our lives there," Aiken said offhandedly. His parents looked at him in dismay again, but he just shrugged. "If that's what it took to get rid of Warman, it would have been worth it."

"Fortunately, after a couple of months of exploring, we accidentally discovered that you can maintain a stable teleport from either end, and applied that to time teleports, and the rest is history."

"Future," Aiken said absently. Nicole swatted him on the arm with her free hand.

"Wait, did you say a few months?" Connor asked.

"Yeah, it took a while before we figured out that the person who goes through a teleport can then hold it open for the person who started it. But it takes teamwork, so we don't have to worry about Warman showing up again," Nicole explained.

"No, what I mean is, you've been gone a couple of months?" Connor asked again.

"Well, it's kind of hard to keep track of how long it's been when you're moving through time," Nicole began. "We had to rest a while after each of the big jumps, because only one of us powers it at once, so there were a few days between each jump."

"We think about a year," Aiken said bluntly. "Certainly no less than nine months, and possibly up to fourteen."

Silence followed this pronouncement. Finally, Ethan said, "So, you're older than me now?" General laughter followed this and the tension lessened somewhat.

"We wanted to be careful we didn't end up too far in the future," Nicole explained, "So we started with huge jumps, because not a whole lot changed between them. We took smaller and smaller jumps the closer we got back here. When we got them down to a century or so, we could do a couple of teleports a day."

"And then the last couple were a decade at a go," Aiken picked up. "I think we did three of those yesterday, then another two today."

Nicole nodded her agreement.

Aiken's mother spoke, "I can't get used to the idea of people jumping around through time like a kid playing hopscotch."

"Well, it's a little more complicated than that," Aiken protested.

"Yeah," Connor chuckled. "You were jumping around through time **and** space."

"Speaking of," Aiken started. "Nicole and I came up with an interesting idea for how to use our abilities to help out the wider world. It'd mean a bit of travelling, but we think it could really make a difference to the future."

Chapter Forty-Two
Thursday, March 4th, 2245

"Do you think they'll be here?" Lieutenant First-Class Rachael Yeung asked, flipping the toggle switches to spin down the massive quantum tunneling drive.

"We know they will be," Captain Sayid Banning answered with a smile. "Anticlimactic though it may be after the voyage we've had, we're already in the history books back home for a successful arrival."

"That whole notion that we're now in Earth's past gives me a headache," Officer Tori Gardener interjected. She checked the astrogation chart to ensure they'd tunneled through the universe to exactly where they wanted to be.

Just then a squawk was heard over the communications channel. The three bridge officers of the E.S.S. Valiant surreptitiously adjusted their uniform jackets before answering.

"Unidentified transport, this is Kepler 62 control. Please identify and state your intentions." A shiver went through the three officers. Someone was waiting for them. It was a good sign.

"This is Captain Sayid Banning of the Earth Space Ship Valiant. We are a colony ship and are expected."

"Shuttle Valiant, transmit the clearance code for shield passage."

The bridge crew looked at each other, mystified. This was not the procedure they'd been trained in.

At that moment, another voice came over the circuit, "Never mind that last. Connor's just having a little fun at your expense. Welcome to the Kepler 62 system. You should be within sight of the fourth planet. We'll meet you once you make planetfall. Kepler 62 control out."

The next few hours were so full of activity, readying the massive colony ship for planetfall that no one had any time to speculate on who would be waiting for them when they touched down on the surface of humanity's newest colony.

The network of satellites that had helpfully been placed in orbit around the planet before their arrival communicated with the ship's computers, identifying the best landing zones on the surface, ranked in order of surrounding habitability.

Seeing no reason to override the selection, Captain Banning ordered the ship put down. Landing the more than three hundred meter long vessel was deftly handled by the computers, with the three bridge crew hovering anxiously; ready to take over if anything went wrong. This was much too delicate a job for the colossal engines that had pushed them from the Sol system, so a network of thrusters over the entire length of the ship guided the vast ship down.

Once the ship had finished settling on the ground in the valley selected by the orbiting satellite network, the Captain gave the order to begin waking the colonists (or thawing the peoplesicles, as Tori irreverently put it).

The programmed sequence would run over the next few days, waking up the five thousand plus colonists for their new start here on 62e. The ship's narrow corridors would soon be bustling with people going about their jobs, preparing the colony to get off to the right start.

The crew, having been the only ones awake through the five-year voyage between two universes, were eager to open the ship up and get out into their new world.

Midway up the port side of the flattened cylinder that was their ship, the airlock cycled and the green light flashed over the exterior door.

The door slid smoothly down into the hull below them, and they could see from their vantage point near the nose of the ship, that the ramp had already deployed, leading downwards at a sharp angle.

Sayid looked left and right through his suit's visor at the other two officers, who each gave him a slight nod. He stepped forward onto the ramp and headed down to the planet's surface.

The trio stopped at the bottom of the ramp and, as captain's prerogative, Sayid stepped alone onto the planet's surface.

"I hereby christen this planet Ostara of the Lucina system. We come representing all humankind to establish a new world built on peace."

The speech that he'd spent so long agonizing over was over before he'd even had a chance to get too nervous about it. The other two now stepped on to the surface.

Tori was looking around in fascination, mentally cataloguing everything she saw. Rachael turned back and looked at the huge ship behind them. She thought she could see the bulges of the latest generation tunneling drive near the stern of the ship, almost three hundred metres away. Those drive nodes were responsible for making the eleven quadrillion kilometre trip possible in just under five years. The Valiant had been the crew's home for the last five years, but it would now be broken down for building material for the new colony.

Tori looked down at the holographically projected readout on the arm of her suit. "Fifteen percent atmospheric O_2 at a hundred and forty kilopascals pressure, just like we expected."

"Breathing is going to be difficult for the first few weeks," Sayid acknowledged. "The extra weight doesn't seem to be an issue, though."

"Looks like the ship's spin increase worked like it was supposed to," Rachael said from behind him.

Just then, three people appeared with a pop that could be heard over the crew's helmet speakers. Two young men flanked a young woman in the center, unintentionally mirroring the three crew of the Valiant. They were wearing casual clothing and had rebreather masks over their mouths. The young woman was holding hands with the taller of the two men, while the other looked on in amusement.

Tori gave a squeak of surprise, and Sayid took a step back, booted foot hitting the ramp back up to the ship. He forced himself to calm down and stepped forward.

"Hello, I am Captain Banning of the Valiant."

"Hello, Captain," the young woman said. "I'm Nicole Spencer, and these are Connor Jacobs and Aiken Drum." She nodded to her left and right as she made the introductions, releasing Aiken's hand as she did, and the officers recognized the trio from their history lessons. They looked to be in their mid-twenties, though, not the towering icons that they expected from reading about their accomplishments.

The two groups stood awkwardly, studying each other, until Aiken broke the silence.

"Anything you'd like to let the folks back on Earth know that shouldn't wait for twelve hundred years?"

Rachael laughed nervously. "Is that how long it would take to get a message back?" *I didn't expect him to be so cute*, she thought.

Nicole's head twitched in astonishment. "What did you just say?"

"Uh, I was just wondering what the transmission time between here and Earth was," Rachael fumbled.

"No, after that," Nicole said. *What did you say?*

Nothing, it was nothing.

The two young men's heads snapped up to look at her sharply. The one on the left, Aiken Drum, gazed piercingly at her, then his eyes refocused, and she felt a tingling sensation on the inside of her skull. What was happening?

"Her brain's been altered. They all have," Aiken said quietly after a moment. He nodded up towards the bulk of the ship curving away above them. "All of them."

Nicole turned to him. "How is that possible? Unless..." she broke off and looked at the Valiant, looming large behind them.

Connor gaped at both of them. "Oh, great. Now what?"

Ian Hecht is a high school teacher, but don't hold that against him. He lives in Saskatchewan, Canada with his wife and three kids. He started writing novels in 2003, when he joined in the National Novel Writing Month. *Crucible* was written largely during the 2006 NaNoWriMo event.

Ian can be found online at his website www.ianhecht.com or on Twitter with the username @ianhecht.